SURVIVING THE END

Crumbling World

Fallen World

New World

SURVIVING THE END BOOK ONE

GRACE HAMILTON

BLURB

Family comes first—and he'll do whatever it takes to protect his from the looming storm.

Even before becoming a husband and father, safety had been Shane McDonald's priority for most of his forty-five years. As a nuclear engineer, it's his responsibility to keep the Sequoyah Nuclear Plant functioning at optimum levels to avoid what protesters fear most—a meltdown.

But when a coronal mass ejection from the sun wipes out power across the globe, stopping a nuclear chain reaction is no longer his primary concern.

Now Shane must trek across hundreds of miles to ensure the safety of his loved ones in a world rapidly disintegrating into lawlessness. Yet with few functioning automobiles and a blind teenage daughter to protect, it'll require careful planning to reach his prepper mother-in-law's and reunite with his family.

His wife has her hands full as well. When her brother's chemo drip suddenly stops working and her son gets stuck in the hospital elevator, all Jodi McDonald wants is the security of her husband's steady presence. But with a weakened brother and inexperienced son to look after, Jodi must remain strong amid the chaos and help guide them to her mother's.

However, even the best laid plans go awry as the miles stretch out between them. Supply thefts run rampant. Those who have necessities prey on those who don't. Minds broken by hardship kill on sight.

But the fatal mistake comes when thugs threaten the McDonald's little girl.

Shane must find the strength to do the unthinkable—or watch his family suffer the consequences.

CONTENTS

1

Violet must have sensed the furious crowd gathered in front of the gate. In the rearview mirror, Shane saw her sit up straighter and cock her head to one side. Ruby, her black lab guide dog, responded to the sudden change in her body language and looked at her with concern. Roughly two dozen people had gathered in a grassy area alongside the entry road to the Sequoyah Nuclear Plant, some of them carrying neatly stenciled signs as they marched back and forth. On the other side of the road two police officers stood watching in front of their patrol car.

"Dad, what's going on?" Violet said. "I can hear a crowd of people. It sounds like they're chanting."

He hadn't intended to tell her about the protestors. He had been hoping to avoid having to explain to his daughter why people were protesting his place of work on Take Your Child to Work Day. She was fourteen, but she was also somewhat naïve. Shane had perhaps sheltered her too much as a child, waiting to protect her from danger, from bullies, from so many possible problems, particularly because of her disability. This had only recently become difficult, as she began to push back, growing into a questioning teen who would no longer accept easy answers.

"Just some people," he said. "Don't worry."

As the car drew up alongside the protestors, the words of their chant became clear.

"Shut it down! Shut it down! Shut it down!"

Ruby had been sprawled across the back seat, but she rose now and placed her head on Violet's lap. Some would have mistaken this for a gesture of affection. Shane recognized it as a protective move.

"Why are they saying that?" Violet asked, pushing her sunglasses up the bridge of her nose. "Is something wrong? They sound angry."

Trying to ignore the hateful stares of the protestors, Shane slowed as he approached the guard station next to the front gate. He fumbled in his shirt pocket for his work ID, trying to think of the best way to explain the situation to his daughter. Violet tended to think the best of people, and he didn't want her to lose that optimism.

"They're just exercising their first amendment rights," he said. "Freedom of speech is a beautiful thing, even if the things being said are questionable."

"So they're protesting the power plant?" she asked.

"Well…yes," he replied, hoping she would leave it at that.

"That happens a lot here, huh?" she said. "A lot of people protest?"

"No, only occasionally. Generally, when we make the news for some reason or another."

"Why are they so mad this time? Did your company do something wrong?"

"They're upset because of the talk about adding a third reactor to the plant. Our service area is growing, and we could use another reactor, but as soon as it hit the news, people in the community started complaining. I imagine they organized some kind of protest gathering on social media, and here they are. It's fine. People are entitled to voice their concerns." He flashed his ID to the guard, who gave him an anxious smile and waved him through the open gate. The parking lot beyond was emptier than usual. At two minutes to four in the afternoon, they were smack-dab in the middle of a shift change. Had the protestors planned it that way, hoping to catch the bulk of the second shift workers as they pulled into the gate? It seemed likely. "If you ask me, they're being rather alarmist. People like this, I don't think they get it."

"They don't get what, Dad?" Violet asked.

He carefully considered his words before answering. Would his daughter think less of him if she understood the controversial nature of his chosen industry? "Well, Violet, sweetheart, nuclear energy is the cleanest and safest form of energy in the world—hands down, no question—but the word *nuclear* makes some people nervous. They assume radiation is seeping into the environment and creating three-eyed fish in the river."

Violet laughed at that. "Is it?"

3

"No, of course not. The radiation is fully contained."

Ahead, the vast gray cooling towers rose on either side of a domed containment building, billowing steam into a crisp late-April sky. Shane could see the curve of the Tennessee River where it slipped behind the plant in a broad arc. It was a sight that never failed to impress him, even after these many years, and he wished his daughter could enjoy it. As he pulled into the closest row of parking spaces, he considered ways he might convey the majesty of this place to her.

"Dad," she said, "we talked about nuclear power in our science class at school. Our teacher said nuclear power plants are dangerous because if they overheat, they can go into a meltdown. She said meltdowns have happened before, and they hurt a lot of people, even poisoned whole cities. Is that true? Could it happen here?"

"It's true. But did your teacher mention that more people die in coal mines *every year* than have ever died from nuclear meltdowns?" Shane said.

Violet persisted. "But a meltdown could happen here?"

Shane grunted unhappily. "That would require a very severe accident."

"But they've happened before," Violet said. "At Chernobyl in the Ukraine, and somewhere in Japan. One even happened in America, she said, at a place called Three Mile Island."

"Don't worry," he said. "Something like that is not going to happen here. The Chernobyl accident was mostly caused by the poor design of RBMK nuclear power reactors. We don't have that problem here.

And Fukushima in Japan was caused by a tsunami, which probably isn't going to happen in the mountains of Tennessee. We're safe."

"But how do you know for sure?" Violet asked.

"Because I'm a nuclear engineer," he replied. "It's my job to know. It's my job to keep everyone safe, and I will. I will keep us safe."

"Promise?" Violet said.

"Promise."

The hallways were emptier than usual because of the shift change, but they met Landon just outside the control room. He was coming from the direction of the break room, his sleek black wheelchair making its gentle *whirring* sound. It had wheels with fat spokes that were slanted inward, a heavily padded seat and backrest, and a sturdy frame. As Landon had explained in the past, it was technically an athletic wheelchair, but he'd gained an affinity for them during his years of playing wheelchair basketball. He was broad-shouldered and strong, a former athlete with a well-built upper body. His legs had atrophied from spina bifida, but this had rarely been an issue on the job.

"Hey there, buddy," Landon said, when he spotted Shane rounding the corner. "I don't usually beat you to the office. What's the holdup?"

"I brought a guest with me this morning," Shane said, "so watch your salty language today."

"What are you talking about?" Landon replied. "I haven't even said my first four letter word of the day."

Shane shuffled slowly down the hall, holding his daughter's hand and guiding her. She came somewhat reluctantly, her other hand sliding along the wall. Passing through security had made her nervous—the great hum and hiss of the metal detector, x-ray machine, and radiation monitor—and she kept fiddling with the small radiation monitoring device hanging around her neck. Like the workers, she had been given an orange hardhat, and it was slightly too big for her head, pushing against the rims of her sunglasses.

To make matters far worse, security had insisted she leave Ruby behind. They'd made a place for her beloved black lab in the security office, but Violet had balked at the idea. It was Shane's fault. He'd pulled strings to get approval for Violet to come to work with him— no easy feat—but he'd forgotten to get clearance for Ruby.

That'll put a damper on the day, he thought.

Fortunately, Violet knew Landon well—he was practically family— so when she heard his voice, she relaxed a bit.

"Hey there, Vivi," Landon said. Only Landon could get away with calling her Vivi. "Where's your furry sidekick? I've never seen the two of you apart." He was particularly fond of the dog.

"They wouldn't let me bring her into the building," Violet said. "Even though she's a trained guide dog, they said it's not safe to bring an animal—any animal—into the plant, so she's sitting back there by herself."

"Not by herself," Shane said gently. "The security team will take good care of her, and we can check on her from time to time. We'll bring her something to eat during my lunch break."

"I don't know what they're afraid of," Violet said. "She never bites, and she doesn't get into anything. She doesn't even bark unless I'm in trouble. If we brought her inside, she would sit quietly and mind her own business all day long, except for pee breaks."

"It's just company protocol," Shane said. "Sorry, I should have tried to clear it first. I didn't realize it would be a problem."

"Don't you worry about it, Violet," Landon said. "I won't let this injustice stand. I'll file a formal complaint. It's not nice separating a kid from her loyal sidekick. If we have to take this all the way to the board of directors, so be it. Policy must be rewritten."

Shane shook his head at Landon. "It's fine. It's only for a few hours. Ruby will be okay. We'll check on her at lunchtime, get her something to eat, take her potty, and everything will be okay."

"She doesn't know that," Violet said. "She doesn't know we're coming back at lunchtime." Finally, Violet shrugged and rolled her head back on her shoulders. When she did, the orange hardhat almost fell off, and she had to grab it. "Oh well, nothing we can do about it, I guess. I'll give her an extra treat after we get home tonight."

"There you go," Shane said. "Great idea."

"I don't know why you wanted to come here anyway, kid," Landon said. "Should've gone to work with your mom at the CDC. You know your dad's job is incredibly boring, right?"

"Dad says his job is to keep everyone safe," Violet said.

"He's not wrong." Landon turned and wheeled toward the control room door, beckoning for them to follow. "But you'd be surprised how boring it is keeping everyone safe."

"Now, now," Shane said, laying a hand lightly on his daughter's shoulder. "Don't undersell the experience, Landon. She's been looking forward to this."

"All I'm saying is you should have gone with your mom," Landon said. "She works with diseases. She's battling deadly viruses on the daily, keeping world-devouring pandemics at bay with nothing but grit and determination."

"That's not exactly true," Shane said. "She does have a lot of grit and determination, though, I'll give you that."

"Centers for Disease Control. That's her place of employment, right? Disease *control*, man. They're protecting us from mutating Ebola and bio-engineered smallpox. Those are the real dangers right there, not some silly old nuclear power plant. Nothing exciting happens here."

"Dad said yes first," Violet said.

"I did," Shane said. "Plus, your mom is technically a statistician for the CDC. She's not battling bio-engineered smallpox, but they do work to prevent diseases. He's right about that."

"It's fine," Violet said. "Except for poor Ruby, I don't mind coming here. I can visit Mom's place next time."

The curve of a long green console took up most of the center of the control room, its surface covered in a complex array of gauges, screens, buttons, and knobs. A low hum filled the room. Violet reacted upon entering the room, perking up and turning her head first one way and then the other.

"The air is different in here," she said. "Feels kind of weird. Sort of electric, if that makes sense."

"Lots and lots of warm electronics," Landon said, wheeling himself up to the console and leaning in close to one of the monitors. "That's what you feel. It kind of smells plasticky, doesn't it?"

"Yeah," Violet replied.

Landon's elbow crutches were leaning against the end of the console. He kept them close, but he preferred using the wheelchair. When Shane took a seat, they started to slide so he caught them and set them on the floor. As Landon began cycling through system menus, Shane called his daughter over, took her right hand, and laid it on the console beside his keyboard.

"You feel that?" he asked. "That's my computer. I spend a whole lot of time at this computer."

"I can almost see it," she said. "The screen is bright right now, isn't it?"

"That's right. The starting screen is a light blue color."

Though Violet was visually impaired, Shane knew she could perceive light. She described bright lights as vague, distant blobs. She could also tell when she was in a completely dark room. Beyond that, she was incapable of perceiving shapes or colors.

"We monitor every system in the station from this room." Shane turned to Landon. "In fact, we can pretty much determine everything that's happening from right here, and we can call other departments if we need to talk to them."

"On rare occasions, we even leave the room," Landon said.

"That's true," Shane said. "In fact, I was thinking about giving her a tour of the facility when the rest of the staff get here. She could meet some of the department heads and hear what they do. What do you think?"

"Sorry, pal," Landon replied. "After the software upgrade, we've got to run through the rest of those scenarios this morning. The tour will have to wait until after lunch."

"Oh, man, I thought we finished those yesterday."

"Not even close," Landon said. "They're being especially comprehensive this time."

Shane guided his daughter's hand to the next seat, and she sat down.

"Sorry, sweetheart, I'll take you on a tour a little later," Shane said. "Just hang out here for a bit while we get some work done. Do you need a drink or anything? I could run to the break room and get you something."

"I'm fine, Dad," Violet replied, feeling the edge of the console and resting her forearms against a spot that was clear of buttons, gauges, or knobs. "Don't worry about me. Just do your work. I don't want to be a bother."

"You're never a bother," he said.

"Brace yourself, Vivi," Landon said. "Running through end-of-the-world scenarios while pretending they can never happen gets dull after a few hours."

Shane almost shushed his friend, but it was too late. The words were out. Violet pushed her sunglasses up the bridge of her nose and frowned.

"End of the world?" she said. "What do you mean by that?"

"Just scenarios," Shane said. "Not real life. We're testing a recent software upgrade by seeing how it responds to theoretical situations."

"What kind of situations?" Violet asked.

But at that moment, a harsh squawk came out of one of the tiny speakers beside Shane's computer console as a window popped up on his screen. A red message flashed brightly: CORONAL MASS EJECTION EVENT IMMINENT TWO MINUTES. It flashed a few times before he registered what he was reading.

"Coronal mass ejection," he said. "Landon, did you start the simulation already?"

Landon leaned back in his chair to get a look at Shane's screen. "I haven't done anything," he said. "I haven't pressed a single button yet." A two-way radio sat near the edge of the console, and he grabbed it. "Let me see if I can find out what's going on. Maybe they're running some kind of remote drill. Is that possible? I mean, it can't be real."

"If it was real they would have given us a lot more than two minutes warning," Shane said, feeling a flutter of anxiety despite his words. "It has to be some kind of test."

"Okay, let me see if I can get hold of someone," Landon said. "If it's an unplanned simulation from on high, I'm going to pitch a fit. We have enough scenarios to run through without the higher-ups messing around. Sometimes, they're too clever for their own good."

"Dad?"

Violet managed one plaintive word before the power went out. Every light and screen went dark, and Shane heard cooling fans winding down.

"Well, that's not good," Landon said. "We just lost everything."

Shane had been trained to handle this kind of scenario—he knew the steps—but having his daughter present changed everything. He could hear her panicked breathing, the squeak of her chair as she fidgeted. It was distracting. He wanted to comfort her, but he also knew they had to act fast.

"Dad, what's happening? What's a coronal…whatever?"

"Coronal mass ejection," Landon said. "A massive burst of plasma from the sun. Causes an electromagnetic pulse which can knock out the power grid, fry electronics, and do all sorts of bad, bad stuff. I'm going to take a wild guess here and say it's not a simulation."

The control room was quiet, too quiet, but Shane heard shouting in the hallway—panic throughout the building just as the second shift was arriving. Terrible timing.

"Backup power's not coming on," he said. "Could the CME have taken out the generators?"

"Doubt it," Landon said in the darkness. He sounded breathless. "If it's a CME, the backup generators might be fine. They're just old-fashioned diesel engines. No electronics in them to be fried. We'll have to start them manually though."

Shane was still half-convinced it was a test, but he didn't like the nervous edge in Landon's voice. The man was usually so calm and collected.

"I'll take care of it," Shane said. He started to rise from his chair, but Violet's hand clamped down on his arm.

"No, Dad. Don't leave. I'm scared."

"It's okay, honey. I just need—"

He heard the whir of Landon's wheelchair. "I've got it. You two stay here. I know the way, and I can move faster than either of you. We need to act quickly."

"No, I'll come with you," Shane said. "It might require two of us to get the generators working. Violet, you can come, too. I won't leave you here by yourself."

"Are we in trouble?" she said. "What happens if you don't get them working?"

"If the main power is knocked out, the control rods drop into the core, and the reactor is flooded with water to drive the temperature down," Shane said. "That can't happen until we get the backup generators on, but we will. It'll just take a minute."

"You're talking about a meltdown," Violet said, her voice quavering, her hand squeezing his arm tighter. "That's it, isn't it?"

"No, no, we have…plenty of time to get things under control." He had to force the words out. *But it's a test, right? It has to be? If it's a real CME, they would have warned us a lot sooner.*

Shane heard the hiss of the control room door as Landon heaved it open and wheeled into the hallway. Shane rose and grabbed Violet's hand. Then he followed after Landon.

He wanted to believe they had plenty of time. He almost did believe it, but he'd never heard Landon sound so scared.

2

M ike sat up in his chair, trying his best not to let the crushing wave of nausea show on his face. It swept over him like a tidal surge, submerging his whole body in sickening pain. It hurt to sit up straight with the massive bandage on the side of his neck. He hadn't dared to look at the incision, so he didn't know how much of his neck they'd cut away to remove the cancer. In truth, he didn't want to know—something to be dealt with later. For now, he just wanted to get this last round of chemo over with.

It wasn't all bad. Though he knew he didn't look his best, not with the patchy hair and the puffy cheeks, the attractive oncology nurse was responding to his best stories and jokes. That almost made the discomfort worthwhile.

"Did I ever tell you about the time I clipped a seagull with a golf ball on the fifth hole at Orchid Island Golf Club in Florida?" he said.

Erica was checking the IV bag, which was almost empty. "Not on purpose, I hope," she said with a smile. She was around his age, maybe a couple of years younger—forty, he would have guessed, though he knew better than to ask. Her blonde hair was cut short in a way that flattered her face. More than that, Mike clung to her sunny personality like a lifeline while he endured these horrible chemo treatments.

"No, not on purpose," he replied. "The seagull lived. It's quite a story actually. I think he helped my game. Got me closer to the green, and I wound up hitting an 88 on a par 72 course. Not too shabby, if I do say so myself."

"Oh yeah? I don't know golf scores. Is that good"

"It's decent. I mean, I'll never qualify for the PGA, but I beat the doofus I was playing with, who got stuck in a sand trap three times. The seagull was just the capper to a great day. I'll have to tell you about it sometime."

"It sounds like you just told me the whole story already," she said. "How much more could there be?"

"You'd be surprised," Mike said. "I'm sure we don't have time right now. Seems like that chemo bag is almost empty." Summoning his courage, he went for it: "Actually, it's the kind of story that goes best over coffee."

"That kind of story, huh?" She checked the drip chamber and the port on his IV. "Over coffee, you say. Not a cold beer?"

"Well, I'll take a beer over coffee any time, of course. I just figured a coffee shop was a better…"

Mike trailed off as another spike of nausea hit him. He groaned, leaning to one side. Erica grabbed a stainless-steel emesis basin off a nearby table and placed it on the arm of the chair under his chin. The wound on the side of his neck made it difficult to lean over so he propped his head against his hand and waited for the waves of stomach-churning pain to subside. His whole torso hurt, his head was pounding, even his feet ached.

His sister, Jodi, was watching him from her chair on the far side of the room, concern on her face. Though Mike was dressed like a slob in an old polo shirt and sweatpants, Jodi looked as crisp and professional as ever. She was a statistician for the CDC, and she always looked the part. Her posture was annoyingly rigid, and Mike often picked on her about it. "You look like you're sitting on a thumbtack," he liked to say, but he opted not to say it now.

Jodi had sent her teenage son, Owen, to the cafeteria in the basement to get some snacks. Owen was a good kid, protective of his family, but neither Jodi nor Mike liked making him witness the harsh reality of the cancer treatments. In fact, he'd insisted on coming today, despite his mother's discouragement. If Owen knew why he was being sent to the cafeteria, he didn't complain about it. Mike had asked for a bag of plain chips, thinking something mild might help his stomach, but he'd now lost his appetite. At the moment, all food seemed revolting. He almost hoped the kid got lost on the way back, so he wouldn't have to see the food

"This is worse than the last time," Mike said with a groan. "I didn't think it was possible to feel sicker to my stomach, but this is it. Erica, put me out of my misery. It's like a belly full of hot death. I can't go on."

"It'll pass," the nurse said. "Just hang in there. We're almost done. You're doing great."

"If I hit the floor, leave me there," he said. "Don't bother picking me up. I just want to melt into a little puddle and seep into the crack."

"Don't talk like that. You're not going to hit the floor, and you're definitely not going to melt. You'll be fine. Just hang in there a little longer. Think about how far you've come. This is your last round of treatment. Think of the future."

"The future…" Mike said in a croak. "Can't quite…picture it…"

Behind Erica, a broad window looked out over a staff parking lot behind the hospital. It was nestled at the base of a row of grassy hills, and above the hills, tall power lines cut across a clear blue sky. Mike fixed his gaze in that direction and tried to imagine a cool breeze against his face.

This has to be the last of it, he thought. *I can't go through this again. God, let this be the last of the chemo for the rest of my life.*

It was theoretically his last round of chemo, but the doctor wouldn't declare him cancer free until he had a PET scan. Mike had often dreamed of hearing those words: cancer free. All of this sickness, the hair loss, and getting a huge chunk of his neck chopped out—all of it would be worth it just to hear the doctor say those words.

"You're doing great, Mike," Erica said. "You're a lot tougher than you give yourself credit for. We're just about done here."

"Yeah, I feel just about done," Mike said, attempting a laugh that became a groan. "What's that old saying? 'Stick a fork in me…'"

He happened to be looking right at one of the transmission towers when he saw a giant shower of sparks burst from it. He almost said something about it, but all the lights and computer screens in the room went dark.

"Whoa, what was that?"

Jodi immediately stood up. "That's not good."

Erica looked around. "Sorry about that. Don't worry. The backup generators will kick in shortly."

"That was quite a fireworks show out there," Mike said. "Did either of you see it?"

"You saw something?" Jodi asked.

"Huge sparks on a transmission tower up on that hill," he said, gesturing toward the window. "Just happened all of a sudden. Almost like an explosion. I didn't see any lightning hit the tower. Wonder what caused it?"

Erica turned to see what he was talking about, but the sparks had stopped. Jodi went to the door and peered out into the hallway. Voices arose from other rooms. Nobody sounded particularly concerned yet, but Mike did hear someone running down the hallway.

"I hope Owen doesn't panic," Jodi said. "What if he was in the elevator? What if he's trapped in there right now?"

"Unlikely," Mike said. "I'll bet he was standing in front of the vending machines, trying to choose between the mini donuts and the pecan spinwheels. He might still be pressing the buttons over and over even as we speak."

"I sent him to get *food*," Jodi said, "not junk."

"Well, whatever the case, he'll be fine."

"I want to make sure," Jodi said.

Mike glanced down at the IV line running into the port in his arm. Being hooked up to the machine with no power made him nervous. "Hey, Erica, I don't suppose we can go ahead and remove this thing. It's bugged me since you put it in," Mike said, lightly tapping the plastic disk that had been inserted into his arm. It was meant to make inserting the IV needle easier, but he'd found it disconcerting having the thing permanently attached.

Erica didn't respond for a few seconds. She was staring up at the ceiling. With a questioning grunt, she shrugged and began removing the IV. "We were done anyway. I'm sure the doctor will be here in a minute. He'll clear us to remove the port."

She removed the IV, working slowly, clearly killing time. Jodi began to pace. Mike was still too preoccupied with the waves of sickness roiling through his guts, the lingering tingle of weakness in his limbs, to worry about the power. The worst part was knowing the most severe nausea hadn't set in yet. The worst of it didn't usually hit until about a day after chemo. That's when the relentless vomiting started.

"What are the odds we'll get the PET scan done today, so he can clear me?"

"Well, I don't know," was all the nurse said

As she always did after a round of chemo, she checked his blood pressure and took his temperature. Jodi continued pacing, occasionally glancing out the door. A full minute passed, and still the power hadn't come back on, and the backup generators hadn't kicked in. Now, the voices in the hallway started to sound concerned. Someone in a distant room was shouting for a doctor.

"Owen's not back," Jodi said, glancing at the clock on the wall. "He probably doesn't know what to do."

"Sis, Owen is sixteen," Mike reminded her, "and he's a smart kid. The power went out. It happens. A transformer blew. The building didn't fall down. He'll be fine."

Erica slid the IV pole away from Mike's chair and looked at the dead computer screen nearby, tapping it a few times as if that might help. "Backup power should be on by now. Maybe another minute."

Jodi paced the room a few more times, which only made Mike anxious. It was just a power outage, no big deal, but something about the situation didn't seem right. The rising tide of voices in the hall didn't help. Mike thought he heard someone crying.

Finally, as if she'd made up her mind, Jodi stopped in her tracks, nodded, and grabbed her purse from the chair. "I'm going to look for him. I'm sure Owen is fine, but…I just want to make sure he can find his way back."

As she moved to the door, Mike felt a flutter of fear. "Be careful out there."

Jodi paused, adjusting the strap of her purse on her shoulder, and gave him a smile. "Don't worry. I'll try my best not to run into people or fall down the stairs."

She meant it as a joke, he could tell, but he merely nodded. No, something about the situation wasn't right, but he couldn't put his finger on it. Erica was chewing on a fingernail, but she moved suddenly to a counter and slid open a drawer.

"Here, you'll need this," she said to Jodi, pulling a small flashlight out of the drawer. "There are no windows in the stairwell. I'm sure the power will come back on before you get there, but…you know, just in case."

Jodi took the flashlight from her and clicked it on. Bright white LEDs cast a blinding beam on the wall beside Mike's chair.

"Thanks," she said. She nodded at Mike, her smile faltering, and left.

The loud click of the door swinging shut broke Mike out of his distraction. He turned his gaze to the window. Below, in the parking lot, a doctor still in his scrubs was getting out of his nice gray BMW X2. He stood beside the door a moment, shaking his head. Then he clapped a hand to his forehead. He walked a circle around the car, started to get back in, then changed his mind and raised both hands over his head. Finally, he smacked the roof of the car and appeared to curse.

"What is going on?" Mike whispered, but then the nausea and anxiety met in the middle, creating a stomach-churning nightmare. He bent over the emesis basin, squeezing his eyes shut.

3

A single window at the end of the hall cast a ghostly light along the doors on her right. It was mid-afternoon, and the sunlight had taken on a heavy quality. Jodi saw anxious faces peering out of many of the rooms. She heard a child crying, a parent trying to comfort her. Nurses spoke words of encouragement.

"Don't worry. The power will be back on in a minute."

"I'm sure it's no big deal. They'll get it all up and running soon."

"Probably just a lightning strike or something."

But a few minutes had passed, and still there was no power, no backup generator kicking in, just shade and shadows in every hallway, room, and corner. Jodi turned the flashlight on again and followed the dim hallways until she reached the elevator. A couple was standing there, staring at the elevator door as if waiting for it to open, but Jodi kept going to the stairs.

Something about this power outage didn't seem normal. Jodi was analytical by nature—it was her profession after all—but she couldn't figure out why this situation bothered her so much.

Sparks on a transmission line on a sunny day. Yes, maybe that was it.

Beyond the narrow beam of the flashlight, the stairs were utterly dark, and the shifting shadows as she descended were unnerving. She moved as fast as she dared and pushed open the door to the first floor. As soon as she did, she heard a nearby commotion—strained voices, some kind of mechanical grinding, and sounds of exertion. She stepped into the first-floor lobby and saw a few maintenance workers in uniforms gathered around the elevator door. One of them had a flashlight pointed at the door. They had two-way radios clipped to their belts, and a multitude of distorted voices kept speaking as problems unfolded throughout the building.

As Jodi approached, one of the workers turned to her, an older gentleman who was sweating profusely.

"Don't get too close, ma'am," he said. "The elevator is stuck between floors. We got some people in there."

Jodi watched as two of the workers pried the door open, and she spotted the bottom half of the elevator near the ceiling. A narrow opening gave a glimpse of the dark interior, and when she shone her flashlight in that direction she saw the soles of shoes moving around. A sick feeling took hold in the pit of her stomach.

"Owen, are you in there?" she called, slipping past the maintenance worker. "It's Mom."

After a second, she heard a panicked reply. "Mom, we're trapped in here. The elevator just stopped all of sudden for no reason." She could tell by the pitch of his voice that he was just barely holding it together.

"It's okay," she said, trying to keep her own voice calm. Actually, she felt a bit relieved to know where he was. At least he was safe. "We're going to get you out of there."

One of the maintenance workers waved her back, so she moved out of the way. She clicked off her flashlight—there was enough residual light from the lobby windows—and dug her cell phone out of her purse.

For a moment, she had the strange idea that her phone wouldn't work, but when she tapped the screen it lit up. She unlocked the screen and dialed Shane's number. He didn't answer. She considered leaving him a voicemail message, but she tried to call again instead. Still, he didn't answer, so she tried Violet.

Her daughter answered on the first ring.

"Hello?"

"Sweetheart, are you there? Is everything okay?"

"Mom, the power went out," Violet said. She sounded terrified, close to tears. Jodi felt her first glimmer of real fear. Was this power outage really that widespread? "The power went out in the whole plant."

"I understand, honey. It's out here at the hospital, too," Jodi said, "but are you and Daddy okay?"

Violet hesitated a second before answering. Jodi heard some kind of activity in the background—running and shouting—but she couldn't make out what they were saying.

"Mom, it's real bad," Violet said. "If they don't get the backup power on soon, this whole place could blow up. Dad said they have to do something with the core to keep it from overheating, but they need backup power to do it."

"*What?*"

"It could blow up," Violet said again, and now she sounded like she *was* crying. "The rods could overheat and melt down and it'll all blow up."

"Violet. Violet, honey, calm down." Jodi felt a stab of icy fear deep in her guts. She listened as her daughter tried to get her crying under control. "Is your father there?"

"Y-yes," Violet said. "We're on our way with Landon to get the generators turned on. I heard them say the core could overheat in *minutes*. In minutes, Mom."

"Look, I'm going to hang up, but I want you to have your father call me as soon as he can, okay?" She fought back her own tears. *Blow up?* Surely Violet hadn't meant it. Surely she'd misunderstood, but Jodi felt utterly helpless. "Can you do that, Violet? Have your father call me."

"I will," Violet replied, voice shaking badly.

"It's…it's going to be okay," Jodi said.

"No, it's not. I heard what they said."

It was the last thing Violet said before hanging up. Jodi was tempted to call her back, but she knew it wouldn't help. Sequoyah Nuclear Plant was all the way in Soddy-Daisy, Tennessee, at least 270 miles from the hospital in Augusta. That made for a huge power outage, and it also meant the possibility that Jodi's mother just outside Macon was affected as well.

With shaking hands, Jodi called her mom. If anyone could handle a situation like this with calm and purposeful intensity, it was Beth Bevin. She was a tough old bird, and she lived to be prepared for catastrophes of all kinds.

Jodi got an answering machine.

She considered calling again, but at that moment the lights came on, and the elevator began to move. The maintenance workers stepped back as the door opened on its own.

"Oh, thank goodness," Jodi muttered, putting her phone back in her purse.

The lights were dimmer than usual, but it was better by far than the ominous shadows. The intercom system throughout the hospital chirped as it came to life, and a voice spoke.

"Ladies and gentlemen, please excuse the inconvenience," it said. "We experienced a brief malfunction with the backup generators, but everything is working now. There is still a widespread power outage in our area, so please conserve power and avoid using the elevators."

Owen hopped out of the elevator as soon as it reached the first floor and ran to his mother's side. He didn't hug her—he was at that age— but she could see the relief on his face.

"Are you okay?" she asked.

"I'm fine," he said. "That was bad timing on my part, you know? I didn't have time to get the snacks." He was dressed neatly for a sixteen-year-old in a button-up shirt and khaki pants. Studious and smart, he favored her, both in looks and temperament.

As soon as the elevator cleared, the maintenance workers taped a large orange 'Out of Order' sign on the door. As they did, they began to chat, and Jodi lingered, trying to eavesdrop without appearing to do so. Owen took a few steps toward the stairs, realized she wasn't following, and turned back. There were three of them: the older gentlemen, a younger man with a wild mop of reddish hair, and a stocky fellow with beady eyes.

The one with the reddish hair was speaking, gesturing dramatically as he did so. "Something fried the circuits and shorted out the electronic control system in the backup generator," he said. "You heard them. They had to bypass the control system to get it up and running. That's not a normal power outage, guys."

"Oh, here we go," said the stocky fellow. "What was it, moon beams or something?"

"Not moon beams," he replied, "but there *is* something that could cause a power outage *and* fry electronic circuits."

"Can't wait to hear it," the older gentleman said with obvious sarcasm. "Doomsday Daryl, tell us all about it."

"Yeah," the stocky fellow said, chuckling. "Tell us, Doomsday Daryl. Tell us what you read on the internet."

"Coronal mass ejection," Daryl said, jabbing a finger in the stocky man's direction. "You know what that is?"

"Sounds like a disease," the stocky fellow said. "Something you get from drinking dirty water."

"It's a massive cloud of plasma from the sun," Daryl said, eyes wide and intense. "It works like an EMP. The shockwave produces a geomagnetic storm that releases terawatts of power that can fry circuits, satellites, and electric transmission lines. We're talking about long-term damage, guys, maybe permanent. You ever dreamed of going back to the Victorian era *permanently?* Dust off your top hats and corsets, because here's your chance. We should check the other buildings in our area to see if they've been affected. I'll bet they have. I'll bet the whole area's been affected."

"Sounds like another form of moon beams to me," the stocky fellow replied as he picked up a toolbox and turned to leave. "Conspiracy stuff. You've rotted your brain on it."

"Yeah, something you read on one of your weird websites," the other worker agreed, shaking his head.

"Well, you tell me, have you guys ever heard of a power outage frying circuits like this?" Daryl said, making a big sweep of his arm. "I mean, *all* circuits across panels throughout the building?"

But the other workers laughed again and started to walk away. Daryl scowled and didn't follow them, crossing his arms over his chest. "It's never happened!" he called out to their backs.

Jodi had listened to the conversation with mounting alarm. When she glanced at Owen, he was staring at the workers with a grimace. She held up a finger to say, "Just a second," and approached the one they'd called Doomsday Daryl.

"Pardon me," she said. "Sorry to bother you. I couldn't help but over-hear your conversation, and I wondered—"

"I'm not crazy," he replied, spinning to face her. "I know what they think, but I've read all about this. I've done my research. Not conspiracy stuff, but real science."

"I don't think you're crazy," Jodi said. "What can you tell me about this…what did you call it?"

"Coronal mass ejection," he said. "It's happened before, you know. In 1989, a CME caused a big geomagnetic storm that knocked out power all over Quebec and caused radio interference. It happened so fast, they didn't see it coming. If I'm right, then everything outside this hospital has been affected by it. Come on, let's take a look."

He beckoned her and rushed over to the windows on the far side of the lobby. Jodi gestured for Owen to stay with her and followed Daryl. From here, they had a broad view across a parking lot to a nearby intersection.

"Do you see any lights out there?" he asked. "Headlights, building lights, anything?"

The first thing Jodi noticed was that the traffic lights at the intersection weren't working. Vehicles were stopped there, as if the absence of traffic lights had left their drivers bereft of purpose and direction.

"But of course traffic lights wouldn't be working," she said.

"You go out there and you'll find most of the cars don't work either," Daryl said, gazing wild-eyed across the city. "Especially the newer ones. A solar EMP would do that. There was no flash in the sky, so it wasn't caused by a nuke. It just happened all of a sudden. Lady, this is worse than you think. It's worse than anyone thinks."

The dread that had begun as a flutter in her belly was now choking her. What would it mean if circuits were fried all the way from Augusta to Soddy-Daisy? She couldn't imagine it. How would they get by? No lights, no power, no electronics. She didn't even want to think about it.

"But wait," Jodi said. She dug into her purse and pulled out her cell phone, lighting up the screen and showing it to him. "If it was an EMP then why is my phone service still working? I was able to call my daughter. I spoke to her. If the cell phone company is still able to provide service, you can't be right."

"Common misconception," Daryl said, wagging a finger in her face. "You see, an EMP at this level doesn't fry everything. Some cell phone providers don't rely on the electrical grid. They've got backup generators of their own, which means your phone service might still work for a while. It'll be spotty. I'm sure there will be network over-load, and eventually it'll stop working altogether, so enjoy it while you can. I'm telling you, lady, I know my stuff. This isn't going away. Everything has changed—you just don't know it yet."

Jodi didn't know what else to say. She wanted to dismiss him, but she had no response. She turned to her son, saw the horrified look on his face, and started back toward the stairs. Daryl stayed by the lobby windows, gazing out across the dead city with wild eyes.

"He's not right, Mom," Owen said. "He can't be…can he?"

She wanted to tell him that Doomsday Daryl was nothing more than an end-of-the-world nutjob. It would have reassured Owen, but she couldn't bring herself to say it.

"Don't worry about it," she said. It was the best she could manage without tweaking her conscience too much. "Let's go back to the oncology unit and check on Mike."

But as they mounted the stairs, moving slowly beneath the dim half-lights, she couldn't shake what Daryl had said.

Everything has changed—you just don't know it yet.

She shuddered. Whatever happened, they had to get Mike and get out of the hospital. Now.

4

Beth's cantankerous little Schnauzer, Bauer, was attempting to hold the line against a large wolf spider that had dared to pass through the line of cabbages at the edge of her garden. His bark was the dog equivalent of an old man hoarsely shouting "You darn kids get off my lawn!" Beth knew he wouldn't actually attack the spider. If it advanced too far, he would back off and resume barking from a safe vantage point.

"Grammy, that's a big spider," Kaylee said. "Does it have poison?"

Beth's garden was diverse, neatly ordered, and well kept, but it required constant attention. She grew vegetables for all seasons, and at the moment, being late April, she was weeding the spring vegetables that had been planted only weeks earlier: cabbages, peas, spinach, turnips, carrots, potatoes, onions, and radishes.

"That spider won't hurt you if you don't hurt her," Beth told her granddaughter, digging up the roots on a patch of persistent crabgrass.

"She's good for the garden. Spiders eat other bugs that want to munch on our cabbages."

"I don't like cabbage," Kaylee said. "Yuck!"

Bauer gave up on the spider and returned to Kaylee's side, sniffing the air. Kaylee giggled and awkwardly petted her back.

"You don't like cabbage, but cabbage likes you," Beth said, standing up, wincing at the creak in her back. "It keeps you nice and healthy."

"I like carrots and peas," Kaylee said. "Cabbage is gross, and spinach is gross."

Beth took in her garden and thought, not for the first time, *I'm ready*. With the many cans and jars in her basement, and a dozen rows of healthy, growing vegetables to supplement them, she had enough food for herself and her loved ones—come what may. Satisfied, she turned to her granddaughter. Kaylee was six, and she loved helping her grandma in the garden—and Beth didn't mind that she would occasionally sneak and nibble some of the veggies right out of the ground.

Kaylee's hands were grubby, and she had dirt on her cheeks and fore-head. Beth hugged her and turned her toward the house.

"Let's go in and wash up," she said.

Her home was an unassuming, typical ranch-style house set in the middle of a nice piece of property in a quiet neighborhood. No one would suspect the fortress she had turned it into. Cans and jars and water and weapons and fuel to last for years. Her husband, Mitch, gone almost five years, had thought her a little bit cuckoo. He'd seen it not as preparedness but as paranoia, but he was gone now. She was unfettered. They went in through the back door behind the dining room, Bauer padding along beside them and continuing to sniff the air as if he'd caught a strange scent. He barked at nothing in particular just before following Kaylee through the door.

Beth reached in and flicked the light switch, but the small chandelier above the dining room table didn't come on. She tried again. Nothing. She realized every light in the house was off.

"Uh-oh, power's off," she said.

"Is it broken?" Kaylee asked, sidling up next to Bauer.

"I'm sure it's fine," Beth told her granddaughter. "I'll check the breaker box and see if we haven't tripped a breaker. You head to the shower, pumpkin. Leave the door open. I'll be there in a minute to help you wash up."

The guest bathroom was just past the living room, the first door in the hallway. As Kaylee approached the open bathroom door, she came to a stop, planting her feet and crossing her arms over her chest in that childish way of hers.

"Grammy, it's too dark," she whined. "I don't wanna go in there."

There were flashlights, batteries, candles, and matches in almost every room. Beth grabbed two flashlights from a shelf in a corner beside the dining room table, turned one of them on, and brought it to Kaylee. Then she escorted her granddaughter into the bathroom, setting her on the padded toilet seat.

"You sit right here with your light," she said. "I'll be back in a second." Bauer padded in after them, whimpering. "See, Bauer's right here with you."

"Okay," Kaylee said softly, shining the flashlight in her own eyes.

Beth left her granddaughter there, making sure the bathroom door was wide open, and went to the breaker box in the utility closet. Every breaker was clearly marked—she'd made sure of that. Because of her meticulous nature, she checked each individual breaker one by one. Even though none of the breakers was tripped, she wanted to be sure.

She shut the breaker box and went to the landline phone in the kitchen. She had a list of important phone numbers scrawled on a piece of laminated notebook paper taped to the counter beside the phone. One of them was for Georgia Power. She lifted the receiver to call them. The phone was an old sturdy piece of plastic with an actual cord, nothing that needed batteries or might readily break from being dropped. Beth loved sturdy and reliable things. However, when she picked up the phone, it was dead—no service, no dial tone.

That was the moment she felt the first twinge of real concern. She set the phone down and fished her cell phone out of her pants pocket, sliding the flashlight in its place. When she unlocked the screen, she saw that her daughter, Jodi, had tried to call twice.

She returned the call. It rang a few times before a voice spoke: "All circuits are busy now. Please try your call again later." The call disconnected.

"Grammy, is it something bad?"

Kaylee was standing in the beam of her own flashlight just inside the bathroom door. Bauer peeked out between her legs and barked again for no particular reason. Beth's first instinct was to comfort her granddaughter, but she refused to lie. She'd never been one to sugar-coat the truth. Instead, she beckoned Kaylee and gestured to the dining room table. Kaylee shuffled down the hall and clambered up into one of the high-backed chairs, pressing her still-grubby hands to the tabletop. The Schnauzer followed and crawled under the chair.

"We're going to figure out what's wrong," Beth said, stroking Kaylee's hair, "and then we're going to figure out how to deal with it, okay? That's what we do."

"Okay." Kaylee seemed to accept this answer and went to work tracing wood grains on the polished tabletop with her finger.

Beth sat down beside her and continued trying to call Jodi. Fortunately, her cell phone battery was almost full—she kept it recharged as often as possible. She kept getting the same message, but Beth was persistent. Finally, she got some crayons and a notebook for Kaylee and brought her out onto the patio.

"You sit here and color," Beth said.

"Grammy, are you trying to fix the lights?" Kaylee asked, sprawling on the patio and splaying her crayons in front of her. "I'm tired of it being dark in the house."

"I know, pumpkin."

Beth paced while she continued to call. *All circuits busy. All circuits busy.* As she listened to the message over and over, she looked in the direction of the nearest house. Mrs. Eddies lived there. She was almost ninety and used oxygen. All the windows in her house were dark.

I should check on her, Beth thought.

But then one of her calls connected, and she heard her daughter's frantic voice on the other end.

"Mom, is that you? Where are you? What are you doing?"

"Jodi, I'm fine. I'm at home." Beth carefully modulated her tone of voice, glancing down at Kaylee, who, upon hearing her mother's name, looked up and smiled. "Calm down, dear. What's going on?"

"Massive power outage," Jodi said. "I'm at the hospital in Augusta with Owen and Mike. Mom, there was a guy here who thinks it might have been an EMP."

"Ah," Beth said. That explained a lot, didn't it? It put all the pieces together in her mind. It also helped her begin formulating a plan of action. Now she knew what she was working with. "What caused it? Tell me we're not at war."

"Coronal mass ejection. You know what that is?"

"I do," Beth replied. "Are you guys safe?"

"For now," Jodi replied, "but, Mom, Shane and Violet are at Sequoyah. The power's down over there, too, and they can't get the backup generators on. Violet said something about an explosion." Jodi's voice started to rise, edging toward panic.

"I'm sure she didn't mean it," Beth replied. "Anyway, Shane will do his best to keep that from happening. Listen, dear, we've talked about situations like this. I know you guys were sometimes only half-listening to me, but we always knew a major event like this was a possibility. What did I always tell you? The key to survival is to remain calm and focused."

"Remain calm and focused," Jodi said, breathless. "Mom, that's a lot easier said than done."

"You remember the plan?"

"In the event of a crisis, come to your house," Jodi said.

"That's right. Get here as soon as you can. We have everything you need right here. We're *prepared.*"

"Okay." Beth could tell her daughter was struggling to calm herself. "Okay, we're prepared. You're right, Mom. Calm and focused."

Beth glanced at Kaylee again. Fortunately, her granddaughter continued to color away, scribbling like mad across multiple pieces of paper. If she'd guessed at the nature of her grammy's conversation, she wasn't giving any hint.

"Mom, we're leaving right away," Jodi said. "We'll get there as soon as we can."

"Do you think Shane will follow the plan?"

"Yes, I think so. If I talk to him, I'll make sure."

"Good," Beth said. "Listen, you're at a hospital. Grab some medical supplies before you leave, anything you can get your hands on, and *as much* as you can get your hands on."

"How am I supposed to do that?" Jodi said. "They're not just going to hand me supplies."

"You're resourceful. You'll find a way. Now, get here as soon as you can. Shane and Violet will follow. Don't dawdle. Things are going to get real bad as soon as people start to figure out how serious the problem is. When people get scared, they make dangerous decisions, even when they mean well."

"Okay, Mom. We'll hurry. Love you."

"Love you, too. See you soon."

Beth hung up the phone, checked the battery life again, and slid the phone into her pocket. She couldn't depend on the phone service. When the cell phone providers lost backup power, that would be the end of it. Hopefully, she'd said all she needed to say to get Jodi and Shane moving in the right direction.

She took a deep breath and settled herself. "This is it," she muttered. "This is what it was all about, all those years of preparation."

"Is Mommy coming here?" Kaylee said.

"That's right," Beth said. "Kaylee, you stay out here for a second. I have to check on a few things."

Kaylee took this in stride and went right on coloring, Bauer sitting beside her. Beth went to the kitchen and pulled open the pantry. It was a generous space, with seven deep shelves, and it was full almost to overflowing. All the staple foods were there, carefully stored, arranged by category, and readily accessible.

Just beside the pantry, a doorway led to the basement. Beth took the flashlight out of her pocket, turned it on, and went downstairs. The broad basement was carpeted and contained a couple of cots, some folding chairs in the corner, and a shelf stocked with tools. But Beth was drawn to the back corner, where a seam was visible in the carpet. She knelt down and pulled back a corner of the carpet, revealing a small recessed handle.

When she pulled it, a section of the floor swung up on hidden hinges, revealing another set of stairs leading to a large subbasement beneath the faux floor. Beth shone her flashlight into the space, revealing a vast cache of supplies. She climbed down the stairs, plucking a clipboard off a nail on the way. Placing the flashlight between her teeth, she took a small pencil from its holder on the clipboard and began to inventory her supplies, going down the list meticulously one by one.

Everything was in place. She had food, water, fuel, tools, even seeds, enough for her family to survive at least three years, and the seeds could help them survive much longer. Although she hoped the loss of power was temporary, a mere hiccup in the grid that would soon be remedied, she looked at the checkmarks on her inventory list and felt reassured. She put the pencil back in place and took the flashlight out from between her teeth.

"We're ready," she said.

As long as her family could get there, they would survive.

5

The backup generators were contained in a row of enormous yellow metal boxes resting on black pedestals inside a large utility room. Shane found the whisper quiet of the uninsulated room nerve-racking. He knew that just one building over, the reactor core temperature was quickly rising out of control.

Landon led the way, forcing the door open with his knees and racing to the nearest generator as Shane caught the door and held it for Violet. He could hear people racing down the hall in both directions behind him. Second shift had just started to arrive, and now everyone was frantic. Landon had a two-way radio clipped to a strap on his wheelchair, and voices smothered in static kept breaking through the quiet.

"Dad, we have to go and get Ruby. She'll be scared and confused sitting there by herself."

"She's safer where she is for now," Shane said, gently moving Violet near the door. "We have to get the power on first. Stay right here. It'll just take a minute."

Violet didn't say anything, but she backed up against the wall and bowed her head. Landon already had the control panel open on the generator, his big plastic flashlight tucked into a space between his thigh and the side panel of his wheelchair.

"Any idea what's wrong?" Shane asked.

"I don't see any obvious problems," Landon replied. "What do you think?"

Shane checked the gauges. Oil level and fuel levels were good. He checked to make sure all the switches were in the right position.

A frantic voice spoke from the two-way. "Get those generators on now! What's the holdup? Are you guys down there yet?"

Landon grumbled under his breath and chose not to respond. He fished around in the circuitry behind the control panel.

"Whoever is at the generator, we need power now," the voice continued. "Is someone on this? We need power *now*!"

"When this is all over, I'm going to find out which mid-management goon that is," Landon grumbled, "and give him a good smack in the face."

"You take the left cheek, I'll take the right," Shane said.

Shane spotted the problem first. A tiny water sensor beneath the control panel. It appeared to have been fried. He tapped it.

"I think this is the culprit right here," he said.

"Good eye," Landon said. "Step back and let me at it. I'll bypass the stupid thing."

Shane stepped back beside Violet. She hadn't moved, still standing against the wall with her head bowed. In fact, she hadn't said a word as they'd worked on the generator. Shane rubbed her back, trying to reassure her, but she didn't react.

"That's it, folks," Landon shouted. "I think we got it. It's showtime."

The generators rumbled to life, each one in succession quickly filling the room with their deep-bellied growl. The lights followed a second later, and then squawks from the two-way that might have been cheers from elsewhere in the building.

Shane and Landon scarcely had a moment to celebrate. They raced back to the control room as fast as they dared, slowed only by Violet, who hugged the wall as she walked. They received cheers from a couple of employees in passing, and Landon gave a dramatic bow in return.

"Yes, yes, we saved the day," he said. "Send a note to human resources."

When Shane got back to his console in the control room, he immediately checked the core temperature and found that while it hadn't significantly dropped, the coolant was flowing. Safe for now. But the generators wouldn't last forever.

While he did that, Landon picked up the phone handset on his console and tried to make a call.

"No phone service," he said, after a moment, setting the phone back down.

Shane opened a browser on his cell phone and navigated to a news website. It wasn't working, so he tried another. This one came up but slowly. He was surprised to find that cell phone service still worked at all. But as soon as he saw the page, his heart sank and his whole body went cold. Splashed across the front page was an image of North America, all of it bathed in red, and two words: *Nationwide Outage!* He clicked the article and started to read.

"Landon, they're saying the power's out across the entire country," he said, struggling to catch his breath. "Much of the European infrastructure is severely damaged as well.."

He tried to click to the second page of the article, but the website crashed. When he reloaded, he couldn't get it back up, and a few seconds of trying other websites revealed the entire internet was down. He turned to Landon, who was huddled in his chair, staring at his own phone. Slowly, he turned and met Shane's gaze.

"They weren't kidding about the CME, I guess," Landon said.

"Yeah, but it must've been huge to affect such a broad area," Shane said. "Landon, we're not prepared for something on this scale. I mean, the country's not prepared."

"You don't have to tell me," Landon replied. "This might have obliterated the entire power grid, knocked out satellites, blasted all kinds of electrical equipment. You know how long it'll take to get the grid back up and running? Months at best. Years, maybe. Heck, they might *never* get it all back up and running." He smacked his forehead. "This is bad. So bad. Look, I'd better check in with the other departments, and I'm not going to shout into the radio like these other idiots. We need to coordinate to keep this place running."

Shane nodded as Landon headed for the door. When Shane turned to watch him leave, his eyes fell on Violet. She had taken a seat behind the console, but she was quiet, too quiet. Shane realized her face had gone extremely pale, and she was biting furiously on her lower lip. Her sunglasses had slid down the bridge of her nose again, and she hadn't bothered to push them back up. Her orange safety helmet was tipped too far back, about to slip off her head.

Shane pushed his chair back and went to her, taking one of her hands. It was cold and clammy, and it trembled in his grip.

"Honey, it's okay," he said.

But her trembling only got worse, and her breathing became fast and shallow. A sheen of sweat broke out on her upper lip.

"Violet, we're okay." He adjusted her helmet. "Listen to me. We're safe now. We got the power back on. The power plant is safe."

When she didn't respond to this, he hugged her, patting her back.

"This is a lot worse than you're telling me," she said, finally, in a tiny voice. "I know what can happen. I know if the core overheats this whole place could explode."

"No, no, that's not going to happen. We're getting the temperature down right now. Everything is fine, I promise. Do you believe me?"

"I guess."

Her trembling had subsided enough that he dared to let go of her.

"You need to talk to Mom," she said. "She wanted you to call. I didn't tell you before because you were busy, and I was scared to interrupt you in case…in case…you know."

As he pulled his cell phone out of his pocket, she pushed her sunglasses back in place.

"Okay, honey, I'll call her right now."

Shane stepped back and dialed Jodi's number. He managed to get her on the first try.

"Shane, finally," she said. The connection wasn't great. Her voice seemed distant. "What's happening? I've been worried sick. Violet said something about the power plant *exploding*."

"We're fine now," he said. "She was a little confused. The plant is not in danger of a meltdown. We've got the backup power running. Have you seen the news? The power outage is all over the place, the entire continent and all the way to Europe."

"Oh my God, Shane, it's that bad?" Jodi replied, pausing a moment, as if struggling to take it in. "You have to get to my mom's outside Macon. We're headed that way. I don't know how Mike is going to hold up. He's not doing well after chemo, and the worst of it probably hasn't even hit him yet. He's exhausted and sick to his stomach, and he said his feet are starting to hurt. All symptoms he's felt before, but worse this time."

"Have you tried to start your car?" Shane said.

"Not yet," Jodi replied. "Let's hope it starts."

"You think it's safe to travel on the highway."

"It has to be. We have to get to Mom's. This might last…a long time."

"Yeah," Shane said, feeling that sinking feeling again. *What if a long time is forever?* "Is Owen there with you? Let me talk to him."

He heard some shuffling as Jodi passed the phone to their son, and then Owen spoke. "Dad, I was stuck in the elevator when the power went out."

"Are you okay?"

"I'm fine. Violet really freaked us out though."

"I know," Shane said. "Listen to me, son. This isn't going to be as simple as a normal drive to Grandma's. No telling what problems you might run into. You have to help your mom and look after your uncle Mike, okay?"

"How can I help anyone?" Owen said.

"You can do it. You're a smart kid. Be safe."

"I'll try, Dad."

"Let me talk to your mom again."

Owen passed the phone back to Jodi.

"Jodi, be safe. What route are you planning to take?"

"We'll take Highway 1 straight to Macon," she said. "Should be a quick drive. It's not an interstate, so maybe fewer people will be on the road. What about you?"

"Interstate 75 down to Atlanta. I'll probably stop by our house on the way and get some clothes and supplies, just in case we're at your mom's for a while. You'll get there before I will. When are you heading out?"

"Right away," she replied. "Please, Shane, get there as soon as you can."

"I will. Love you."

"Love you, too."

He hung up the phone, glanced at the screen, and wondered how much longer cell phone service would hold up. *What if that was the last call?* He put the thought out of his mind and went to his daughter.

6

Shane cycled through menus, checking to make sure everything was in order. The temperature in the core continued to drop, though not quite as fast as he would have hoped. Violet waited for him by the door, her back pressed up against the wall, one hand holding the rim of her orange hardhat.

"You said we might run into problems, Dad. What did you mean by that? You told Owen it won't be a simple drive."

"Well, I'm not sure," Shane replied, exiting out of the menu and stepping away from the console. "I just want them to be cautious, that's all. Speaking of which, we'd better head out."

"But you can't just leave the power plant," Violet said. "It's your job. What will happen if you're not here to keep an eye on it?"

"We'll figure it out. Let me worry about that."

"What about Landon? We should invite him to come with us. He doesn't really have a family of his own."

Shane grabbed his daughter's hand in passing, pulled it away from her hardhat, and headed for the door. "Let's go find him."

"He doesn't have a wife or kids," Violet reminded him. "He doesn't even have his parents anymore. You'll invite him to come with us, won't you? He might be lonely staying here all by himself."

"Yes, sweetheart, he can come with us, if he wants to."

They found Landon in a file room just off the main entry hall. Most of the small space was taken up by a set of large metal shelves stacked from end to end with books and fat plastic binders. Here, the company kept maps, diagrams of the facility, and paper copies of all documentation. Landon had one of the binders open on his lap. When Shane and Violet came up behind him, he was furiously flipping through pages.

"We're leaving," Shane said.

Landon slammed the binder shut, jammed it back onto the shelf, and turned his wheelchair to face them.

"My mother-in-law has a place just outside Macon," Shane continued. "She's a prepper, always has been. We used to think she was a bit…over the top, but it looks like she was the smart one. We can hold out at her house for a long time, whatever happens."

"Sounds like a good idea," Landon said. "Violet doesn't need to be here while everyone's running around in a panic."

"You can come with us," Shane said. "You wouldn't be imposing."

"Grandma has plenty of food," Violet added, "and she won't mind. Kaylee and I can double up, so you can have the guest room. Plus, Ruby knows you, and she likes you."

Landon nodded—somewhat sadly, Shane thought—and made a sweeping gesture with his hand. "We can't leave the plant unattended. Even if we get it properly shut down, a skeleton crew will need to stay behind to keep an eye on the place for a while and monitor the system. I suspect most of the team will head home once they realize how bad it is out there." He grabbed another fat binder and dragged it onto his lap.

"Landon, this is not your responsibility," Shane reminded him. "Let the supervisors handle the long-term safety protocols. Come with us."

Landon shook his head as he flipped open the binder. "Can't do it. Don't trust the suits to do the job properly. We need someone here who knows the equipment, someone who is up close and personal with it every day…someone who doesn't have a family to worry about. I'm staying. It might as well be me."

"Are you sure?"

"Yeah," he said. "I mean, hey, the entire building is pretty much wheelchair accessible so it's easier for me here than anywhere else. But you can do me a favor, if you like." He glanced up at Shane and grinned. "I'm a bit of a prepper myself. Got a whole bunch of stuff in the back bedroom. Would you mind heading over to my house and bringing back as much of it as you can stuff into my Volkswagen?"

"You don't have to stay," Violet said.

"But I am, kid," he said. "Don't worry about me. Shane, the Volkswagen is a '72. It shouldn't be affected by an EMP." He dug into his shirt pocket and produced a couple of ancient keys on an oversized key ring, tossing them at Shane. "Everything is packed together in plastic buckets and labeled, so you won't have to sort through it. Just load up and come back. You know where my house is. It's not far."

Shane held the keys. He hated leaving Landon here. What if things got worse, far worse? Still, it was clear he wouldn't be talked out of it.

"Okay, Landon, if it's what you really want. We'll make sure your van is stocked, so you can hold out a long time. If you change your mind—"

"Thanks," Landon said, cutting him off. He turned his attention back to the binder, flipping through pages. "Good luck, guys. I'll be fine. Everything will be fine."

He didn't sound like he meant it, but Shane took Violet's hand and left.

Ruby was as nervous as Shane had ever seen her, but this was partly due to the fact that Violet wouldn't stop hugging her. The guide dog kept looking around, trying to see out all the van's windows at once, as if she sensed an unseen threat.

"Don't squish her," Shane said.

"Poor girl, she was all alone when the power went off," Violet said.

"The security guys stepped out of the office and left her there. She probably thought I abandoned her."

"I'm sure she was fine, but you're kind of making her nervous right now."

"I can't help it, Dad."

The parking lot was half empty, but Shane spotted a few employees fiddling under the hoods of the vehicles. Just as Landon had said, his old '72 Volkswagen Westfalia was unaffected by the EMP. It was a sturdy old thing, a boxy van from a different era, with faded red paint and a white top. Landon had several modifications on it for his own use, including hand controls for the brake and accelerator, which Shane had disconnected and stored in the back.

The back of the vehicle had a wheelchair dock with straps poking through slits in a carpeted floorboard. Plenty of space to load up supplies for Landon. He could hold out as long as he wanted, though Shane hoped he wouldn't settle in. The nuclear power plant should be fine once it was powered down and the reactors cooled. Still, Shane hated the thought of leaving his friend behind. It didn't seem right.

"Are we really going to abandon him?" Violet asked, as if reading his thoughts. "Poor Landon. He doesn't have anyone."

"We can't force him to come with us," Shane replied. "When Landon makes up his mind, there's no talking him out of it. Trust me. The best we can do is make sure he's as prepared as possible for any situation."

"Well, I don't agree," Violet grumbled, leaning back in her seat and finally detaching herself from Ruby's furry neck. They'd left the hardhats behind, and she reached up to angrily sweep her bangs off her forehead. "We should try to make him come with us. People don't always know what's best for them."

"He wants to keep everyone safe," Shane said. "That's a brave thing to do. Don't you think?"

"I guess so," she finally conceded.

Most of the protestors were gone. Either they had scattered when the power went out—possibly expecting a meltdown, like Violet—or else they had been cleared out by the police. A few lingered, but they'd discarded their signs and were wandering about, confused.

Beyond the gate, Shane spotted a number of stalled cars clogging the roads. Landon lived a few miles from the plant, but it didn't look like it was going to be an easy drive. A few people were thumbing rides by the side of the road, but Shane avoided eye contact. He hated leaving anyone behind, even strangers, but he was on a mission.

Sorry, folks, he thought. *Good luck.*

Sequoyah Access Road, which cut right through the heart of the town of Soddy-Daisy, wasn't too bad. However, when he reached the downtown area and turned onto the highway, he saw stalled vehicles everywhere. He cut away from the highway and used Dayton Pike, a much smaller road that cut through town. That proved to be a mistake. He almost got stuck near downtown when a pickup truck pulled in behind him at a blocked intersection. As stranded drivers glared at him from the sidewalk, he waved the pickup truck back and made a three-point turn.

"Well, this is a mess," he muttered. "The CME zapped most of the newer model cars. They're just two-ton obstacles now."

"Are we stuck?" Violet asked.

"No, but it has become a lot trickier getting anywhere."

He finally resorted to driving through neighborhood streets. Landon's home was located at the end of a long, forested road in the nearby town of Falling Water. However, as he turned onto the street, Shane saw a brand-new 2019 Blazer, a beautiful blue vehicle, stalled across both lanes with the driver's door wide open. The driver was nowhere in sight.

"Hang on," he told Violet. "This might be a little bumpy."

Violet grabbed Ruby's harness with one hand, an armrest with the other. Shane hesitated a moment before turning the van and driving up onto the sidewalk. The old Volkswagen already rode rough, so the bounce of the curb nearly threw him out of his seat. The lap belt held him in place, but he felt the top of his head brush the ceiling.

He tried to swerve back onto the road, but there was a second car stranded behind the SUV. A mailbox on a brick post was straight ahead, so he swerved further off the road instead. The van jounced violently over a small flowerbed, annihilating a few rows of pretty petunias, and then cut across a driveway.

Looking into the rearview mirror, he saw the residue of the obliterated flowers and felt a twinge of guilt. Fortunately, the road opened up again, and he thumped over the curb again to get back in their lane.

"If I make it back this way someday, remind me I owe those people a few bucks for a new flowerbed," he said.

"Dad, what did you do?" Violet said, rocking her head back in the way she did when she was annoyed. "Did you drive through someone's yard?"

"I had to make a new road," he said.

"Dad!"

"I know. I know."

The lanes were open the rest of the way to Landon's house. Landon had half an acre of property surrounded on three side by tall trees. He kept his grass neatly trimmed, and he'd installed broad paved paths between the driveway, the house, and a large storage shed in back. The property was, of course, fully wheelchair accessible, with low-angle ramps to every door and extra wide doorways.

Shane parked close to the house and walked around the van to make sure he hadn't done any damage to the tires or bumpers. He noticed grass and flowers ground into the treads.

"Well, we didn't bust up Landon's van," Shane said. "That's the good news."

Violet let herself out of the van. Ruby instinctively took the lead and started moving toward the front door. They'd been to Landon's house a few times over the years. The dog seemed to remember it.

Shane unlocked the front door and let them into the house. The living room was well kept and sparsely decorated, but the walls were cluttered with shelves and cabinets. Led by Ruby, Violet felt her way to the nearest couch and sat down.

"It'll just be a couple of minutes," Shane told her. "Wait for me here."

Shane went down a short hallway to the back bedroom. Though he'd been at the house before, he'd never gone into this particular room, and when he opened the door, he gasped. The walls were lined with sealed plastic buckets stacked almost to the ceiling. Landon had scribbled the contents of each, along with the date of packing, in permanent marker along the side of each bucket: food, water, first aid supplies, water purification tablets, tools, and much more.

He should've spent some time with my mother-in-law, Shane thought. *They would have had a lot to talk about. They've both been preparing for the end of civilization.*

As Violet waited patiently in the living room, and Ruby curled up on the cushions beside her, Shane began taking supplies out to the van. He couldn't carry more than two buckets at a time—Landon had a lot more upper body strength, and he'd packed them for his own use. By the time Shane dumped his fourth load into the van, his upper arms were screaming in protest. He took a moment to massage each arm, then headed back into the house.

"How much longer, Dad?" Violet asked.

He paused in the foyer to catch his breath. "A couple more minutes. Sorry. It's a lot more work than I expected."

He blew his breath out, gave his left shoulder a gentle squeeze, and started across the foyer.

That's when he heard the distinctive sound of a gun being cocked behind him. It came from the open front door, a loud click followed by a single heavy footfall on the smooth tile floor. Immediately, Ruby rose and turned toward the door, hackles raised and growling. Violet grabbed her harness with both hands and held on tight to keep the dog from leaping off the couch.

Shane scarcely had a moment to think. Acting on instinct, he stepped between Violet and the front door.

"Don't you dare move," came the gruff voice from behind him. "I'll blast you right here and now, I swear to God."

7

E ven though Mike's chemo treatment was done, Erica hadn't left his side. Jodi found them when she returned to the oncology room. Mike was slumped against the arm of his chair, pale and sweating, as the nurse crouched beside him. They both turned as Jodi and Owen entered the room.

"There they are," Mike said. "The lights came back on while you were gone, but it looks like someone sucked out half the wattage. These flickering half-lights might be creepier than full-on darkness. They kind of make me feel like I'm losing my mind. They sure don't help my nausea any."

Owen lingered by the door, but Jodi approached Erica. She wasn't comfortable asking for help, but it couldn't be avoided. They needed medical supplies, and the friendly nurse was the only possible source.

"I think we know what caused the power outage," she said. Something in the sound of her voice must have struck them, for Erica rose, and Mike sat up as best he could in his chair. Jodi proceeded to tell them the story shared by Doomsday Daryl. She held nothing back, painting a bleak picture, and as she spoke, Erica's frown got deeper and deeper

"So, the power could be out for months?" Erica said softly, wringing her hands. "Is that what you're saying?"

"They will have to rebuild the entire power grid," Jodi said. "I have no idea how long that might take, but it won't be easy. It seems to me the best thing anyone can do is find a safe place stocked with supplies and wait it out." She paused a moment before getting to the point. "Speaking of which, we need your help, Erica. I'm taking my family to my mother's house. She has plenty of food and water, but we need medical supplies. Especially with Mike in his current condition."

"What kind of medical supplies?" Erica asked.

"Whatever you can spare," Jodi said. "Bandages, disinfectant, medicine, a bit of everything."

Erica looked from Jodi to Mike and back to Jodi, chewing on a fingernail. "I don't know. I can't just give you medical supplies. I'd be putting my job on the line."

"Maybe not under the current circumstances," Jodi said.

"Under any circumstances. I doubt they'll suspend all of the hospital rules just because the power is out."

"But you believe Daryl's story?"

"Well, it's not completely crazy," Erica replied, "and I agree you can't travel with Mike in his condition. The next couple of days will be hard on him."

"I knew you cared," Mike said weakly, trying to muster up a laugh.

"If we get caught, I'll take the fall," Jodi said. "I'll make up some excuse to get you off the hook."

Erica regarded her silently for a moment. Finally, she nodded and said, "Okay, follow me. Let's do this quick. Maybe no one will notice."

She headed out of the room. Jodi patted Owen in passing and followed her.

"Just act like nothing weird is going on," Erica said over her shoulder.

"Got it," Jodi replied.

Erica led her down a long hallway and around a corner toward a nurse's station. When she greeted a few hospital staff members in passing, she practically whimpered, having trouble following her own advice. She first led Jodi to a small closet just past the nurse's station. Inside, a large cardboard box was piled high with clothing. Someone had scrawled the word *Unclaimed* across the front of the box in black marker.

"This isn't quite what I had in mind," Jodi said from the doorway.

Erica dug into the pile, rooted around, and produced a small duffel bag. "You'll need something to carry the supplies," she said, thrusting the bag at Jodi. "I might as well load you up, so you don't run out of basic first aid supplies. I'll feel better sending Mike out of here if you're prepared to take care of him."

Jodi took the duffel bag from her and glanced left and right down the hallway, making sure they hadn't drawn any undue attention. Everyone seemed engrossed in their own concerns. When she turned back around, she saw Erica wrestling a much larger rolling suitcase out of the bottom of the pile, scattering jackets, hats, shirts, and blankets all over the floor. She extended the handle and slid the suitcase toward Jodi.

"That should do it," she said. "This is the easy part. Nobody's going to wonder why we're getting stuff out of the lost and found. The next part is tricky. I can't let you into the hospital pharmacy, but we have shelves of stock meds and supplies in a small alcove near the nurses station. It'll have to do. I'll let you grab stuff from the shelves while I keep an eye out, but you'll only have a couple minutes. Do you know what you need?"

Jodi worked for the CDC, but not in any sort of medical capacity. Still, she thought she had enough passing knowledge to identify basic medical supplies. "I'll figure it out."

Erica gave her a probing look, lips pressed tightly together. "I'm only doing this because I'm worried about your brother. I don't like the idea of setting him loose into the chaos. But…it's still a dumb thing to do. Don't dawdle. Grab what you want and get out of there fast."

"I know," Jodi said. "I appreciate it. I really do. If you need anything from us…money maybe…"

"No, I don't need money. Well, I *do* need money, but it seems like if I take money for the supplies it makes this all a lot worse. Come on."

Erica pushed past her and went further down the hall. Just as she'd said, the alcove was located near the nurses station, and it contained a few shelves stocked with standard meds and medical supplies.

"I'll be back in two minutes," Erica said. "Try not to be seen, and make as little noise as possible."

The duffel bag in one hand, the rolling suitcase in the other, Jodi approached the shelves. As she walked along the shelf, she grabbed anything that looked useful and shoved it into the duffel bag. She took plenty of bandages and gauze, syringes and antiseptic, and pain relievers like Tylenol and ibuprofen, anti-nausea meds, cold medicine, and copious amounts of antibiotic creams. Once the duffel bag was full, she started filling up the suitcase.

At one point, she heard people right outside the room, and she ducked back out of sight, waiting until they passed.

Finally, a voice spoke.

"Okay, time's up. You need to go."

Jodi dared a glance at the door and saw Erica standing there, beckoning her with both hands. Mike and Owen were with her, Mike leaning heavily against the doorframe. Jodi approached them, handing the duffel bag to Owen.

"Are we planning on opening our own pharmacy?" Owen said, hoisting the duffel bag onto his shoulder. It was practically bursting at the seams.

"We might have to," Jodi replied. "Are you ready to leave?"

Pale as milk, Mike stepped away from the door and made a show of standing up straight. "Ready as I can be."

"I'm ready," Owen said. "Let's please get out of here, Mom."

Erica shut the supply room door, leaning against it for a moment, then turned to them. She looked at Mike, her hands on her hips.

"Are you not going to wait for the doctor?" she said. "I'm sure he's just running behind. We can knock out that PET scan and make sure you're all clear. Wouldn't you feel better hearing it from him?"

"Under the circumstances," Jodi said, "I don't think we should wait."

Mike frowned at Jodi, then nodded. "Yeah, I think it's best not to stick around much longer. Let's pretend like we know I'm cancer free. Just say the words for me, would you?"

Erica gave him a puzzled look. "What do you mean?"

"It would be nice to hear the words before I leave," he said. "*Cancer free*. Just say it, even if we don't know for sure."

"Um…cancer free," Erica said with a shrug. "You're cancer free… most likely."

"Nice." Mike smiled. "That'll do. Thanks."

"You're welcome, for what it's worth," Erica said. "Good luck, guys. Be careful out there."

"Why don't you come with us?" Mike tried to reach for her hand, but then he wobbled and leaned against Owen for support. "Things might get bad here. When people go nuts and start getting hurt—or hurting each other—they're going to descend on the hospital in droves. You don't want to be in the middle of that, do you? Where we're going, we're all set up for the end of the world. We've got a stockpile of food, water, and supplies. There's room for one more in the house."

"I'm sorry, I can't leave," Erica replied, with a sad shrug. "I have to stay here and help. If I abandoned my patients, I would feel awful."

"Well…" Mike ducked his head. "At least let me give you the address of where we're going, just in case you change your mind later."

Jodi was tempted to protest. It wasn't a good idea to spread the news of their location. When people got desperate, they would start looking for those with plenty of food. Still, Erica had risked her job to help them. Mike produced a scrap of paper from his wallet, and Erica pulled a small pencil out of her pocket. As he scribbled the address to their mom's house, Jodi bit her tongue.

"If you need a place to go, you know where to find us," Mike said. "If your GPS doesn't work, just make your way to Macon and ask around. Someone will point you in the right direction."

"Thanks," Erica said, sliding the paper into her pocket. "Maybe it won't get too bad."

"I hope you don't get in trouble because of us," Jodi said.

Erica waved off the comment. "What's done is done. Can't change it now. If things are chaotic enough, maybe no one will notice. Otherwise, I'll be fired, and maybe I'll use the address you gave me. Good luck out there."

We'll need it, Jodi thought

In the parking garage, they saw a few frustrated drivers who couldn't get their cars to start. An early '80s model Good Times van rattled its way to freedom, but it was one of the exceptions. Jodi's truck was a newer Dodge Durango. She was quite fond of it, but getting Mike into the passenger seat took some work. He had leaned on Owen all the way through the hospital, and by the time they reached the garage he seemed quite weak. In the end, they had to bundle him into the seat like a sack of potatoes.

"Don't break anything, please," he said, grimacing in pain. "I'm feeling sort of brittle."

"Sorry, Uncle Mike," Owen said, clicking Mike's seatbelt into place. "Are you okay?"

"I'm hanging in there, kid. Feet hurt, head hurts, stomach hurts, neck hurts, and I have this dumb plastic thing stuck in my arm, but it could be worse. Thanks."

When Mike was settled, Jodi and Owen loaded the medical supplies into the back seat, then Jodi slipped in behind the wheel.

"Cross every finger that it works," she said, sliding the key into the ignition.

She turned the key, and the truck did nothing. Absolutely nothing. She tried again. When it still didn't work, she pulled the key out, took a deep breath, and tried a third time.

"Why are all the cars dead?" Mike asked, gripping his forehead.

"An EMP damages electronics," Jodi said. She looked around. Another older car—it appeared to be a 2002 Pontiac Grand Am—was happily circling down the parking garage toward the exit. "Mostly on really new cars, apparently."

"Mom, what are we going to do?" Owen said. "We can't walk all the way to Grandma's. Do you have any idea how long that would take?"

A nice, new blue Mustang was parked next to them. The hood was up, and a young man was bent over the engine. Jodi opened her door and rose, clearing her throat to get his attention. He looked up at her, grease smeared across the bridge of his nose.

"Pardon me," she said. "When you're done, would you mind taking a look at my truck? It seems to be having a similar problem. I'm willing to pay you for your time."

The young man groaned, shook his head, and slammed the Mustang's hood shut. "No point," he said. "It's dead, just like mine. All the electronics got zapped when the power went off. Unless you're driving an older model, you're not going anywhere. Brand-new cars are toast."

Jodi felt someone tugging on her sleeve. When she turned, Mike pointed out his window. An older Ford F-150 pickup was slowly backing out of the space on the other side. The man behind the steering wheel looked gaunt, pallid, and glassy-eyed. He had thin patches of hair on top of his head and a small bandage on his left temple.

"I know that guy," Mike said. "He's been getting chemo treatments. We've chatted a few times in the waiting room. I'm sure he'll remember me. Get his attention quick!"

Jodi stepped out of her car, turned toward the pickup, and waved both hands until the driver glanced in her direction. He seemed disinterested until Mike opened his door and gave him a thumbs-up. He rolled down his window and leaned out.

"Hey, Mike, are you stranded here like all the rest of these people?" he said. He had a sickly wheeze.

"Yeah, Bill, can you believe the timing?" Mike replied. "I was just on the verge of puking my guts out when the power went off. Are you safe to drive?"

"I'm fine," Bill replied, with a mischievous smile. "Don't tell the nurses. They think I got picked up by a friend. I suppose y'all want a ride?"

"We'd sure appreciate it," Mike said. "I promise not to throw up on your seats."

Bill shrugged and gestured for them to get in. "Hurry up and get in before everyone else wants to pile in with you."

Mike took the front seat, while Jodi squeezed onto the narrow bench in the extended cab with Owen, the medical supplies squished between them. As Bill pulled away, she noted quite a few disgruntled looks from stranded drivers, some of them openly hostile.

"How far you guys need to go?" Bill asked.

"Just as far as you're willing to take us," Jodi said. "We don't want to be a bother."

Bill said nothing to this as he pulled out of the parking lot into a narrow street that ran along the side of the hospital. Problems became apparent almost immediately. As they approached an intersection, they saw vehicles stalled all over the place. Traffic at the intersection was at a dead standstill. The Good Times van they'd seen earlier was inching along a strip of grass between the road and a fence.

Muttering curses, Bill stopped and turned around, taking them through a large neighborhood. Even then, they were forced to divert at one point when they encountered a large sedan that had plowed into a streetlight and spun sideways across a narrow street. Bill was forced to go well out of their way, taking a meandering course through the neighborhood to get around the blockage.

"It's like everyone forgot how to drive," Bill muttered. "Can't hardly get anywhere."

The residential streets eventually emptied onto another major road half a mile away from the hospital, but it was blocked in both directions with cars. Bill managed to go around a few of them by driving on the sidewalk, then he turned down another side street. Here the congestion was only marginally better, and he kept having to jump the curb and take to the sidewalk. Each time, the shocks on his F-150 squealed like they were in agony.

In the space of half an hour, Jodi estimated they made it about three miles from the hospital. Bill's pickup seemed to be riding rougher already. It clearly wasn't built for the constant bumping and thumping. Finally, Bill pulled into a parking lot in front of a liquor store and killed the engine.

"I can't take you any farther than this," he said. "It'll take us the rest of the afternoon just to get across town."

"Are you sure?" Mike replied. "Can you at least get us—?"

"My home's not far from here," Bill said, speaking over him, "and I can't afford to run my truck into the ground just trying to get you guys somewhere. I'm sorry; that's the way it is. I'm afraid the ride's over."

Scowling, Mike started to say something else, but Jodi leaned forward and laid a hand on his shoulder. "It's fine," she said. "At least he got us this far. Thanks, Bill. We'll take it from here."

"Good luck," Bill said. "I'm sure someone's running some kind of taxi service. You'll catch another ride before too much longer. Stick your thumbs out, and…" The rest of what he meant to say was lost in a fit of coughing and retching as Bill clutched his belly and curled over his steering wheel. Mike leaned over, as if to help him, but Bill waved him out of the truck.

As they climbed out of the truck with the bags, Owen gave his mom a horrified look. As soon as they were out, Bill slammed the passenger door shut and drove away, leaving them at the edge of the parking lot in the middle of Augusta in a vehicle graveyard. Jodi looked at Mike, at Owen.

"My God, Jodi, what do we do now?" Mike asked. "We're still smack-dab in the middle of Augusta with no form of transportation except our aching feet."

Jodi tightened her grip on the handle of the suitcase. "We walk," she said. "I'm afraid there's no other choice. Are you up to it?"

"My feet hurt, but they still work," Mike said. "I guess we'll just see how long I can last."

"I'm sorry," Jodi said.

"I don't blame you," Mike said. "I blame the sun. First, it gave me skin cancer, and now it's trying to destroy the world." With what appeared to be a forced smile, he shook his fist at the sky.

"If you need to stop, let me know," Jodi said.

Pulling the suitcase along behind her, she headed in the direction of the nearest highway, though it was well out of sight. Mike, clinging to Owen's shoulder, fell in beside her. Jodi tried not to let the abject fear show on her face. They were at least 125 miles from her mother's house with no easy way to get there. Mike was weak and sick, and they were lugging two heavy cases full of medical supplies.

We'll never make it, she thought.

8

Poor Mrs. Eddies didn't make it out of her house much these days, and her little statuary garden beside the front porch was overgrown with weeds. A concrete angel was slowly being consumed by green, its face peering out of a tangle of vines. Beth knew Mrs. Eddies had a couple of grandsons who were local, but they rarely visited. A home care provider also stopped by a couple of hours each day, but there were no vehicles in the driveway at the moment.

Beth held Kaylee's hand as they approached the front door. They'd left Bauer at home, and Beth could hear him barking furiously in the distance. The little Schnauzer didn't like being left behind.

"Is Mrs. Ebby coming to our house?" Kaylee asked.

"She might," Beth said, "if she's able. I expected to see her caregiver here. You'd think the agency would send someone out to check on clients, especially the ones with special medical needs."

"What kind of needs, Grammy?"

"Well, Kaylee, Mrs. Eddies has a problem in her lungs called COPD," Beth said. "It makes it hard for her to breathe."

"Is that like asthma?" Kaylee asked. "There's a girl at school that has asthma, and sometimes she can't play at recess."

"Yes, it's something like that," Beth said. "Mrs. Eddies used to smoke, and even though she quit, the cigarettes did damage to her lungs. Eventually, it caught up to her."

"It caught up to her?" asked Kaylee, clearly confused by the expression. "She didn't run fast enough?"

"She didn't quit soon enough," Beth corrected, "and now she has to do breathing treatments. Let's hope she's okay."

A large welcome mat took up much of the porch. Beth stooped down, bracing herself against the front door, and lifted a corner of the mat to reveal a hidden house key. She retrieved it and unlocked the door. Easing the door open, she poked her head inside and was immediately assaulted by stale, musty air. A wooden coat rack sat in a corner of the foyer, a dusty yellow raincoat hanging from a hook. Beyond the foyer, a dim hallway stretched toward the back of the house. Mrs. Eddies' bedroom door at the end of the hall was ajar.

"Mrs. Eddies?" Beth called. "It's Beth Bevin. Mrs. Eddies? Are you here?"

The whole house was utterly quiet. Slipping through the front door, Beth pulled Kaylee along behind her.

"Mrs. Eddies, are you alright?" Beth called, as she moved down the hall. "I just stopped by to see if you need anything."

"It smells yucky in here," Kaylee said. "Like old soup. Maybe she had lunch and forgot to clean it up."

"I don't know, Kaylee. Let's just hope she's okay."

"Maybe she needs help with the dishes," Kaylee suggested. "We could help her."

"I hope that's all she needs," Beth said.

When they reached the end of the hall, Beth pushed the bedroom door open, but she couldn't see Mrs. Eddies' bed from this angle. She stepped into the room and turned to the far corner. A portable oxygen machine sat on a nightstand beside the bed, a breathing tube running toward the pillow, where Mrs. Eddies' tuft of white hair was just visible above the blanket. The power light on the machine was dark, as was the electronic alarm clock beside it.

As Beth approached the bed, Kaylee ducked behind the bedroom door and peered around the edge. Maybe she sensed something was wrong. Beth grabbed the blanket and eased it back, steeling herself. For Kaylee's sake, she dared not react.

She uncovered Mrs. Eddies' face, and it was immediately clear the older woman was gone. Based on the yellowish color of her face and her half-lidded eyes, she'd been gone a while. Beth pressed a finger to her neck and checked her pulse anyway. Nothing.

"Is she taking a nap?" Kaylee said.

Though normally not one to hide the truth, in this instance Beth didn't think it a good idea to tell Kaylee she might be in the presence of a corpse. Her granddaughter still felt relatively safe, and it seemed wise to keep it that way.

"That's right," Beth said. "Taking a nap. Let's be really quiet so we don't wake her."

Kaylee pressed a finger to her lips and made a shushing sound. "I'll be super quiet, Grammy. I promise."

I should have checked on her sooner, Beth thought. But, then again, what could she have done? She didn't have a spare oxygen machine in storage.

She pulled her phone out and dialed 911, surprised to find that cell service still worked. It took a few rings before the dispatcher answered.

"Nine-one-one, what is your emergency?"

Beth quickly informed her of the situation, careful how she worded it for Kaylee's sake. "She's been without her oxygen for a couple of hours. I'm not sure what you can do for her, but I just thought someone should take a look."

"It sounds like your friend may already be gone, but if you want, you can attempt to give her CPR. Do you know how?"

"I do," Beth said, "but it's too late for that. Believe me, it's too late."

"I'm sorry to hear that, ma'am. We'll send someone when we can, but I can't tell you how long that'll be. We only have a couple of func-tioning vehicles at the moment. None of our newer ambulances are working. There have been numerous reports of electrical fires in homes and businesses across Macon. We're trying to get to everyone, but we're simply forced to triage our responses."

"I understand," Beth said. "There might not be anyone here when they arrive, so I'll leave a key under the mat. Thank you."

She hung up and laid a gentle hand on Mrs. Eddies' stomach.

"I'm so sorry, dear," she said. "Sorry you were here all by yourself. Sorry I couldn't help. I don't want to think about what it must've been like, but you certainly deserved better."

She pulled the cannula out of Mrs. Eddies' nose and set it on the nightstand beside the oxygen machine. Then she laid the blanket over her face and turned away. She left the room, snagging Kaylee's hand in passing.

"I don't have to take a nap, too, do I?" Kaylee asked, as they walked back down the hallway. "I'm not tired."

"No, not now. We'll get a good night's sleep tonight." They passed a framed photograph of Mrs. Eddies from many years earlier, when she'd been a robust and sharp-eyed woman. Beth felt a moment of sharp regret—regret and guilt—as she hurried past.

She stepped outside and shut the front door, setting the deadbolt. Then she slipped the key back under the welcome mat.

"Grammy, who did you call?" Kaylee asked.

"Just some people," Beth replied. When that didn't seem to satisfy Kaylee, she added, "Some people who can come and check on Mrs. Eddies later." She knelt beside the garden and pulled some of the weeds away from the concrete angel. It seemed appropriate somehow. Thinking aloud, she said, "I wonder how many people across the country have experienced a similar fate? Just think of all the sick and elderly who are alone with no one to help them."

"What are you talking about?" Kaylee asked.

"Oh, just thinking about all the people having problems," Beth said. She took Kaylee's hand and started back toward her house. "We're going to have to help them. With the power not working, there are going to be a lot of people in need."

"We have lots and lots of flashlights," Kaylee offered.

"Yes, we do." Beth managed a laugh. "Yes, we sure do."

"We can share."

"That's right," Beth said, hugging Kaylee. "It's good to share with people in need. I love your attitude."

They walked back to Beth's house and met a frantic Bauer at the sliding glass door in back. While Kaylee petted and reassured the dog, Beth went to the refrigerator. She'd gathered up all the meat from the big freezer in the garage, piled it on a platter, and covered it in plastic wrap. She pulled the platter out now, straining under the weight of all that meat. Stepping carefully, she carried it to the propane grill on the back porch and set it down.

As she opened the grill, she noticed Kaylee staring back across the yard to Mrs. Eddies' house. The little girl seemed to be deep in thought, as if she was trying to figure out a puzzle.

"Grammy, was something wrong with her?" she asked. "Was Mrs. Ebby hurt? Is that why you called someone? You told the person on the phone, 'It's too late for that.' What is it too late for?"

Instead of answering, Beth waved her over. "Come here and help me prepare lunch."

Kaylee persisted. "Was it because of her lungs? Did she get so sick in her lungs she needed a doctor?"

"Mrs. Eddies has been sick a long time, yes," Beth replied. "Now, stop worrying about it and come help me."

This finally seemed to satisfy her, and Kaylee bounded over to the porch.

"Pull the plastic wrap off the meat for me, would you?" Beth said. "Be careful not to drop any of the meat on the ground."

As Kaylee struggled to get the plastic wrap off, Beth lit the burner on the grill. The platter was piled high with steaks, burger patties, sausages, and chicken wings. Kaylee looked at it and scrunched up her face.

"That's a lot of food, Grammy," she said. "We can't eat all of it. That's, like, a hundred steaks. Daddy can't even eat that many."

"Well, honey, I don't want all of this meat to go bad," Beth explained. "It'll spoil unless we cook it, cure it, or smoke it, and the first option is the easiest at the moment. It'll keep longer if it's cooked. Maybe we can have a big dinner when your mom and dad get here. How does that sound?" She removed a large set of tongs from a hook on the side of the grill and began laying the meat in neat rows over the fire.

"It'll take a long time to cook," Kaylee said.

"It will," Beth agreed, "and I'll cook it all. We're going to save as much as we can before it all goes bad. That's all we can do, pumpkin. Just save as much as we can before it all goes bad."

9

Shane tried his best to remain calm, the sound of the gun being cocked lingering in his mind. Ruby was pulling against her harness, trying to lunge over the armrest of the couch and leap at the front door. He had never seen the dog so desperate to attack someone.

"Ruby, calm down," he said. "It's okay, girl."

In a last-ditch attempt to stop the dog from attacking, Violet wrapped her arms around her neck and buried her face against her back. The unseen attacker spoke again. He sounded gruff, half-crazed with either fear or rage.

"Turn around very slowly," he said. The man had a hint of Georgia twang. "Keep your hands where I can see them. I have no qualms about blasting you in the back."

Shane turned, holding his hands out to either side, trying not to make any sudden movements. He felt his heart pounding in his throat, in his temples. How could he get Violet out of this situation safely?

Give the man whatever he wants, he thought.

Their attacker was a gnarled old man with flinty blue eyes and a scruffy gray beard covering his cheeks and chin. Despite his age, he looked quite strong, upper arms straining against the sleeves of a green Members Only jacket. He was also holding an old Browning shotgun with a shiny black barrel pointed directly at Shane's chest.

"We don't want any trouble," Shane said.

"You *got* trouble," the old man said. "I watched you pull up in that van. You didn't think nobody would notice, but I live right next door. You've got about three seconds to tell me what you're doing loading up on Landon's stuff."

"You're a neighbor," Shane said. That was better than he'd feared. "Sir, we're not robbing the house. I work with Landon."

"Prove it," he said.

Shane's only proof was his work ID, which was in his wallet. Would this crazy old man shoot him if he went for it?

"I can show you my ID from Sequoyah Power Plant," Shane said. "It's in my back pocket. Landon sent us to get supplies for him, so he can stay behind and keep an eye on the place for a while."

"Show me," the old man said. "Pull it out real, real slow. I'm ready for any funny business, so don't think you can get the drop on me."

Violet whispered calming words to Ruby, who was alternating between growling and barking. Moving slowly and deliberately, Shane reached back and drew his wallet out of his pants pocket. Seeing the great black eye of the shotgun barrel pointed at his chest made his skin crawl. He was one twitchy finger away from being killed in front of his daughter.

"Don't you know what's happened out there?" Shane said. "Have they told you anything about the power outage?"

He flipped open his wallet to reveal his work ID. When he did, the neighbor leaned in close to get a look, and the cold barrel of his shotgun pressed against Shane's chest.

"No one's told me a thing," the neighbor replied, "but it all seems fishy to me. My lights went out, my TV went out, even my laptop died, and it was on battery power. Sounds like the government's up to something. Who else can destroy a laptop that's running on battery power? Some kind of satellite weapon, that's my guess."

"It wasn't the government," Shane said. "It was a geomagnetic storm caused by the sun. The whole power grid is fried."

The neighbor grunted. "Seems like a story the government would tell. Personally, I'm skeptical about whatever all this is. But your ID seems legit," he said, lowering the gun. "I guess you're okay."

"Thanks for the approval," Shane said bitterly. "Does that mean you're not going to murder us in cold blood?"

"Hey, I thought you were robbing the house," the neighbor said with a scowl. "We look out for each other in this neighborhood. It's a small town, and we don't put up with funny business. Strangers stand out like a sore thumb."

"You didn't recognize Landon's van?"

"You could have stolen it."

"I could have, but I didn't," Shane said, fear giving way to anger. "What if you'd shot me by accident?"

The neighbor gave him a troubling half-smile. "It wouldn't have been an accident. If you were up to no good, I'd already be burying you in the backyard. Good thing you had ID. Now, we get to be buddies."

"Okay, that's fine," Shane said. "If you don't mind, I'm kind of busy. Landon is waiting for us back at the power plant."

The old man uncocked the shotgun, setting it down in a corner of the foyer. "If this really was caused by the sun, what does that mean for the big picture?"

"It means the power is going to be down a long, long time," Shane said. Ruby had ceased barking, but Shane could tell by her wheezing breaths that she was still on edge. "The power plant is shutting down, the reactors being cooled, but Landon is staying behind to keep an eye on things. We're bringing him supplies at his request. We're not robbing him."

The neighbor extended a hand to Shane. "Okay, I got it. I'm Larry. Sorry if I startled you."

Somewhat reluctantly, Shane shook his hand. "You could have asked a few questions before you pointed a gun at me," he said. "Maybe your first reaction shouldn't be shooting people."

"What are all those big plastic buckets you're putting in the van?" Larry asked, ignoring his comment.

"Come on out to the van. I'll show you."

"Dad, are we safe now?" Violet asked.

"You're safe, girl," Larry said. "Y'all can't blame me for assuming the worst. People have been jumpy all afternoon. I heard people screaming in the street, yelling at each other, and making all kinds of noise."

"Stay right here, honey," Shane said. "I'll be right back."

Shane almost led Larry down the hall to the back bedroom, but then he thought better of it. He didn't know Landon's feelings about this particular neighbor. Maybe he wouldn't want crazy Larry rooting around in his house. Instead, Shane slipped past him and went to the van, showing him the rows of plastic buckets he'd stacked in the back. He pointed out the neat writing on each of the buckets.

"Ol' Landon had all these stored in his house?" Larry said, leaning into the van to get a good look.

"Yeah, and more," Shane replied.

Larry took it all in and whistled softly. "That's a lot of food." He began reading labels out loud. "Rice, flour, wheat, MREs, water tablets, powdered eggs...wow, it's like Y2K all over again. My grandpa had a closet full of MREs back then, and he never needed it. We threw it all out after he died."

"You're going to wish you had a closet full of MREs like your grandpa," Shane said. "You'll definitely need them now."

Larry waved off this comment. "I had no idea Landon was a hoarder," he said. "Looks like he was prepared for the end of the world."

"Seems like all the smart people were," Shane replied.

"I don't know about smart," Larry said, "The man's got no wife or kids. How much food did he think he was going to need? It's a little bit crazy for a man who lives alone to have so much, don't you think?"

"This morning, I might have agreed with you, but to be honest, it doesn't seem so crazy now."

"Well, if you say so," Larry said. "Maybe the hoarders had it right all along. Let's hope Landon plans to spread the wealth a little bit."

"That's for him to decide," Shane said.

"You still loading up the van?"

"Yeah, I can fit a few more buckets in here," Shane said, moving back toward the house. "I want to take as much as I can. No telling how long he'll be stuck at the power plant."

"Need some help?" Larry asked. "I'm kind of interested to see how many rooms he's got packed to the gills."

Shane's heart was still racing. He'd never had a gun pointed at him before, and it wasn't an easy feeling to shake off. Larry seemed a little too curious about Landon's stash, and quite frankly, Shane was ready to be rid of the guy. He couldn't go from someone shoving a shotgun in his chest to being their buddy the next minute.

"To be honest, Larry, I'd rather handle it myself," Shane said. "You should probably head back home and see to yourself. We'll be out of here soon. Sorry about the confusion."

Larry gave him a look that was half-annoyed, half-disappointed. He followed Shane back to the house, and for a moment Shane feared he might come inside and root around anyway. Instead, he grabbed his shotgun from the foyer and tucked it under his arm.

"When you see Landon again, tell him I said good luck not getting us all irradiated," Larry said. "If anyone can make sure the reactors are safe, I suppose he can. Maybe I'll trade him for some food later on, if he ever makes it back this way. One of my antique guns should get me a bucket of rice or something, I would think."

Shane couldn't tell if the man was joking, so he nodded. "I'll mention it, but I'm not sure when Landon will make it back this way. He has a lot of work ahead of him."

With a final disappointed look into the house, Larry turned and walked away. Shane watched him head across the yard to the house next door, but he didn't breathe a sigh of relief until the neighbor went inside.

"Sorry about that," he said to Violet. "I didn't consider the possibility that we would look like looters."

"He didn't just point the gun at you," Violet said. "He cocked it like he was really going to shoot you. I heard it."

"He did," Shane confessed.

"Is everyone going to become paranoid now?" Violet said. She was still holding tight to Ruby, but the dog had ceased growling and started panting instead. "Is everyone going to assume the worst?"

"I hope not, but…we'll be more careful from now on. I shouldn't have let him sneak up behind me like that. From now on, I'll be a little more careful."

"Dad, please hurry and load up the van," Violet said. "I don't want to be here anymore. What if there are more weird neighbors like that?"

"I'll work as fast as I can," Shane said. "Is Ruby okay?"

Violet petted Ruby and hugged her again. "She's better. She really wanted to bite him. I've never seen her get so mad before, not at the mailman, not at anyone. I guess she knew Larry was dangerous."

"I'm glad she's protective of you," Shane said, "but I'm even gladder you held on tight."

He hurried to the back bedroom and resumed loading up the van. He made three more trips, filling up the back of the van. The last thing he grabbed was a small tool chest, which he slid in behind the driver's seat next to a rolled-up blanket that Landon had stored there. Then he escorted Violet and Ruby to the passenger seat, locked Landon's house up tight, and got behind the wheel. He still felt shaky from his encounter with Larry, and it took him a couple of tries to get the key into the ignition.

"Dad, are you okay?" Violet asked, clicking her seatbelt in place.

"I will be," he replied. "Just trying to shake off the memory of my new buddy Larry."

"He had a creepy voice," Violet said. "Even when he was trying to be friendly."

"Yes, I know what you mean."

He got the van started and backed down the driveway. As he pulled away from the house, he noticed Larry staring at him from the living room window of the house next door, the shotgun still tucked under his arm.

On the way back down the street, he was forced once again to mount the curb to avoid the stalled vehicles. This time he was careful not to tear through the flowerbed, cutting around the yard instead and sparing the dozen or so petunias that had survived his last pass.

The drive to the power plant was worse than the drive to Landon's house. More people had learned the hard way that their vehicles didn't work. Many were under their hoods trying to figure out what was wrong. Others were standing in the streets, as if waiting for someone to come along and make everything work again.

Shane knew enough this time to avoid the highway, but it made little difference. People and stalled vehicles were everywhere, and many of them waved at the van in passing, trying to flag down a ride. At one point, they passed a young mother with a baby in her arm and a toddler clutching her skirt. They were standing on the curb, and it was clear they'd all been crying. The mother made a half-hearted wave at the van, but Shane had no room for them. The back was packed with supplies.

"These poor people," he muttered. "What are they all going to do? There must be hundreds, if not thousands, stranded across our area. I can't imagine the domino effect of something like this—people who can't get home from work, sick people who can't make it to the hospital, police and EMTs who can't go anywhere. What a mess."

"I can't wait until we're at Grandma's," Violet said. "I can hear people shouting and cussing through the windows. Just now, I thought I heard someone crying. The world sounds...nervous. It makes me uncomfortable."

"Sorry, Violet. We'll get underway as soon as we can."

When he finally reached the front gate of the plant, he saw a few protestors still lingering in the grass. All of their signs had been discarded on the ground, and they seemed mostly to be stranded now. A couple of them were hiking down the middle of the road, and they glared at Landon's van in passing. Another was smacking a cell phone and shouting curses. Maybe he'd lost cell service.

The world was bad enough already, but Shane dreaded a world without functioning phones. As he pulled up to the gate, the anxious guard recognized him and waved him through.

Try not to think too far down the road, Shane told himself. *Concentrate on what's next.*

That was easier said than done when the world was full of people on edge.

10

The cooling towers and containment building looming in front of the river seemed ominous now, a vast powder keg being held together by generators in a closet and a relentless engineer in a wheelchair. Shane spotted a few employees in the parking lot, some still working on their cars, others wandering off into the distance. He was alarmed to see a couple members of the security team walking away.

Nice to know when the world's falling apart most people will abandon their posts, he thought. Then again, hadn't he done the same?

He pulled up to the wheelchair ramp in front of the double-door entrance to the power plant and put the van in park. He sat there a moment, considering his next step, then pulled the key out of the ignition.

"Violet, I'm going to do something that would definitely get me fired under normal circumstances," he said, though he knew it was probably a mistake to say it. "I'll be right back. Sit tight."

"That doesn't sound like a good idea," Violet replied. "Are you sure? You might need your job again after all of this is over."

"I doubt anyone will hold it against me under the circumstances. I'm doing this for Landon's sake. Be right back."

He reached back behind the driver's seat, sliding his arm alongside Ruby's big fuzzy body until he found the tool chest he'd grabbed from Landon's house. Opening it, he fished around inside until he found a screwdriver. Then he hopped down out of the van and approached the front entrance. Normally, only one of the doors was unlocked, but there were crash bars on both of them. On rare occasions, when they needed to move some large piece of equipment into or out of the building, they would open both of them. It was a large opening, certainly wide enough for the Westfalia.

Just inside the entrance, a large open lobby gave way to the security area. Though Shane had seen employees scattering across the parking lot, he was still shocked to see no one staffing the area.

Why would management let the security team leave? he wondered. *Especially now.*

Maybe they hadn't asked.

Shane used the crash bars to open both doors, then set the door stops in place. There was a mullion separating the two doors, but Shane had seen it removed before. Fortunately, the mullion wasn't keyed, so removing it was as simple as unscrewing a few screws from the top fitting. As he did this, he kept glancing over his shoulder, expecting someone to come running from the security office to curse him out. But the metal detector and x-ray machines sat there in the hallway like abandoned relics of an earlier age.

With the screws removed, he pulled the vertical bar out of its frame and set it to one side, then he hurried back to the van.

"Can you please tell me what's going on?" Violet asked. "I heard some kind of clanking sound."

Shane started the van, backed up, and circled around. "I'm trying to get the van into a safer location so Landon is less likely to be looted or have the vehicle stolen. It'll also make it easier to unload the supplies."

He backed up toward the wheelchair ramp then kept going, bumping up onto the sidewalk and then backing right through the open doors into the lobby.

"Are you driving *into* the building?" Violet said. "It sounds like we're inside. Can you do that?"

"I just did it," he replied, "but under normal circumstances security would chase me out of the building if they saw me doing this."

"Dad!"

"We don't have a choice. Landon may be living out of this van for a while. It's going to be the only halfway comfortable place to sleep. I don't think there's a single padded chair or carpeted floor in the entire building. We can't have our friend lying on cold tiles at night."

"I guess that's true," Violet said. "We should have got him a pillow from the house. What's he going to lay his head on, Dad?"

"I didn't think about that," Shane said. "Maybe he can use one of those big plastic binders from the library."

"That's not the same."

He backed the car all the way across the lobby, easing it into a far corner near the hallway. Then he killed the engine and went to close the lobby doors again. As he screwed the mullion back in place, he noticed some people far across the parking lot watching him, a few of the idle protestors from before. He shut the doors and went back to the van.

As he opened the sliding door on the side of the van, he heard the distinctive metal sound of wheels coming down the hallway. When Shane stepped around the back of the van, he saw Landon passing through the security area.

"Hey, buddy, I thought I heard some funny business going on down here," Landon said. He spotted the van then and gaped in amazement. "Wow, you got that whole thing in here. Impressive. Looks a little bit like the showroom at a used car lot. I'll give you fifty bucks for the crappy old van."

"Hey, this crappy van is one of the only working vehicles on the road," Shane said. "You chose wisely."

"I just needed something to haul the wheelchair around," Landon said, "and I didn't want a full-size van."

"Well, it's pretty bad out there," Shane said. "People are stranded all over the place."

"Yeah, I heard a few rumors from other employees who've been in contact with family. Sounds like things are quickly turning into a big, miserable mess."

Shane began unloading the buckets, lining them up along the wall in the lobby. As he did, Landon retrieved a flatbed handcart from a closet near the security office, pushing it ahead of his wheelchair.

"You have a lot more supplies at your house," Shane said. "I can bring a second load if you want. You might need them."

"Nope, this'll last quite long enough," Landon said, as he began stacking the buckets on the handcart. "If things aren't resolved by the time I run out of food, we'll be in a lot bigger trouble here at the plant. More food won't much matter at that point. Tell you what, I want you to go back to my place and take the rest of the supplies with you, then get Violet somewhere safe. Your family could use the stuff, and I don't want it to go to waste."

"I can't take your emergency supplies," Shane said, helping him load the handcart. "Why don't you come with us? There's no need to stay here. Why should you accept all the risk? It seems like everyone else has fled."

"Most of them, yeah," Landon said, dragging the last of the buckets onto the handcart. "Management called an impromptu meeting, and most of the employees complained about wanting to go home and check on family or pets. They almost had a mutiny on their hands, so they agreed to leave a skeleton crew in place and let everyone else leave…except then most of the skeleton crew left, too. So, you see, it's more important than ever that I stay. Anyway, as I said earlier, the world outside is not a convenient place for a guy in a wheelchair. I have the run of this place. It's my domain."

Shane gave his friend a concerned look. He hated to leave him. Imagining Landon roaming the halls by himself, trying to keep the whole plant in check, was a disquieting thought, but it seemed unavoidable now. Finally, he shook Landon's hand.

"Be safe," he said.

"Same to you," Landon replied. "Violet is your priority, friend, okay?"

"Yeah, I sure hate leaving you alone here."

Landon shook his head. "I want to do this. You're not leaving me. Now, quit feeling guilty about things that aren't your decision and get out of here."

Reluctantly, Shane went to the van and opened the passenger door. Violet was stroking Ruby's head and rocking back and forth. She was clearly getting nervous again. Shane took her hand in both of his.

"He's still not coming with us," she said.

"No, but he'll be okay," Shane said. "He has enough food, water, and supplies to last for months and months, and by then, they'll have the power back on."

"Months and months," Violet whispered, shaking her head.

Her sunglasses had slid down her nose again, and Shane gently pushed them back in place. Then he pulled her out of the van. Ruby dutifully padded along beside them as they left the building. Shane had parked his car in the front row of the parking lot, his nice, shiny Jeep Cherokee sitting in the midst of two dozen other nice, shiny vehicles that had been abandoned. As soon as he went to load Violet and Ruby into the back of the car, he noticed a problem—when he opened the door, the interior light didn't come on.

He tried to start the vehicle anyway, climbing into the driver's seat and turning the ignition. Nothing happened, but he turned it a few more times just to be sure. He considered checking under the hood, but he knew it would be useless. The car was as dead as a brick.

"Next time I buy a car, remind me to buy an old clunker," he said, smacking the steering wheel in frustration. "I don't think we're going anywhere in the Cherokee."

"If we can't leave," Violet said, "does that mean we're stuck here? Are we going to have to stay in the power plant with Landon?"

Shane considered their predicament. Unfortunately, there was only one other option, but he hated to do it. Still, he had to get Violet to safety, and he'd promised Jodi he would head to Macon. Already, they were wasting time, and within a couple hours of losing power, the world had become less safe.

"We're not stuck here," he said, finally. "Come on. I know what we need to do."

He led Violet and Ruby back into the building. Landon was lining up the handcart to push it through the security area when they stepped into the lobby.

"Let me guess," Landon said, glancing at them over his shoulder. "Your car has breathed its last, and you need a ride."

"So it would seem," Shane replied. He led Violet back to the van and let her sit inside, shutting the passenger door.

Landon spun the wheelchair around and grinned at him. "Well, I'll spare you the awkwardness of having to ask, old pal. You can take the van. I *want* you to take it, but only on one condition."

"What's that?"

"Promise me you'll go back to my house and take the rest of the supplies with you," Landon said. "Someone needs to use them, and if they just sit there in the house, they'll get stolen sooner or later."

Shane thought of gnarled old neighbor Larry and shuddered.

"Okay, fine," he said. "We'll do it. Sorry, I hate to leave you without a vehicle."

"Hey, I'm not going anywhere," Landon said.

"Where are you going to sleep at night?" Shane asked. "I assumed you would use the van."

Landon wheeled over to the van and opened the side door. "I've got a solution to that." He leaned inside and dug in between the driver's seat and the toolbox, pulling out a rolled-up blanket. He unrolled it, revealing that it was actually two blankets. They were handwoven of some coarse fabric, probably souvenirs from a trip south of the border. He laid one over the handle of his wheelchair and stuffed the other one back behind the driver's seat.

"This is all I need for a good night's sleep," Landon said. "Believe me, it won't be the first time I've slept in rough conditions. Now, let's get you on the road." He dug into his pants pocket, pulled out his wallet, and retrieved a small, folded piece of paper. He glanced in Violet's direction and then, speaking softly, he said, "Here, you'll need this. It's the combination to the gun cabinet in my bedroom.

Take everything in there. Don't let some scumbag break in and steal my guns."

"I'll bring a few back here," Shane said, taking the piece of paper. "You need a way to protect yourself."

"I'm already protected." Landon wheeled to the back of the van and opened the door. Then he grabbed an edge of the carpet inside and rolled it back, revealing a custom storage space beneath. It was empty. "While you were outside, I unloaded the cache right here." He shut the back door and jerked a thumb over his shoulder at the hand-cart. Shane could see the edge of a rifle stock poking out from between the buckets, and he signaled for Landon to keep his voice down. He didn't want Violet to overhear them discussing guns.

"I've got an AR-15, a Glock 19, and my trusty Remington shotgun, along with plenty of ammo," Landon said, speaking softly. "An army could storm the power plant, and I'd be able to hold them off right here in the lobby. Fill the space in the van with the guns from my cabinet."

"Wow, I never knew you took this prepper business so seriously," Shane said. "I have to tell you, Landon, I don't really know how to shoot. I don't have much gun experience. I'm sure my aim is terrible."

"Well, then, get over here." Landon wheeled back over to the hand-cart. "I've got two more AR-15s and a Glock 17 in the gun cabinet. I'll show you the basics of the rifle and pistol before you go."

Landon picked up the Glock and dropped the magazine as Shane approached hesitantly. In truth, the guns unnerved Shane a bit. He'd never actually held a pistol in his hand. He'd only seen them in movies. Landon pulled the slide to eject the final bullet, then handed him the gun.

"The Glock 17 is a little bigger than this," Landon said, "and it holds a couple more rounds. Otherwise it's about the same. There are holsters for it in the cabinet, so you can keep it handy at all times. Make sure you take the boxes of ammo. The Glock uses 9mm, and the AR-15 uses 223 Remington. Not sure if you knew that."

"I do now." Shane held the gun lightly, the grip cold against his palm. It felt heavy and awkward to him. "To be honest, I'm not sure about this. Can't remember the last time I held a gun in my hand. I might accidentally shoot myself in the foot."

"My friend, it's time to get comfortable with guns," Landon said, sternly. "If the looting hasn't started already, it will soon enough. You know how people are. This is our world now, okay, and you have to be ready for it. Keeping a gun handy might just save your life and the lives of your loved ones."

Shane grunted, still uncomfortable but seeing the truth. "You're right. Show me what I need to know."

11

"What were you guys talking about?" Violet asked. "Landon sounded serious."

Shane breathed a sigh of relief that she hadn't heard them talking about the guns. He'd made an effort to keep his voice down, even as Landon showed him how to load and unload, assemble and disassemble, the pistol and rifle.

"Just discussing the rest of Landon's supplies," Shane said. "We're going to head back to his house and pick up the remaining buckets to take with us to Grandma's. Landon doesn't want all that food to go to waste."

"We have to go back there with that creepy neighbor?"

"Don't worry about Larry. He won't bother us this time, and if he does, I'll be ready for him."

Violet twisted her lips to one side in an expression that suggested she didn't quite believe him. Shane retrieved the screwdriver from his pocket and proceeded to remove the mullion from the double doors. Then he edged the van out of the lobby and went back to screw the mullion back in place. By then, Landon had returned from taking the supplies to his office, and he gave Shane a final wave.

"Good luck out there, buddy," he said. "Stay sharp. Be ready for anything."

"I will be," Shane said. "Thanks for your help. Look after yourself, Landon, while you're looking after this place."

"I always do."

Shane shut the doors and walked back to the van. Wondering if he would ever see his friend again, he climbed into the driver's seat and pulled away. At least he knew the best path to Landon's house now, though he was troubled to see many of the same people waiting in the same places as before. Everyone seemed lost, unsure of what to do next in a world with no easy transportation. They sat on curbs, sat in their vehicles, roamed, or stood gazing at nothing.

As Shane pulled into the town of Falling Water, it occurred to him to check the fuel gauge—just over three-quarters of a tank. Would it be enough to get him to his mother-in-law's house? He wasn't sure. He didn't imagine that Landon's Volkswagen van got great gas mileage. It was a little over 200 miles to his mother-in-law's house, but if traffic was bad, he might burn more fuel than usual, especially if he was weighed down by a bunch of heavy supplies. Stopping for gas seemed like a daunting prospect. The one gas station they passed outside of Soddy-Daisy was swarmed with vehicles and people carrying gas cans.

He pulled onto Landon's street and made a third pass through the same neighbor's yard. The wheels spun for a second in the ruts of their previous passage, and Shane gunned the engine to ensure they didn't get stuck. As they thumped down onto the street again, he looked in the rearview mirror and saw the wheels had dug through the grass down to the soft soil beneath.

There won't be much of that yard left by the time I'm done here, he thought.

He approached Landon's house and pulled into the driveway, relieved to see that things were as he had left them. Only when he stepped out of the van did he notice a problem—the front door was ajar. Had he left it open? As he thought back, he was pretty sure he remembered locking up. When he moved closer to the door, he saw splintered and gashed wood along the edge of the doorframe. Someone had forced the door open, tearing the deadbolt out of the doorframe in the process.

Shane went to the passenger door and opened it. "Violet, stay here," he said. "I'll be right back."

"Why?" she asked, immediately grabbing the handle of Ruby's harness. "What happened?"

"Nothing happened," he said. "Just stay here."

"I'd rather come inside with you. I don't like the idea of sitting out here in this van."

"Ruby is with you," Shane reminded her.

"Yeah, but can't I come in and help?" Violet. "I can be useful, you know."

Shane couldn't decide if it was more dangerous leaving her out here in the van or bringing her inside. Either way, he would have to check the house first to make sure Larry wasn't lurking about.

"Okay, you can help me," he said, "but first, I'm going to take a quick peek inside the house."

"Why? Is someone in there?"

"I hope not, but I just want to make sure."

She frowned at this. Shane locked her door and shut it, then slowly approached the house, straining to hear any unusual sounds. When he reached the front door, he leaned in, but the house beyond seemed utterly still. He eased the door open as slowly as possible, creeping into the foyer, ready to bolt at the first sign of trouble. In the dimming light, the living room seemed just as he'd left it. Shane moved across the room, stepping lightly, and down the hall.

The back bedroom door was wide open. He couldn't remember if he'd closed it. He leaned around the doorframe, peering into the room. The first thing he noticed was a bucket tipped on its side beside a stack that had clearly been moved. It seemed much of the remaining stash had been stolen.

I guess Larry decided to help himself as soon as we left, he thought

What if he was still in the house somewhere? What if he saw the van in the driveway and came back? Either thought was alarming. Shane didn't want to linger. It wasn't worth the risk. He headed for the master bedroom, fishing the folded piece of paper out of his pocket. He opened the door slowly. The shades in the master bedroom were pulled on the windows, creating deep shadows around a king size bed. He spotted a tall dresser, a desk in the corner with a laptop, and finally the gun cabinet beside the bed.

Shane hesitated a moment before entering, just in case a crazed Larry lunged out of the darkness. When the stillness persisted, he went to the gun cabinet. It was a sturdy steel cabinet, the handle held shut by a heavy combination padlock. He spun the dial as fast as he could, though he fumbled and had to start over a few times. Finally, he opened the lock and tossed it onto the bed. Pulling the cabinet open, he saw two AR-15s sitting upright beside a stack of shelves. The Glock was on the top shelf. The others were full of ammo boxes, leather holsters, and other accessories he couldn't identify.

He picked up the Glock 17 first and checked the magazine. It wasn't loaded, so he grabbed a box of 9mm ammunition, pushed it open, and dumped it on the bed. Then he proceeded to awkwardly load the magazine, counting the rounds as he did. He managed to get thirteen bullets into the magazine, then he slid the magazine into the handgrip.

He found a suitable leather holster and slid the pistol into it. It had a clip that attached to his belt, though it took him a second to figure out how it worked. This put the gun out in the open.

Am I breaking the law by openly carrying a handgun? he wondered. He had heard of open-carry laws, but he wasn't sure if Tennessee was a participating state. Gun laws weren't something he'd ever had a reason to pay attention to.

The gun felt heavy and strange against his hip, and when he practiced drawing it, he found that he was clumsy. Still, Landon had taught him the basics. He hoped it would be enough.

He grabbed both rifles next and slung them over his shoulder. Then he grabbed as many boxes of ammo as he could carry—9mm for the Glock, 223 Remington for the rifles—and made his way back to the van.

"Dad, can I help you now?" Violet asked, rolling down her window. "I've been sitting here a while. I'm starting to get nervous. What if that creepy neighbor comes back?"

"You can help me," Shane replied. "If creepy guy comes back, I'll deal with him. He's not getting the jump on us this time." He hoped it wouldn't come to that. Could he actually shoot someone if he had to? He wasn't sure, but he would certainly try if Violet's safety depended on it.

He quickly loaded the rifles and ammunition into the hidden storage space under the carpet, then opened Violet's door. Ruby hopped out first and guided her back into the house. As Shane went after them, he glanced at Larry's house next door, but there was no sign of the neighbor.

Ruby pushed through the open door, leading Violet inside. She bumped against the doorframe, felt the splintered edge, and paused. For a moment, it looked like she was going to say something, a scowl on her face, but then she continued into the house.

Shane moved past her and headed to the back bedroom. Greedy Larry had only left five buckets. Apparently, he had a huge appetite for dehydrated food and MREs. Shane brought one of the buckets to Violet and asked her to carry it to the van.

"Oof, that's heavy," she said, picking it up. "What has he got in here? Feels like a bucket of lead."

"That one is full of rice," Shane said, reading the label on the side. "Looks like it's enough rice to feed a village for three days."

"I don't even like rice that much," Violet said.

"Yeah, but it'll stay fresh a long time. That's the point."

Violet could only carry the bucket a few steps at a time, alternating carrying and dragging it down the hall, as Ruby led her back to the front door. Shane didn't help. He could tell when she wanted to do something by herself. As he loaded up the rest of the buckets, Violet slowly worked her single bucket to the van and hoisted it inside. When she was done, she smiled and shook her aching hand.

"I didn't drop it," she said proudly. "The handle felt like it was cutting my fingers off, but I never let go."

"Good job, sweetheart," Shane said. "Thanks for the help."

"Do you need my help with anything else?"

"Not right now. We're almost done here."

Shane finished loading the rest of the buckets into the van, trying to be ready at a moment's notice to drop a bucket and grab the Glock. When he was done, he made a final pass through the house. He found a few cabinets open in the kitchen, a drawer open in the bathroom, and the refrigerator door ajar.

He hated that he couldn't lock the place up again. He went outside, pulled the front door shut—though it no longer fit snugly in the splintered doorframe—and got back inside the van. Violet had taken her seat and clicked her lap belt into place.

"Are we leaving now?" she said.

"We're on our way," Shane said. "The next stop will be our house in Resaca, and then on to Grandma's."

"Good. I can't wait to get there."

He started the van and backed out of the driveway. As he drove away, he caught a glimpse of movement out of the corner of his eye. Looking at the side-view mirror, he saw a stooped shape in a Members Only jacket loping across the yard like some primeval creature. Larry had a black plastic trash bag dangling from his right hand as he ran toward the front door.

"That sneaky little scumbag," Shane said.

"Is it Larry?" Violet said.

"Yeah, he didn't even wait until we were out of sight," Shane said. He watched as Larry kicked open the busted front door and slipped into the house, trailing the trash bag behind him. "He doesn't seem to have the shotgun with him. I'm tempted to go back there and scare him off. Poor Landon."

"Don't do it," Violet said. "It's not worth the risk, Dad. Just tell Landon about it, and he can report Larry to the police."

"I doubt the police will prioritize a burglary," Shane said. "I imagine they are overwhelmed at this point with more serious problems."

"If police won't help people when they're getting robbed, then we're all in big trouble," Violet said. "What are we supposed to do? I guess people just have to police their own property."

Shane's right hand slid down to the holster at his hip, his fingers brushing the cold metal of the Glock's slide. "Maybe so, but we will. Don't worry, we will. At least we got the last of the food."

And the guns, he thought, but did not say.

12

Mike made it two blocks past the liquor store before he began violently heaving. They'd stopped at the liquor store to buy him a bottle of water, and it crinkled as he crunched it in his fist. He finally managed to vomit, then he took a swig of water. Instead of swallowing, he spat the water at his feet. Jodi stood beside him, resting a hand on his back, but she knew there was little she could do. He always got sick like this after chemo treatment, even when he was resting at home.

"Give me a minute, guys," Mike said, patting his face with the hem of his t-shirt. He took another swig of water, swished it around his mouth, and spat it out. "Can't even swallow. Just makes me want to puke again."

"Take it easy, Mikey," Jodi said. "Try to relax."

"Relax, she says. I doubt I could relax if I was in a pine box buried six feet under."

"Don't talk like that," Jodi said.

Owen finally caught up to them then, but his attention was fixed on his cell phone. "I keep losing signal," he said. "Sometimes I can send a message, and sometimes I can't." The duffel bag hung from his forearm so he had easy access to the phone.

Mike finally rose and signaled for Jodi to continue walking. "I think I've got the puking out of my system for now. Actually, I've moved beyond vomiting to fainting, but let's see if we can make it another block or two."

"Just take it at your own pace," Jodi said. "I don't want you to collapse."

"My own pace would be standing still," Mike said, "but that won't do. Remember when we were kids, how I was the athletic one and you were the brainy kid? The tables have turned. Well, no, my table collapsed. You're still the brainy one. I'm now the useless one."

"Mike, stop it," Jodi said. "Stop putting yourself down. It's fine."

They moved at a snail's pace past a shopping center. Jodi couldn't imagine how they were going to keep this up. There was no possible way Mike would make it all the way to Macon on foot. Or the rest of them, for that matter. On top of that, she was beginning to feel hungry. Owen had been on his way to get snacks when the power went off, but now it was edging toward dinner time.

"If you guys have to leave me behind..." Mike started to say.

"Don't even suggest it," Jodi replied. "Nobody is getting left behind. You have to stop talking like that."

"I'm just not going to make it much farther," he said. "That's my point, sis. Everything hurts. I can't think of one part of my body that isn't feeling some amount of discomfort."

Ahead, Jodi spotted a Walmart Supercenter. The store was open, and people seemed to be gathering there. According to a sign on the outside of the building, there was a small fast-food restaurant just inside the entrance. Jodi pointed in that direction.

"I'll tell you what," she said. "Let's head inside the Walmart. You can rest for a while. Owen and I will get something to eat, and then we'll find a way to proceed when you're ready."

"Take me to the camping supplies in the back of the store, lay me down on a sleeping bag, and leave me," Mike muttered.

"Stop that," she replied. "We will find a solution that doesn't involve abandoning you."

"You say that now…" Mike left the thought unfinished.

"I should have bribed Bill to take us farther," Jodi said. "That was my mistake. I'll bet he had his price, and I've got the cash."

"Bill wasn't much company anyway," Mike said with a wave of his hand. "Even when we used to chat in the waiting room, all he ever did was complain about stupid stuff in his life."

"I will endure bad company if it can get us to Mom's house."

She stopped and turned in the direction of the store. As she did, she heard Owen frantically shuffling to one side, as if to avoid someone. A second later, a young man on a bicycle flew past them, forcing Jodi to grab Mike and move him out of the way. The bike rider said nothing. He came within inches of knocking Mike down and kept on going in a blur. Jodi watched him do the same to numerous other pedestrians as he pedaled away.

"That was rude," Owen said.

"Yeah, but I think he's got the right idea," Mike said.

They made their slow and agonizing way to the Walmart entrance and pushed through the crowd. The restaurant inside had a long line, but an employee was moving up and down the line with a hastily scrawled sign in her hands that read, "Cash Only—No Credit Cards—No Checks—Limited Menu." Dragging the suitcase, Jodi moved to the back of the line.

"Mike, are you okay to be here?" she asked. "I just thought if we got some food, we could sit and relax for a while, let you recover some of your strength."

"I'm not hungry at all," he replied, joining her at the back of the line, "but I wouldn't mind sitting for a few hundred years. I'm wiped out. Honestly, I'm surprised people are willing to wait patiently in line like this. They're running each other down on the sidewalk out there, but—surprise, surprise—inside the local Walmart, a last vestige of civilization hangs on by a thread." He managed a weak laugh.

As Jodi thought of the bicycle rider, she got an idea. "We should get bicycles while we're here," she said. "It would certainly be better than walking. Mikey, do you think you could ride?"

"I'm willing to give it a try," Mike said. "It's been a few years since I was on a bicycle, but they say you never forget."

"I mean, in your present condition."

"In my present condition, blinking and breathing are a challenge," he said, "but riding a bicycle might be easier than walking. Taking the weight off my feet would be nice."

Owen was still trying to get his cell phone to work, but he perked up at her suggestion. "Can we afford bikes, Mom? Even a cheap bike is going to be over a hundred dollars. My Schwinn was almost three hundred."

"I don't have more than about forty dollars in my pocket," Mike said. "That might get me a single tire."

Jodi patted her purse, which was hanging by its strap from her right shoulder. "I have plenty of cash to cover three bikes," she said, speaking quietly enough that the person ahead of them in line wouldn't hear.

"Why are you carrying around hundreds of dollars in your purse?" Mike said.

"Thousands," Jodi said. "I'm carrying thousands of dollars."

Mike glanced at Owen and shook his head in disbelief. "Do you always lug around unreasonable amounts of cash? That seems unsafe."

Jodi hesitated a moment before answering. Of course, telling him the truth didn't much matter now. The money was there for a purpose, but it seemed their priorities had shifted. "I hate to spoil a surprise, but Shane and I were going to buy you a used car so you could drive to your doctor's appointments. We know money has been tight while you're going through treatment, and you keep paying for Uber."

Mike stared at her, his mouth hanging open. "Sis, you didn't have to do that. Paying for rides is a pain, but it's nothing compared to the medical bills that are piling up."

"We found a seller on Craigslist last night," Jodi continued. "I was going to surprise you by meeting with the guy after your treatment today."

Shaking his head in amazement, Mike started to say more, but no words came out. He seemed on the verge of tears.

"That's what family is for, Uncle Mike," Owen said.

"Well, in that case," Mike said, "let's forget about this restaurant business and go buy a few bikes." He gave Jodi a feeble hug, gave Owen a hearty pat on the back, and got out of line. "You guys can eat cold hamburgers later."

They found that people were behaving in a less civilized manner throughout the store. Shelves were quickly being emptied, baskets piled high with food and drinks. The bread aisle seemed to be the epicenter of the worst behavior. Jodi spotted two women wrestling over a loaf of bread, shouting and cussing each other and smashing the bread to oblivion in the process. The soft drink shelves had also been picked clean.

"Can't face the end of civilization without plenty of Wonder Bread and Sam's Choice Cola," Mike noted with a chuckle.

Jodi didn't quite find it amusing. Didn't people realize how much better it was to take nutritious food with a long shelf life? Dried grains and beans, canned meats and vegetables, and rice would last longer and be more beneficial than white bread and soda. Jodi was no expert on survivalism, but she'd learned a little bit from her mother over the years.

Later, they passed a hostile crowd fighting in the shoe department, and Jodi made sure they walked well clear of it. An old man lay on the ground, covering his head with a shoebox, as a store employee pleaded with people to calm down. People were also fighting over cell phone accessories in the electronics department.

"People need to consider their priorities," she said. "Long-term survival over short-term enjoyment."

"If they're fighting over electronics," Mike said, "they haven't accepted that this is a long-term problem."

"They're thinking about immediate opportunities rather than lasting necessities," she said. "This is why things are going to get so much worse. They'll have shoes, cell phone plugs, and moldy bread, and then the desperation will set in."

When they reached the bicycles, Jodi found the aisle relatively neglected. Owen pointed out the ten-speed models beyond the kid bikes. As they were examining the various models, an exasperated worker came around the corner, fanning her face with her hands.

"Can I help you?" she asked.

"Would it be possible to buy some bikes off the rack?" Jodi asked. "We also need three helmets."

"Well, first of all, our credit card reader isn't working," the worker said, sounding half-dead with exhaustion.

"That's fine," Jodi said. "We have cash."

"Great," the worker replied, "but, second, we don't sell bikes preassembled. They come in pieces in a box. You have to put them together yourself. You can get tools from the hardware aisle."

"I know," Jodi said. She unzipped her purse and fumbled around inside. "I'm asking you to make an exception." She found her money clip near the bottom and worked out a single bill, thrusting it at the worker.

"A hundred dollars?" the worker said, giving Jodi a puzzled look. "What's that for? Three bikes will cost a lot more than that."

"It's a tip," Jodi said. "For you. If you'll accommodate us."

"Wow, big tipper," Mike muttered.

The worker pulled a face, as if debating internally, then she snatched the money and shoved it in the pocket of her jeans. "I can't say no to that, I guess, but don't tell anyone. I'll get in big trouble. Okay, pick out what you want, and I'll let you take it off the rack. Hurry up before my manager sees."

Jodi followed Owen's recommendation and selected three Schwinn mountain bikes, pulling them right off the rack. Then they selected three bike helmets. The worker, glancing around nervously, led them to the cash register. Since the register wasn't working, she added up the total on a calculator, took a big wad of cash from Jodi, and wrote them a receipt (that did not include the hundred-dollar tip).

"Thanks," Jodi said.

"Good luck," the worker replied. "Don't tell anyone you gave me a hundred bucks. Not an employee, not a customer, not anyone. Word gets around in this store."

"I won't say a word."

Walking their bikes back through the store proved a challenge. At first, they were side by side, but people wouldn't get out of their way. They received a few exasperated stares from an increasingly hostile crowd, and saying, "Excuse me," didn't make the situation better. Finally, they resorted to single file, with Jodi in front and Owen bringing up the rear.

The cell phone accessories were still a war zone, as workers tried desperately to defuse the situation, so Jodi cut through the clothing department. It wasn't much better there. Children's clothes had become ground zero for a group of screechy shoppers.

"Man, it doesn't take long for people to start fighting over trivial things," Mike said.

"Avoid eye contact and keep moving," Jodi said.

It took Jodi a moment to realize that the screeching had moved very close. She heard someone angrily cursing just behind her. When she turned around, she saw Owen wrestling with a stranger. Some bearded fellow in an old heavy metal t-shirt had come up behind him and grabbed his bike, and he was currently trying to pull it away. Owen grabbed the handlebars and held on for dear life.

"I'm taking it," the stranger said with a snarl. "Let go. I need it! I said let go."

Owen had clearly been caught off guard, and he was being pulled forward off his feet. Jodi stepped past Mike, intending to help.

"Stop it," Owen shouted. "We already paid for these."

"I don't care," the stranger said. "I need it. Let go before I smack you."

"You can't have it!" Owen let go of the bike with his right hand, reared back, and took an almighty swing at the man, punching him square in the mouth.

Jodi was shocked at the strength of her sixteen-year-old son. The stranger flew backward, sputtering and flailing his arms. He hit the ground on his back, his head bouncing off the hard floor, and rolled onto his stomach.

"Wow, the kid's got a mean right hook," Mike said. "I don't think that punk is getting up again."

Owen looked at his mom, eyes wide in amazement. Jodi was tempted to scold him—*You didn't have to punch him. It's just a bike. It's not worth a man's life*—but under the circumstances, it didn't seem right. She gazed at the stranger, now sprawled facedown on the floor, legs crossed awkwardly from the fall. His shoulders rose and fell—he was still breathing—but he was out cold. A trickle of blood ran from his nostril onto the floor.

Jodi debated whether or not to help the man. Already, people were looking in their direction. Finally, she made eye contact with an employee, beckoned to him, and pointed at the man on the floor. It would have to do. She didn't want to risk being delayed. As the worker approached, she resumed pushing her bike.

"We'd better get out of here," she said to Mike and Owen. "The employees will have to deal with him."

"I wasn't trying to kill him," Owen said. "He said he was going to smack me."

"Nothing wrong with sticking up for yourself," Mike said. "He had it coming, kid. I hate punks like that. I've had my run-ins with his type before, and a good fist to the jaw is more than they deserve."

They rushed out of the store as fast as they could, keeping an eye out for any other would-be bike thieves. When they got back to the parking lot, they put their helmets on and mounted their bikes. Jodi wasn't sure what to do with her suitcase, but she finally managed to prop it on the frame in front of her and hold it in place with her arms as she gripped the bike handles.

"It's been a few years since I've ridden a bike," Mike said. "To be honest, I prefer the motorized kind. A big Harley hog would be nice. People would definitely get out of our way."

"Regular old bicycles will have to do," Jodi said. "Let me know if you have any trouble."

Once they got moving, Mike seemed to handle the bike just fine. Still, Jodi kept a close eye on him as they cut diagonally across the parking lot.

"Where to next?" Mike called.

"Macon, I suppose," Jodi replied.

"My place is a heck of a lot closer," he reminded her. "We could regroup and maybe take another rest. It'll help me. Maybe I'll get a second wind."

Jodi almost said no. She felt an urge to get on the road and just keep going all the way to Macon, but it was 130 miles. How would they ever make it?

"Okay, we'll go to your place," she said.

Mike's small apartment was a couple of miles from the Walmart. She headed in that direction.

They made it about a mile before Mike came to a stop beside a street-light and proceeded to retch his guts out again. He fell off the bike, went down on his knees, and grabbed the pole to prop himself up. He was wheezing hard now, every breath coarse and wet. Jodi and Owen stopped.

As Jodi stood over him, she heard the rising tide of panicking people on all sides. Crowds had gathered in open spaces all over town. Many seemed to be complaining or arguing. As the afternoon wore on, and the light changed, Augusta was starting to look and feel like a scary place. Jodi couldn't imagine what it would be like once night fell.

"How much farther to Mike's apartment?" Owen asked, watching a fight break out across the street.

"A few blocks," Mike replied, miserably, clutching his stomach with both hands. "Mile at the most."

"We have to get off the streets," Jodi said. "Mike, can you push through the pain? If you can get to your apartment, we can come up with a game plan to get to Mom's."

"Just a second," Mike said. "Give me just a second."

And then another round of violent heaving took him.

13

"Do we have to stop at our house?" Violet asked. "Can't we just keep going to Grandma's?"

"We need clothes and other personal items," Shane said. "Ruby needs her stuff, too. We might be at Grandma's a long time. You don't want to wear that same shirt every day for the next year, do you?"

"I guess not," Violet conceded, stroking Ruby's head. "Ruby will sleep better if she has her doggy bed. Otherwise, she's kind of restless at night."

"Exactly. Plus, we've got a lot of food that will go to waste in our pantry. Might as well bring it with us. It won't take long. Don't worry."

It was about 60 miles from Sequoyah Power Plant to their house, then another 70-ish to Atlanta, and finally another 85 or so to Macon. Living so far from his place of work wasn't ideal, but it had been a necessary compromise since Jodi worked at the Centers for Disease

Control in Atlanta. Shane thought the Westfalia could make it to Macon, but he wasn't sure. They had passed a few gas stations, but each one had absurdly long lines, and Shane was worried about getting stuck in the crowd.

He followed Hixson Pike south from the power plant, but stalled cars were everywhere. Shane kept having to slow way down to weave around them. It got much worse once they reached the highway outside of Chattanooga. Dead vehicles littered the road like confetti after a New Year's Eve party, and stranded drivers and passengers lined the shoulders—some walking, some with their thumbs out, others sitting as if they'd already given up hope. Shane saw numerous wrecks as well, and in places, the lanes were choked with scattered debris and damaged vehicles.

Violet must have sensed the chaos, because she perked up from time to time, tilting her head to the side as she did when she was listening to some strange sound. Near the Chattanooga airport, Shane spotted a group of people treating a seriously injured woman who was lying on the shoulder of the road near an overturned SUV. Farther along, another woman was limping, a makeshift bandage wrapped around her forearm. Just past her, there was a much larger pileup, apparently caused by a semi swerving from the passing lane into a row of cars. One of the vehicles was a blackened husk, and smoke still rose from the wreckage.

"What a mess," he said. "How is anyone ever going to clean all this up?"

"I can tell we're going really slow," Violet noted. "It must be bad out there, especially since you're not describing it to me."

"Just a lot of stalled cars," Shane said, "and a few wrecks. I'm glad we weren't on the highway when the event happened. I hope there's still some kind of emergency response, because I feel bad that we can't stop and help anyone."

"Can't we?" Violet said.

"We probably shouldn't," Shane replied. "Your grandma is expecting us, and we have a long way to go." *And I don't want to put you in harm's way*, he thought. *You're the priority.*

Shane saw a few functioning vehicles on the road. When they turned onto Interstate 75, he saw a mid-80s Chevy Caprice the size of a small tank rattling its way north. One of its headlight covers was shattered, and the hood was rusted, but the car still worked. The irony of a rusty piece of junk rolling past all of these lovely, useless vehicles didn't escape him. Not long after, he saw an old man puttering along on an antique scooter, a massive green military sea bag on his shoulders.

Not every functioning vehicle was an antique. He saw a few newer models that appeared to be working, and he wondered what made the difference. Why had some survived, while others had not? It was as if the EMP had been simply flipping a coin with every vehicle on the road.

Rounding a bend just before the East Ridge exit, they came upon a section of the highway that seemed impassable. Two semis were spread across the southbound lanes, a large sedan blocked the right shoulder, and an overturned coupe blocked the left. Guardrails ran along either side of the highway, preventing Shane from taking to the median. A large crowd had gathered in the area, some chatting, some fiddling with their phones, others settling in as if they expected to be there a long time.

Shane stopped well clear of the blockage. As soon as he did, a large man in a tank top began rather aggressively trying to get his attention from the shoulder, wagging his thumbs over his head, as if trying to hitch a ride.

"Are we stuck?" Violet asked.

"Yeah, for the moment."

The hitchhiker started coming toward them, approaching on Violet's side of the van. He was shouting something, but Shane couldn't make it out yet. Checking the rearview mirror to make sure the lane behind him was clear, he put the van in reverse.

As he backed away from the hitchhiker, the man went from waving both hands to flipping him off.

"Someone's yelling at us," Violet said. "I can hear him.'"

"I know, honey," Shane said. "I know."

"He sounds mad."

"Well, he looks mad," Shane said.

"He shouldn't be mad at us," Violet said. "We didn't do anything to him."

"I'm sure he's just frustrated."

Shane backed up until he reached a spot where there was no guardrail on the left side, then he put the van in drive and cut across the median. The van bounced across high grass and rough terrain, the plastic buckets rattling in the back. Shane turned onto the shoulder of the northbound lanes, moving south against traffic. Driving against traffic seemed rather foolish, but he couldn't see an alternative. The northbound shoulder was open beyond the traffic jam. Still, he drove slowly, his gaze fixed in the distance.

Much of the crowd turned to watch him as he drove past, some pointing. A few tried to get his attention, but he kept going. When he was well beyond the blockage, he cut back across the median into the southbound lanes. He dared a bit more speed, pulling away from the crowd.

"Rough ride," Violet said.

"Sorry, had to get around the blockage," he said.

"Hopefully, we don't break Landon's van. It feels worse now. I think I heard something metal fall off."

She was right, though he didn't like to admit it. The van was taking a beating. Landon kept the vehicle in decent shape, but Shane wasn't sure what shape the shocks were in. It just wasn't meant for all this harsh treatment. The idea of being stranded on the highway miles from home with Violet and Ruby terrified him. What would he do? They could hunker down in the van for a while. They at least had food and water here, but it didn't seem safe with all the milling and meandering people.

A few miles on, just before the town of Ringgold, Georgia, he came to another blocked section of the highway. It looked like a Camaro had left its lane and hit the side of an older Impala, driving it into the guardrail. This had turned both vehicles, positioning them across the shoulder and both lanes. Other vehicles had then come to a stop behind them. Only the inside shoulder was open, so Shane slowed down and eased toward it.

"Dad, Ruby is going to need to stop soon," Violet said. The dog kept getting up from the floorboard, gazing out the window a few seconds before sitting down again. "I think she needs to use the bathroom."

"Okay, but let's find a…" He almost said *a safer place*, but he caught himself. "Let's find an open spot."

"She's a good girl," Violet said. "She won't complain, but if she really needs to go, eventually she'll just pee on the floor."

"I know. I'll keep my eyes open. Maybe when I get past this next little section."

An old motorcycle went flying past them then, zigzagging from the left lane to the right then cutting back over to the shoulder to pass the stalled cars at an alarming speed. It startled Shane, and he came to a stop for a second before proceeding. He watched the motorcycle disappear into the distance, zipping around stalled vehicles.

"What was that sound?" Violet asked.

"A crazy person in a big darn hurry," Shane replied.

After a moment, he let his foot off the gas and pulled onto the shoulder, checking the rearview mirror to make sure no one else was coming. When he looked forward again, he spotted a man and woman stepping out from behind the Camaro. They were a rough-looking pair, young but emaciated and unwell. The man wore a faux-leather jacket and had a baseball cap turned backward on his head. The woman wore an ill-fitting tube top and ripped jeans.

The man held up his hands, palms out, as if he were a cop directing traffic. The woman seemed distressed, grimacing as if in pain. Could they have been injured in the crash? Shane would have swerved out of the way, but he was blocked on either side now, stalled vehicles on the right, a guardrail on the left. There was no going around them. The man began patting the air, mouthing the word, "Help! Help!" As Shane slowed down, the pair moved toward him. The woman gripped her side as she walked, wincing with each step.

"More people shouting at us," Violet noted. "Are they in trouble?"

"They *are* trouble," Shane replied.

He considered backing up, but he didn't want to stop and give them time to reach the van.

"Stop your vehicle," the man said, sternly. "We need help right now!"

He considered stopping the van and helping them—maybe they just needed some first aid supplies—but only briefly. Already, he found himself not trusting people, and while he hated to admit it, he knew what he had to do. Gripping the steering wheel tighter, he leaned into the accelerator and picked up speed.

"Sorry, folks," he muttered. "This is the way it has to be."

As the van barreled toward them, the man and woman held their ground, the man now jumping up and down as he shouted.

"Please move," Shane said quietly. "Please move."

"Dad."

"Please move!"

The woman, still gripping her side, stumbled out of the way, falling against the side of the Camaro and flopping onto the hood. The man held his ground a second longer, and Shane braced himself, fully expecting to plow into him. With about five feet to spare, the man finally leapt over the guardrail, landing in a heap on the grass. The van blew past him, still picking up speed. Shane thought he heard both of them shrieking curses at him as they faded into the background.

"We almost hit them, didn't we?" Violet asked.

"Yeah, but they're fine," he replied, hating the little tremor in his voice. Had he almost just run down two desperate, possibly injured, people? He felt sick to his stomach. "I didn't know what else to do," he said, speaking to himself as much as to his daughter.

Violet was silent for a couple of minutes before she said, "Can we stop and let Ruby pee now?"

"Let me get a little more distance."

He didn't want to pull over now. Too many desperate people on the highway, but he knew he couldn't put off Violet indefinitely.

Just a little farther, he thought.

14

Their house was located in the small community of Resaca. By the time they reached the exit and left the highway, it became clear to Shane that they weren't going to reach Macon today. Progress had been much slower than he'd anticipated, and they were still over 150 miles from Beth's house. The sun had started going down, and the light was beginning to fade. Shane didn't like the idea of trying to avoid all the stalled and wrecked vehicles at night. Plus, the van had consumed far more gas than he'd expected. At best, he figured it was getting gas mileage in the mid-teens.

After a brief stop by the side of the road, Ruby had fallen asleep between the seats, but Violet was wide awake, fidgeting constantly with her sunglasses. Somehow, she could tell when they reached their neighborhood, and she finally perked up. Their house was a nice upper-middle-class home, two stories with generous front and back yards. However, as Shane pulled into the driveway, the dark windows made the familiar place seem uninviting.

"We're home," Violet noted.

Shane was always amazed at the way she could tell their own driveway just by the sound. "Yes, finally," Shane said. "We'll have to spend the night here. The sun is already going down. In the morning, I'll try to find some diesel for the van, and then we'll set out for Grandma's. It'll be safer that way."

"Will it?" Violet asked.

He let the question hang as he got out of the van. He wasn't sure. Traveling at night certainly wasn't safe, but people might become more desperate by morning. After manually raising the garage door, he got back behind the wheel and pulled the van inside.

There are few enough working vehicles that this old van will be a temptation, he thought, as he pulled the garage door shut. *Even in this neighborhood.*

When they went inside, the kitchen seemed too quiet and too dark. Shane retrieved a flashlight from a junk drawer and turned it on, setting it on the counter. Violet was aware of the darkness, and hung back, leading a sleep-addled Ruby.

"What if someone like Larry got into our house?" she said. "What if they're hiding in one of the bedrooms or in a closet?"

Moving his right hand close to the pistol grip at his side, Shane tiptoed across the kitchen. Beyond the center island, he had a view through the dining room to the hallway. All the doors were closed, the whole house utterly still.

"Are you sure we can't just get back in the van and drive to Grandma's?" Violet asked.

"Not tonight, Violet. Sorry. We'll set out first thing in the morning."

"Can we at least call Mom and let her know we're not coming?"

"I doubt I have cell service," Shane said, "but I'll check if it will make you feel better."

"It will, Dad. Thanks."

Shane pulled out his cell phone and unlocked the screen. He still had over half his battery life. He made sure the volume was up so Violet could hear him dialing Jodi's number. The phone rang and rang, but Jodi never picked up.

He was about to apologize to Violet, but he decided on a whim to call his mother-in-law. He dialed her number so his daughter could hear it. To his surprise, Beth answered on the third ring.

"Shane!" She practically shouted his name. Shane heard her little Schnauzer barking like mad in the background. "Where are you? Are you on your way? Tell me Violet is with you."

He was so shocked to be connected that he didn't answer right away. A couple of awkward seconds of silence passed before he said, "Beth, we made it to our house in Resaca. The roads are a lot worse than I expected, but we're settled in for the night. Yes, Violet is here. She's fine."

"Is it safe there in Resaca?" Beth asked.

"I think so. We'll try to get some fuel in the morning, so we can head out. Maybe the highway will be a little clearer by then. What about you?"

"I'll be up all night canning stuff from the garden," she replied. "Trying to save as much food as I can. It will add to our reserves. Listen, first thing you should do is fill your bathtub with water. You never know when you'll lose water service."

"Good advice," Shane said. "Thanks. Hey, why don't you talk to Violet for a minute. She's had a rough day."

He passed the phone to Violet, who seized it enthusiastically and pressed it to her ear. "Grandma, it's so good to hear your voice! So many scary things happened to us."

While she spoke to her grandmother, Shane took the flashlight and went down the hall to the bathroom, turning on the tap to fill the tub and putting the stopper in the drain. There was no hot water, of course, and the water that came out was ice cold. He let the tub fill almost all the way to the brim just to be safe, then he headed back to the kitchen. Violet was just finishing up her conversation with Beth, and she already sounded better.

"You're right, Grandma," she said. "I'll keep that in mind. Okay, good night. See you tomorrow."

She held the phone out to Shane, and he took it from her, shoving it back in his pocket.

"Grandma told me the most important thing to do in a situation like this is to keep our emotions in check," Violet said. "She said you have to choose not to panic, so you can think clearly."

"Sounds like good advice," Shane said. "Why don't you and Ruby settle in. I'll get some of our stuff together so we can leave right away in the morning."

"Okay, Dad."

Violet knew the house well enough to move with confidence from room to room. She grabbed the handle of Ruby's harness and walked with her through the dining room and down the hall. A moment later, Shane heard the sound of her bedroom door.

Once she was gone, Shane started going through the cupboards and the pantry, grabbing anything he thought they could use. He stacked cans on the counter, then dragged the big half-full bag of Ruby's favorite dog food out from under the sink. He reached for the refrigerator door, intending to see what could be salvaged, when he heard a shriek.

Violet! Ruby began barking. Shane stumbled backward, slammed into the center island, and grabbed for the Glock. He fumbled at the holster, trying to get the snap undone, but the shock of Violet's cry had made him clumsy. He grabbed the flashlight and raced out of the kitchen, his heart pounding.

I should have checked the whole house, he thought, cursing himself. *I should have made sure no one else was inside.*

When he reached the hall, he found the bathroom door was wide open. He finally got the Glock out of its holster, but he almost dropped it in the process. Pointing the Glock at an angle toward the floor, he sidestepped to the bathroom door and shone the light inside, ready to confront whatever faceless enemy had attacked them.

He found Violet standing in the middle of the bathroom in her pajamas, her arms wrapped tightly around herself, one bare foot on the edge of the bathtub. Ruby stood in front of the toilet, ears pointing straight up.

"What happened?" he said. "Are you okay? Were you attacked? Where is he?"

His shouting startled her, and she uttered a squeal and spun toward him. "Dad! The water is *so* cold. I was going to take a shower, but I stepped into the tub and it was like *ice*."

"Oh, gosh," Shane said, shaking his head. "I thought…well, never mind what I thought." He holstered the pistol. "Sorry, the water heater's reserves are probably gone by now, so cold water is all we've got."

"Maybe I'll just wash my face and go to bed," Violet said.

"That's fine. Let's try not to scream unless there's a real problem."

"I didn't plan on it," she said.

"I know." He took a deep breath and let it out slowly. "Would you like something to eat first? We never really had dinner."

"I'm not hungry," she said. "I'm just tired."

"Okay, well, get a good night's sleep," he said.

He started to leave when she added, "This was some Take Your Child to Work Day, huh?"

"Not quite what you expected?" he said.

"No, I thought it would be a lot more boring," she said. "Sorry, but I did."

"I wish it had been," he replied.

He left the bathroom, trying to settle his racing heart. After all he'd seen that day, he felt jumpy and restless. Finally, he went to the dining room, set the flashlight on the table, and opened the sliding glass door, stepping into the backyard to get some fresh air. Shane and Jodi had a large stonework porch with tiki torches planted at the far corners. He knew there was a lighter in a small metal trunk beside the grill, so he dug it out to light one of the torches. The single flame did little to cast out the darkness.

He paced for a bit, still trying to calm down. The whole world felt threatening now, filled with dangerous people ready to hurt his family. He hated thinking the worst of people, but he'd seen enough that day. Pacing didn't make him feel any better about it, so he finally spent some time practicing what Landon had taught him about the gun. Assembling and disassembling the Glock proved the biggest challenge. It was a bit like putting together a puzzle.

He tried it a few times until he was halfway decent at it. He removed the magazine and ejected the final bullet from the chamber so he wouldn't accidently discharge the weapon. Then he practiced drawing the pistol out of the holster repeatedly. He just couldn't do it smoothly —it always took him a few seconds to get a firm grip on the gun. How much worse would it be when he was dealing with real danger?

For a good thirty minutes, he practiced drawing the gun, gripping it correctly, and aiming it into the dark, then holstering it. By the end, it started to feel a bit more natural. It would have to do. He suspected that tomorrow, as people awoke in a powerless world, the desperation would really start to set in.

I need to practice my aim, he thought. He didn't dare practice shooting. The whole neighborhood would panic at the sound.

He slid the magazine back into the pistol grip. When he blew out the tiki torch, he was amazed at the depth of the darkness filling the landscape on all sides of the house. No streetlights, no house lights, no headlights, only a brilliant splash of stars across the sky. Though he knew it would take him a long time to fall asleep, he decided to head in and attempt it. It seemed wise to be as rested as possible.

He pocketed the lighter and reached for the sliding glass door. As he was about to step inside, however, something caught his eye—a faint shimmer of light at the edge of his vision. When he looked for it, his gaze was drawn to the northern sky. Hovering above the horizon, a hazy white light, edging toward green, rose above the dark land. Shane found it ghostly, like great vapors drifting toward the stars.

Though he'd never seen them in person, he knew what they were— northern lights. They were not quite as green as the photographs he'd seen of them, but they were still an amazing sight to behold. What were they doing filling the sky all the way down in Georgia? What did it mean?

"Nothing good, I'm sure," he said.

Despite this, it was a breathtaking sight, and he stood there for a while. It made the world seem like an alien place.

Who knew the end of civilization as we know it could look so beautiful? he thought.

15

Mike's apartment was located in a run-down complex in a rather sketchy neighborhood. He'd settled on it after his cancer diagnosis because of its proximity to the university hospital. Jodi hadn't thought to complain about the location at the time, but now, as they turned their bikes onto his street, it seemed like a bad idea. A large crowd of people was gathered in the middle of the road. Two men in the center seemed to be on the verge of a full-blown fist fight as the others shouted and laughed and egged them on.

Jodi steered her bike across the street before she reached the crowd, putting as much space between them as she could. She slowed down to let Mike catch up. Owen had stayed right with his uncle the entire time. They pulled into the parking lot of the apartment building and came to a stop alongside the first building. Jodi's arms were sore from propping the suitcase on her bike frame, and as she climbed off the bike, she didn't have the strength to catch the suitcase before it fell.

"That's no way to treat our medical supplies," Mike said, coming to a stop behind her. He had a sickly pallor to his face, and his eyes were bleary. The relatively short ride from Walmart had been brutal, requiring multiple stops, and he looked much worse now. Sweaty patches of hair clung to his forehead and skull, and he'd soaked through his t-shirt.

Unfortunately, his apartment was on the second floor. Jodi gestured at the stairs. "You think you can make it?"

"Not sure," Mike replied. "Guess I have to. I tried to get a first-floor apartment when I moved in, I really did, but nothing was available."

"I'll help," Owen said. He'd hung the duffel bag from his handlebars, and he plucked it off now and hoisted it up onto his shoulder. "Lean on me, Uncle Mike. We'll get you up there."

"What a helpful kid," Mike said. "I remember holding you when you were a tiny little guy. Never thought the day would come when you'd have to lug me around like dead weight."

"It's not a problem," Owen said.

"We don't dare leave the bikes out in the open," Jodi said, "not in this neighborhood."

"Sis, you're slandering my neighborhood," Mike said with an exhausted smile. "I wish I could disagree, but people will steal the shoes off your feet while you're walking in them around here."

"Yeah, and under the circumstances they might just steal the person wearing them. Owen, help Mike to the apartment and then come down and help me with the bikes. We'll store them in the apartment while we're taking a break."

As Jodi extended the handle of her suitcase, she glanced in the direction of the apartment dumpsters, where a group of young men were huddled. They seemed to be deep in conversation, casting occasional furtive glances in all directions. Under other circumstances, Jodi would have assumed they were simply hanging out and chatting, but at the moment she couldn't help thinking they were planning some crime.

Is it wrong that every group of people looks like trouble to me? she wondered. *Am I just assuming the worst about everyone now?*

Owen helped Mike hobble up the stairs. Jodi heard Mike gasping for air with every step, muttering curses in between. Owen helped him inside the apartment, then he came back down to help Jodi with the bikes. Owen took a bike under each arm and practically ran up the steps. She marveled at his energy. How was he not on the verge of total collapse? She followed him up the stairs, but she had to awkwardly wheel her bike on the steps. She just didn't have the remaining strength to carry it, and she was still lugging the suitcase, which thumped along behind her.

Once inside the modest apartment, she found Mike collapsed on the couch.

"Sorry, guys, I'm pretty close to useless," he said. "Next time the sun decides to end life as we know it, ask it not to pick a chemo day."

"Just rest a while," Jodi said, propping her bike against the wall. "We'll set out in an hour or so and see if we can't make it a little farther today."

"Mom," Owen said, lining the bikes up. "Uncle Mike can't travel any farther today. Look at him. If we keep pushing him, he'll wind up back in the hospital, and then we'll be stuck in Augusta for who knows how long. Shouldn't we spend the night at his apartment so he can get a full night of rest? We could set out in the morning, and then we wouldn't be riding in the dark."

Jodi hated to do it, but she could see by the sickly look on Mike's face that they had little choice. "I suppose you're right. I just wish…" *I just wish we weren't in this neighborhood.* She felt bad thinking it, much less saying it, so she changed the subject. "You know, if this was a normal day, we would all be home by now. Shane would be home from work. Violet and Kaylee would be there."

"One more day, Mom. That's all it'll take."

"You're right," Jodi said with a nod. "One more day."

"Hey," Mike said, rousing himself, "don't you work for the CDC? Call your coworkers and see what's going on in the world? They're all probably home by now."

"Mike, the Centers for Disease Control and Prevention handles biological issues," she reminded him. "My coworkers wouldn't know much about the power grid."

"Ah yes, but they're a federal agency," he said, "with plenty of high-level connections. Someone will know something."

"Assuming cell service still works," she said.

"The doomsday guy at the hospital told you some cell phone providers would have service for a while because they have their own backup generators," Mike said. "Well, it's only been a few hours. Give it a try. It's worth finding out how long this awful situation is going to continue, isn't it? Personally, it's already feeling stuffy in this apartment. I would love to be able to run the AC. It sucks to lie here all sweaty and miserable."

"Okay, I'll see what I can find out," Jodi said.

She set her purse on a table in the corner and dug out her cell phone. Scrolling through her contacts, she came upon the name of her boss, Dr. Emmett. If anyone had meaningful government contacts, it would be him. She was surprised when the phone rang, and even more surprised when he answered, his basso profundo voice coming in strong.

"Jodi, where are you calling from?" he said. "Are you okay?"

"I'm in Augusta," she replied. "I'm with family, and I'm fine at the moment. Dr. Emmett, we have a basic understanding of what caused this situation, but did anyone know it was coming? Was there any sort of warning? It seems to have caught everyone by surprise."

Dr. Emmett hesitated a moment before answering. "I've been in touch with some key people, but I won't say who. Yes, we received an advance warning here at the office, and I know the same warning went out to most government agencies and affiliates. You've probably heard by now that it was a solar event—what's called a coronal mass ejection—and while similar events have happened in the past, this is by far the worst. A CME fried telegraph lines in 1859, but this one seems to have knocked out electronics across half the planet."

"Any prospects for getting the power up and running?" Jodi asked.

"I'll be blunt, because I know you can handle it," Dr. Emmett replied. "It will take *years* for the world to recover from this, and more modernized and electronic-based countries will be even further behind."

"Can't they just rebuild the damaged power grid?"

Mike was watching her intently from the couch, Owen pacing back and forth across the living room. Waiting for good news, perhaps bracing for worse.

"Jodi, from what I've been told," Dr. Emmett continued, "every major city will need several new transformers. Power companies generally have one replacement transformer on standby, if that. For the rest? It takes ten to twenty months to manufacture a transformer, and the work is done overseas. Cargo ships would have to deliver them, and most of those ships rely on electronic systems that will need to be either replaced or bypassed somehow. Do you realize how long that's going to take?"

"So it's what I feared," she said. "We're in this for a very long time."

"And we may never recover completely," he said. "There are economic, social, and political consequences that will be far-reaching and difficult to predict. I'll tell you what I've told every other employee I've talked to: find a safe place to settle in for the time being while we wait to see how this unfolds."

"I'm on my way to a place right now," she said. *If we can only get there.* "What about you?"

"My wife and I own a cabin near Black Rock Mountain. I plan to head there with my family as soon as I leave the office," he said. "Unfortunately, I can't get out of here yet. The CDC is implementing a shutdown protocol to destroy all of our bio samples before the backup power goes down. Not sure how long that'll take, but I can't leave until it's done."

The thought of all that research being destroyed made Jodi physically ill. Much of the data might never be recovered. So many years of work for nothing! It took her a moment to collect herself before she continued.

"The roads are bad," she said. "Be careful out there."

"I will. Thanks. Good luck, Jodi."

"Good luck to you, too, Dr. Emmett. Hopefully, I'll see you again sometime soon."

She hung up the phone and tossed it onto her open purse. Then she turned to Owen and Mike and relayed the information she'd just heard. Owen stopped pacing and collapsed onto the couch beside Mike, his head in his hands.

"He said get to a safe place," Owen said. "This doesn't feel like a safe place. Sorry to say it, Uncle Mike."

"You're not wrong," Mike replied, "but staying here for the night is still better than getting stuck out there in the dark on our bicycles. The wolves will come out when the sun goes down."

"Looters, you mean?" Owen said.

"Yeah, and worse."

Jodi had to resist arguing with him. Spending the night here still felt like a waste of time. The sooner they got to her mother's house in Macon the better, and it seemed wise to get there before traveling became too dangerous. Still, Mike was right about *looters and worse*.

"Let's get plenty of rest tonight," she said. "We'll set out as early as we possibly can, assuming you feel up to it, Mike. If we hit the road just after sunrise, we might avoid a lot of problems."

"I never sleep well after chemo," Mike said, "but I'll try. I'd get a warm beer out of the fridge, if I could keep anything down. Maybe I'll get one anyway. I'll enjoy it for the few minutes it stays in my belly."

"It's not a bad idea to eat and drink," she said. "Tell me you keep some groceries in this place."

"Cereal, water, milk, beer, a few snacks," he said. "Nothing that requires cooking. I have to admit I usually eat fast food. I know it's not good for me, but it's convenient."

While Jodi went through the cupboard that Mike used as a pantry, Owen wandered into the kitchen. Mike had an old battery-operated FM radio sitting on the windowsill, and Owen picked it up and began to fiddle with it. He turned it on and got static, so he spun the dial.

"Turn it to 106.3," Mike said. "Classic rock. That's my station."

"I already dialed past that," Owen said. "Nothing there."

"Dang. I can't imagine a world with no classic rock stations on the radio."

Suddenly, a station came in loud and clear, but it wasn't classic rock —or music of any kind. Instead, they heard a distinctive voice speaking in somber tones.

"Folks, that's our esteemed president," Mike said. "He's giving us the official version of the bad news, I assume."

"I encourage everyone to remain calm," the president said. "The next few days are going to be a little rough, so work with others in your communities. Help each other, and we'll get through this. Don't give in to fear. Don't make decisions out of frustration or anger. Remember, we're all in this together. As I speak, every government agency is hard at work finding solutions to the current crisis."

"That's a whole lot of cliched encouragement," Mike noted, "and very little practical information."

A little rough, he'd said. It was such an understatement that Jodi was disgusted by it. Still, she understood why they wouldn't admit the magnitude of the problem. Of course, the government would try to keep everyone calm.

"Don't give in to pessimism or conspiracy talk," the president continued. "This is not the end of the world. We will rebuild and bounce back stronger than ever. If you can, go to work, live out your ordinary lives as best you can, and avoid the temptation to overreact or panic. This will aid in the recovery, and it will contribute to peace of mind. Folks, it's not the end of the world. I promise you, we're going to rebuild our nation better than ever."

"Live out your ordinary lives," Mike echoed with a bitter laugh. "Has he stepped outside and taken a look at the streets? The world looks about as ordinary as a fever dream. Who can do their work when there's no power and cars won't run?"

"But what else can he say?" Owen asked. "He has to try to keep people calm. He's the president. It's his job."

"If everyone wakes up tomorrow and tries to go to work like it's a regular day," Mike said, "it's not going to generate peace of mind. He's making it worse, in my humble opinion."

They listened to the full address, and none of them felt better afterward. Then Jodi encouraged Owen to turn off the radio to save the batteries. They might need to tune in for information later, assuming the radio station hung in there somehow.

Jodi packed the radio, along with some of Mike's food. Then they ate, and Mike did indeed enjoy a warm beer from the refrigerator. He didn't even puke it up, at least not right away. Jodi tried to call Shane and Violet a few times throughout the evening, but she couldn't get through. She hoped and prayed they'd fared better on the road. Poor Violet. She was a sweet and gentle girl, but she usually assumed the best about everyone. How would she handle this new world unfolding around them?

16

Violet awoke to the sense of light and knew it was morning. Though she couldn't distinguish shapes or colors—bright objects appeared to her as amorphous blobs—she saw a kind of shifting glow that seemed far away. She assumed it was sunlight streaming through the blinds. She sat up in bed, kicking back the covers, and grabbed her forehead. Poor sleep had given her a splitting headache. Ruby stirred nearby, and Violet held her hand out so the dog could find it. She scratched Ruby behind the ears.

"Good morning, girl," she said. "I hope you slept better than I did. I had a lot of bad dreams. You probably need to go outside, huh?"

The whole horrible day came back to her then. Was the world still broken? Maybe someone had fixed it overnight. She had a small fan on the nightstand beside her bed, and she reached over to turn it on. The power switch clicked, but the fan didn't respond.

Nope, the world's still broken, she thought, feeling a sinking in the pit of her stomach.

She bent down, hunting around on the floor until she found her socks. One by one, she pulled them on, then she stumbled out of bed and moved across the room, Ruby padding along beside her. The layout of the house was fixed in her mind. She could move from room to room without Ruby's help, but she still let the dog guide her.

Grabbing the harness off the dresser, she slipped it over the dog's head, latching the straps under her belly. Then she grabbed the handle and let Ruby lead her to the bedroom door. She heard noises coming from the kitchen, and she recognized them as items being removed from shelves, along with the familiar sound of her father muttering under his breath. It sounded like he was packing things into cardboard boxes.

"Hey there, Violet," he said, as she moved into the dining room. "Did you get enough sleep last night?"

"Not really," she replied. "I had bad dreams where people were shouting at us and trying to break into the van. They kept waking me up. I don't feel very good this morning."

"I'm sorry to hear that," her father said. "I didn't sleep well either. With the power off, it's too darn quiet in this house. I can't wait to see your mom tonight. For once, her snoring will be a comfort."

"Yeah, Mom snores," Violet said. "I hear her sometimes all the way in my bedroom."

"Well, so do you."

"I do not," Violet protested.

"Just a little bit."

Violet went to the back door and let Ruby loose in the backyard. The dutiful lab ran to the grass to relieve herself, then came straight back to Violet, positioning herself so the handle of the harness brushed against her outstretched hand.

"Good girl," Violet said. "Dad, can I help?"

"Certainly," he said. "I'm clearing out the pantry and boxing up anything worth taking. Here's an empty box. You can pack the bottom shelf."

She heard him pat the side of an empty cardboard box, so she approached, felt for the edge of the pantry door, and sat down. Pulling the box toward her, she reached into the bottom shelf. As she did, she heard her dad sliding a filled box across the kitchen toward the laundry room.

"I was standing on the back porch last night after you went to bed," he said, "and I saw the northern lights."

"Aurora borealis," Violet said. "I've read about them."

"That's right," her father said, moving back to the pantry.

"Aren't they supposed to be up at the North Pole?" she said. She felt small boxes on the bottom shelf. When she shook the nearest one, it sounded like it was full of instant rice, so she pulled it out and put it in the cardboard box.

"Yeah, usually," he said. "I've never heard of anyone seeing them this far south. I'm sure it has something to do with the solar event, but I'm not sure what it means."

"You could look it up online," she suggested, grabbing a second box. This one sounded like instant potato flakes. She put it into the box.

"I already tried," her father said. "No internet."

"Are you sure?" she said. "I thought the internet would still work. We learned in class that the internet can survive all kinds of disasters because it's not based in any single location. Our teacher called it a *distributed network*."

"Well, technically, you're right," he said, sliding another box toward the laundry room. "In fact, the internet was designed by the Department of Defense specifically to survive nuclear war, but I'm guessing enough of the infrastructure was damaged to make it impossible to connect. The 'net is still there; we just can't get to it."

"There's got to be a way to a connect," Violet said, dragging a bag of beans out of the pantry and setting it in the box. "I'll bet Landon would know."

"You're probably right," her father replied, "but we'll leave him to his work. He has enough to deal with."

"No internet, no lights, no appliances," Violet said. "Soon, we'll be back in the stone age."

"Not quite," Dad said. "More like the early industrial age."

"Well, it's bad either way." She grabbed the last item on the bottom shelf, a bag of potatoes, and set it in the cardboard box, then closed the lid, folding the flaps together to keep them shut. "What if we can't get any gas today?"

"Let's worry about one problem at a time."

She heard him sliding the heavy box across the kitchen, so she rose and felt her way to the dining room table.

"I'll tell you what," her father said. "Let's have some breakfast. The food in the fridge will spoil anyway, so we might as well make the most of it. How does bacon on the grill sound?"

"I don't know," Violet replied. "I never had grilled bacon. It doesn't sound very good."

"Okay, let's see what else we have."

She heard him fishing around inside the fridge, bottles clanking together as he pulled items out. He set some things on the counter.

"We've got a bit of ham as well," he said. "Orange juice. The milk is pretty warm, so I don't know about that, but here are some bagels and cream cheese."

"I'm not super hungry, to be honest," Violet said.

"You should eat anyway," he said. "You'll feel better afterward."

"Okay, if you say so, Dad, but not ham or warm milk. I could stand a bagel, I guess, and orange juice would be fine."

"Coming right up."

After a moment, Violet heard the sound of orange juice being poured into a glass, so she felt for the glass and grabbed it. She took a drink and tasted pulpy orange juice, the kind her parents preferred. She wasn't particularly fond of the texture. Instead of complaining, she set the glass down and gently pushed it away from her.

"How early in the morning is it?" she asked.

"About an hour after sunrise," he said. "Eat something, please. We don't know what the day will bring."

She heard a plate sliding across the tablecloth, so she reached for it and felt along the edge. It was a plate of bagels. When she grabbed one, she found her father had already smeared it with cream cheese. She wished he hadn't. Though she knew he was trying to be helpful, she preferred to do small tasks by herself.

"After you eat, I want you to gather up anything from the house that you'd like to keep," her father said. "We might be at your grandma's for...a long time."

She could tell by the tone of his voice, and the slight hesitation in the way he said it, that he'd meant to say something else. *He doesn't think we're ever coming back*, she thought. An awful thought, but she didn't ask him about it. She didn't want to hear him say it out loud.

After forcing herself to eat most of the bagel, she went to her bedroom to get dressed. Then she began to gather up her things. There was so much she didn't want to leave behind, she didn't even know where to begin. First, she grabbed Ruby's dog bed. When she did, Ruby brushed up against her and began sniffing the bed, as if to say, "Where are you taking that?" Placing the dog bed on her dresser, she went through her clothes, picking out her favorite shirts, jeans, shorts, and pajamas, selecting a few of her skirts and blouses from the closet. She folded and piled them all neatly on top of the dog bed.

She snagged a couple pairs of sunglasses off her nightstand. Kids at school had made her self-conscious in the past about the way her eyes moved around, so she often wore sunglasses when she was out in public. She didn't find them particularly comfortable—she hated the way they pressed against the bridge of her nose—and she had trouble finding a pair that fit well. However, she preferred the discomfort to worrying about whether or not people were staring at her.

She also grabbed her guide cane from its place in the corner. She didn't need it in familiar places, and she often didn't need it in public when she was with Ruby. However, it seemed like a good time to cover all her bases. She folded it up and pushed it into her back pocket.

Finally, she grabbed a few of her Braille books, some mementos she'd collected from family trips, and even a few of her childhood toys. There were still so many things she would have to leave behind. Even the house itself, which had become so comfortable to her. The familiarity of the house gave her such a feeling of safety and security. Feeling the sting of tears, she gathered up all her things and carried them into the dining room, dumping them on the table.

Her father was moving back and forth from the laundry room to the garage, lugging what she assumed were the cardboard boxes. After five or six trips back and forth, he came into the dining room out of breath.

"Is that everything you want to bring?" he asked.

"No, but I guess it's enough," she replied. "We can't bring my whole bedroom. I wish we could. It's not that I want to stay here. I don't. I'd rather hurry and get to Macon so we can be with Grandma and Mom and Kaylee, but…you know, it's my room."

"Sorry, sweetheart." She heard him rearranging her stuff, probably stacking it better on top of the dog bed. "You don't want to bring your digital audiobook player?"

"What's the point?" she said. "It's plugged into the wall. Even if Grandma has batteries, there are probably more important uses for them. Braille is fine."

She heard him hoist her great pile of belongings off the table. As he started back into the kitchen, she thought of something.

"Dad, shouldn't you bring our photo albums?" she said. "You and Mom might want to look at them sometime, and…well, you can't look at the pictures on social media anymore."

"That's good thinking," he replied. "Very smart of you, Violet, especially considering the fact that you—"

He left the comment unfinished, catching himself suddenly, but she knew what he meant. *Considering the fact that you can't look at them.* It bothered her more that he hadn't said it. Her father being embarrassed on her behalf was far worse than any embarrassment caused by the truth. Just in case she was blushing, she knelt down beside Ruby and pretended to fiddle with the harness. The dog sniffed her face and touched her cheek with her wet nose.

"Let's load up, Violet," her father called from the laundry room. "I'll get the photo albums, and then we'll be ready to hit the road."

Violet moved through the dining room and kitchen, trying to enjoy her last moments in the house. When she reached the cold garage, she felt her way to the van. Ruby turned her at the last second, so she didn't bump into the back of the vehicle. Finally, she reached the passenger door and opened it. She pulled the folded cane out of her back pocket and tucked it under the seat. Then she climbed inside.

Ruby hopped up onto her lap then lay down on the floorboard beside her.

She sat there in silence for a minute, feeling a low, trembling dread at the day ahead. If only they didn't still have so many miles to go. She'd always thought her grandma lived close by, but now it seemed like she might as well be on the other side of the ocean. When she heard the loud squeal of the garage door being opened, she flinched.

How much worse can it possibly be out there? she wondered, knowing that she would soon find out.

17

The line at the gas station turned out to be far longer than they'd anticipated. Violet knew it before her father told her by the way his breathing changed. He whispered a curse that was almost inaudible as the van came to a slow stop.

"How bad is it, Dad? I hear a lot of cars."

"I didn't think there were so many working vehicles on the road. I guess they're all here. The line goes across the parking lot and almost a block down the street. It's a mess, but I don't see another way. If I don't fill up the tank, we won't reach Macon, and the last thing I want to do is get stuck on the highway somewhere."

Ruby had risen from her place on the floorboard and laid her head on Violet's leg.

"Dad, Ruby has to go potty," she said.

"I thought she went at the house," her father said.

"She went number one. I think she needs to go number two now. She always does both in the morning, but she doesn't like to do them both at the same time. Ruby is weird that way."

"Can she wait until we get a little closer?" he asked.

"I guess."

They crept forward one car at a time, Shane impatiently tapping out a rhythm on the steering wheel. Ruby finally rose and put her paws on Violet's leg, sniffing at her face.

"Dad, she really has to go," Violet said.

"Okay, we're just about to turn into the parking lot," he said. "There's a big grassy area outside your door. Let Ruby lead you, but be careful. Don't step onto the pavement. There are cars on both sides."

"Got it," Violet said. "We'll be fine. Ruby will keep me safe."

She felt the van make the turn into the parking lot. As soon as it stopped, she opened her door, picked up her cane from the floorboard, and unfolded it by flipping the end outside. She felt her way down to the grass, and Ruby leapt over the seat and landed beside her. The dog began to pace back and forth, the way she did when she was looking for a place to do number two. Violet grabbed the handle of her harness in her free hand and let Ruby lead her, using the cane to make sure she didn't step onto the road.

"Stay with Ruby," her father said. "I'll come get you when I'm done pumping gas."

"Okay," she replied. "We won't go far."

Ruby began to move in one direction, leading Violet farther from the road. Violet could tell they were moving behind a building. As they went, they passed some people who were either kneeling or sitting on the grass. She heard them talking to each other quietly. Ruby was good at maneuvering through crowds, but Violet accidentally bumped one of them with her cane. She apologized.

"Watch yourself," a man said in an unfriendly voice.

Finally, Ruby found a spot that she liked, and she stopped. Violet touched her flank and felt her squatting down. She hadn't thought to bring a bag to clean up the mess. She was just thinking about going inside the gas station to get some paper towels when she heard strange, furtive movements behind her. In the absence of vision, she had learned to react to any sound that was out of the ordinary, especially when it came from somewhere nearby.

As she started to turn toward the source of the sound, someone grabbed her shoulder. Instantly, Ruby was alert, pulling against her harness as she turned to confront the person. Violet heard a growl building in the dog's throat.

"Hey, watch where you're swinging that stick, dummy," a man said. It sounded like the same one she'd bumped into. "You could put an eye out with that thing."

She jerked away from the hand that had grabbed her, and two men began to laugh. This was a sound she knew—mocking laughter from young men.

"I didn't mean to," she said. "Sorry."

"It looked intentional to me," the second man said. He had a higher, sharper voice.

"I think you're right," said the first. "She swung it right at my head. What a rude little runt."

"Hey," Violet protested. "I'm not a *runt*."

One of the men kicked her cane and nearly knocked it out of her grasp. Another poked her in the stomach. She smacked the hand away from her stomach, and it made one of the men laugh harder. The moment felt surreal. She was standing in a busy place surrounded by cars and customers. Why would perfect strangers start bothering her?

"Please, leave me alone," she said. "My dad is right over there." She pointed in the direction of the van.

"Ooh, her daddy is right over there," the first man said in a taunting voice. Something sounded wrong with him. Was he drunk? High? "Did you hear that? Her daddy is right over there."

"Right over there," said the second. Definitely high. "Help me, daddy. Please, daddy, I can't see! I'm so scared, daddy."

Ruby was growling and gnashing her teeth at them. Violet heard one of the men dance away, apparently just avoiding a bite, his laugh becoming a momentary shout of alarm. Violet tightened her grip on the harness and tried to pull Ruby back, but the dog wanted to leap at their throats.

"Down, girl," she said. "Down. You know you're not supposed to bite people. Stop that."

"That damn dog just about took my fingers off," one of the men said. He was still laughing, but it sounded forced now. "Did you see that? That thing looks rabid, man."

"Please, go away," Violet said, fighting as Ruby pulled the handle of the harness taut. "You're upsetting her."

And then Violet heard the sound of a hard shoe connecting with Ruby's ribs, the sudden expulsion of the dog's breath followed a moment later by a pained *yip*.

"I'm gonna kill that stupid dog," the man said. "It tried to bite me. It's a dangerous wild animal."

"She didn't mean it," Violet said. "You're making her nervous."

"Well, *I* mean it," the man replied.

A gunshot filled the air, so close and so loud that Violet went momentarily deaf. Her ears ringing, she dropped down beside Ruby and threw her arms around the dog, trying to protect her.

"No, no, please," she wailed. "Leave her alone. Don't hurt us."

But through the screen of white noise, she heard the men shouting in terror as they retreated. No longer laughing, they sounded terrified, and soon their shoes hit the pavement as they fled across the parking lot.

"Dad, is that you?" Violet said. "Did you shoot them?"

A second passed before someone answered. Not her father, but a woman's voice. "No, I'm not your dad. Are you okay?"

Violet felt a hand on her back, and she flinched.

"Don't worry," the woman said. "I won't hurt you. I scared them off. Fired a round into the sky. Those were some rough-looking lowlifes, let me tell you, but you're safe now. They're hightailing it down the street. You gotta know how to deal with people like that—speak their own language."

Stroking Ruby's side to calm her, Violet rose and turned to the woman. "Who are you?"

"My name's Debra," she said.

"I'm Violet. I don't know why those guys started bothering me."

"Just a couple of tweakers looking for trouble," Debra said, "and they found it. Violet, you said your dad is nearby. Where is he?"

"He's getting gas," Violet said. She was still shaking from the encounter, fighting tears. "He's in the Volkswagen van."

"Come on," Debra said. "I'll take you to him. Don't cry, honey. Those losers are long gone, and if they come back, I have no problem aiming right between the eyes next time."

Debra sounded a little rough herself, but in this moment, Violet was glad for it. A gentler person might not have confronted the men. When Debra grabbed her forearm, Violet allowed herself to be pulled off the grass and across the parking lot. Shane must have seen them coming, as he shouted her name in the distance.

"Violet, what happened?" he said. "I heard a gun? Are you okay?"

"A couple of druggie losers were picking on her," Debra said. "I scared them off. Don't worry. Nobody got hurt."

"Oh, gosh, Violet, I'm so sorry," her father said, giving her a hug. "I shouldn't have let you go off by yourself."

"I wasn't by myself," Violet said. "Ruby was with me."

"Still, I have to be more careful," Shane said, and then to Debra, "Thank you. If something had happened to my daughter, I never would have forgiven myself."

"You're more than welcome," Debra said. "I enjoyed scaring them. They looked like trash."

"My name is Shane McDonald." Violet heard her dad and Debra shaking hands. "I owe you big time for this."

"I'm Debra," the woman replied. "I'll be honest with you, Shane McDonald. I live here in town, but I came to the gas station hoping to find a ride to Sandy Springs. My son is staying at a camp there. I don't know if you're headed that way."

"Sandy Springs," Shane said. "That's somewhere close to Atlanta, right?"

"Just north," Debra said.

"It's not too far out of our way, I suppose. Okay, we'll give you a ride. It's the least we can do after what you did for Violet."

Violet didn't know how she felt about this. As her father and Debra discussed the route they should take to Sandy Springs, she fought an urge to complain. It seemed like a bad idea to divert to another city, and Debra was practically a stranger. It made Violet uncomfortable, as strangers and new situations often did. Still, she might have just saved Ruby's life. How could they refuse to help her?

Debra and Shane finally settled on a route that would take them around Atlanta, and then Shane went back to finish fueling up the van.

"Don't worry, I won't be a bother," Debra said to Violet. "I'll bet you've had a rough time since the power went out, huh?"

"Yeah, driving on the highway was kind of scary," Violet said. "So many stalled cars, and we almost ran over some people."

"On purpose?"

"Sort of. They tried to force us to stop."

Debra laughed at this. "Sometimes you gotta do what you gotta do."

Violet heard her dad speaking to the gas station attendant, so she fell silent. Her father sounded annoyed.

"Cash only?" he said. "It's not like anyone can draw money from an ATM."

"Sorry, sir, we don't have a choice," the young-sounding attendant said. "My boss doesn't trust checks, and our card reader doesn't work."

"You're charging ten dollars a gallon for diesel," Shane said. "That's practically stealing. You're taking advantage of people in a time of crisis."

"No, sir," the attendant replied. "The higher price is because we're working harder. We have to hand-pump the gas, so it's more labor-intensive. It's only fair we make a little more money for the trouble."

"I hand-pumped my own gas while you were helping other customers," Shane said.

"But the price is the price, sir. I didn't set it, and I can't change it."

"Well, I've only got thirty dollars in my wallet," Shane said, "so I don't know what you expect me to do."

"Sir, you have to pay," the attendant said. "We've already had some people try to drive off. That's why we've got security in there."

Debra cleared her throat. "Young man, there's not a problem here. I've got him covered." Violet heard the sound of crisp bills being flipped through. "How much does he owe you?"

"Where the heck did you get all that money?" Shane asked.

"Until yesterday, I was a bartender," Debra replied. "Before I left work, I raided the till and the tip jar. Oh, don't give me that look. No one else was there. Anyway, the money would've been stolen by some other employee or customer eventually. All the bars will end up getting looted, mark my words. Shelves stacked with free booze—scared people will want their liquor."

"Stealing's not right," Violet said. She said it out loud before she could catch herself.

"Desperate times call for desperate measures," Debra said. "I have to get to my son, and, hey, it just paid for your gas. So we've all benefited, haven't we?"

The attendant took the money and thanked her.

"Did you top off the tank?" Debra asked Shane.

"Not quite," Shane confessed.

"Top it off," she said. "I'll cover it."

"Thanks," he said.

"It's my pleasure," Debra said, "and the least I can do for the ride. You seem like nice people. I was afraid I would have to hitch a ride with some filthy creep. You know how that would've gone."

Violet didn't feel right about the use of stolen money. And it bothered her that her father went along with it. Another sign that the world had changed for the worse. She bit her tongue to avoid saying anything else and climbed into the van.

18

S tanding at the kitchen counter, bent over a row of canned
sausages and vegetables, Beth almost fell asleep. On the verge,
her knees buckled, and she snorted herself awake. She rose, rubbing
at her face, and went to the kitchen sink. She'd spent hours canning,
then slept a little bit, and woke up again to can some more. She was
sleep-deprived, her mind foggy, and her whole body ached, but she
figured she could catch up on sleep later. For now, she had to prepare,
and she was determined to preserve as much food as possible before
it all spoiled.

She had filled the sink with water from the tap and put the stopper in
place. Scooping up some of the water now, she splashed it on her face
then patted her face dry with a towel. As she did, she saw movement
in the distance through the small window above the sink. Two men on
motorcycles were pulling into the driveway of Mrs. Eddies' house.
The riders were skinny fellows with bad skin, one in a denim jacket,
the other in a ratty old t-shirt.

As far as Beth knew, EMTs had never come to the house, which meant no one had ever collected the body. These guys certainly didn't look like they were from the local funeral home. The guy in the denim jacket climbed off his bike and approached the little statuary garden, kicking through the weeds as if to see what was there. The other one approached the front door and began knocking on it with a closed fist.

Wanting a closer look, Beth went outside and watched the men through a gap in her fence. The guy in the denim jacket picked up one of the small statues from the garden, a fat-bellied cherub speckled with mold. He turned it over, examined it, then tossed it unceremoniously back into the weeds. The guy in the t-shirt stopped knocking on the front door and went to the garage door, peering through one of the dusty windowpanes.

Clearly, they were looking for a way in. Beth thought about going back inside to get her gun, but she stopped herself. Being armed might make matters worse. Better to adopt a friendly approach at first. She walked through the gate and started across her yard. When the guy in the t-shirt looked at her, she gave him a neighborly wave.

"Hey there, gentlemen," she said. "Good morning."

Denim-jacket guy stopped kicking through the weeds and stepped up beside the other one. When they stood side by side, Beth saw clear resemblance between the two. They both had long, lean faces and high foreheads. For a couple of seconds, they said nothing in response to her greeting, and she considered retreating back to her yard.

"Hey there," denim-jacket guy said finally.

"Good morning," said the other.

She considered approaching them and trying to get them to shake hands. If they accepted, it might defuse the situation a little more. However, it didn't seem safe, so she stopped at the edge of the property and fixed a smile on her face.

"I'm glad to see someone's finally come to check on Mrs. Eddies," she said. "I called 911 yesterday, but I don't think they ever came. I'm sure they have plenty of other emergencies to worry about, but still...I'd hoped someone would come out here eventually."

"Someone did come," said t-shirt guy, tapping his own chest. "Us."

"My name is Beth Bevin," she said. "Nice to meet both of you. Are you friends or family? Maybe I can help you with something."

"Family," denim-jacket guy said, with a weird thrust of his chin. "I'm Greg. Greg *Eddies*, and this is my brother, Travis. This is our grandma's house."

"We just came for a visit," Travis said. When he spoke, Beth noticed he was missing one of his upper canine teeth. "Figured someone ought to check on her and see if she needed anything. Poor Granny, we tried for years to get her to move closer to us, but she was stubborn."

Mrs. Eddies had mentioned her grandsons on more than one occasion during casual conversations, and, as Beth recalled, she'd always spoken of them with a note of disappointment. She'd never said their names, but the phrase "my grandkids" had always been accompanied with a deep sigh or a shake of the head.

"Greg and Travis," Beth noted. "Guys, I hate to be the bearer of bad news, but your grandma passed away yesterday. I went to check on her and found her in the bed. I'm so sorry."

Greg and Travis looked at each other, frowning. Then Travis dropped his gaze and scuffed the toe of his sneaker against the concrete.

"Well, that's a shame," Greg said, crossing his arms over his chest. "That's a darn shame. Grandma was a nice old lady. She always helped us when we were in need, and she was a good cook. Even when she didn't feel like it, she hobbled into the kitchen and made us whatever we wanted. We should've come here sooner, I guess, but we had our own problems to deal with. Plus, it ain't easy getting gas, and it's expensive as heck. Highway robbery is what it is."

"Poor Grandma," Travis said. "We were hoping to have a nice…a nice conversation over a home-cooked meal."

"Everyone's been dealing with their own problems," Beth said, "so I understand. Since EMTs never came to the house, I'm afraid that means her body is still in the bed."

Travis made a disgusted face and walked over to his motorcycle, but Greg took this news in stride.

"Thanks for telling us," he said. "We'll deal with the body. Do you know if she had a spare house key? She used to have this fake rock in the garden with a compartment inside, but I didn't find it. Maybe she moved it. I don't know."

Beth hesitated a moment before telling them. She was afraid they might force their way in. "Under the welcome mat."

"Thanks," Greg said, and made a beeline for the front door. "That's so obvious, I didn't think of it."

Travis scuffed his sneaker again and followed his brother. Beth didn't stick around. No reason to develop any kind of friendly relationship with these two. She walked back to her own house but paused at the fence, watching them for a minute. Instead of pulling back a corner of the welcome mat, Greg picked up the whole thing and chucked it into the weedy garden, covering the angel as if with a shroud. Travis stooped down to grab the exposed house key, but Greg pushed him away and grabbed it himself. As Beth watched, they unlocked the front door, and Greg threw it open hard enough that it bounced off the door stopper with a loud thud.

The brothers looked at each other, and Greg said something to Travis that Beth couldn't hear. Whatever it was, Travis laughed loudly, shook his head, and strode inside. Greg followed.

They certainly don't seem like grieving grandsons. They're just going to trash the house looking for valuables, she thought. Maybe she was wrong—she certainly hoped so—but she felt nervous around them. It didn't seem right to let them loose in the house, even though Mrs. Eddies was gone and even though they were family.

Beth went back inside her own house and found Kaylee sitting at the kitchen table and Bauer wagging his tail nearby. Kaylee had serious "bed head," her hair piled high to one side and matted against her cheek. She'd found some crayons and an old coloring book, and she was hard at work making people and things the wrong colors.

"Good morning, pumpkin," Beth said, trying to comb her granddaughter's hair with her fingers. It was little use, and Kaylee began squirming. "How are you doing today?"

"The lights still don't work," Kaylee said. "I already tried them. They don't work in my room, and they don't work in the hall, and they don't work in the bathroom."

"I know," Beth said, leading Bauer into the kitchen. "They're going to be broken for a very long time, but it's okay. We'll be just fine."

"Do we have to use candles and flashlights all the time?" she asked.

"Just at night," Beth said. "You'll get used to it."

"Okay, but I don't think so."

Beth poured some dry dog food into Bauer's stainless-steel bowl, and the dog began to noisily eat. Beth filled up his water dish as well from the stoppered sink. Then she pulled her cell phone out of her pocket.

Can I squeeze one more call out of this thing? she wondered. If so, she knew who she ought to call. She went to the list of phone numbers beside her landline phone and looked for the local sheriff's number. The number for his office was listed, but she wanted to speak to him directly. She'd made sure to maintain personal connections with law enforcement over the years. It made things a lot easier.

She dialed his personal number. Sheriff Cooley answered on the first ring.

"Beth Bevin," he said. "So nice to hear from you. Where are you? What's going on?" The connection was poor, and his voice kept popping and cracking.

"Sheriff Cooley, I'm glad I caught you," she said. "I'm sure you must be busy."

"Call me James, please," he said. "I wish I didn't have to say that every single time. We've known each other long enough, haven't we?"

"I suppose so," Beth said. "James."

For some reason, this made him chuckle. "To answer your question, yes, I'm incredibly busy. You wouldn't believe how many problems people have when the power goes out. Complain, complain, complain. Everybody thinks it's the end of the world. I keep encouraging them to help each other. Neighbors have to support neighbors, or we're all sunk."

"Well, I don't want to keep you from your duty," Beth said.

"Now, now, I've always got time for you," he said. "What's going on?"

"Speaking of neighbor supporting neighbor," Beth replied, "I'm afraid the sweet woman who lives next door to me passed away yesterday."

"Mrs. Eddies?" he said. "I'm sorry to hear that. Do I need to come over there and deal with the…uh, remains?"

"Actually, her grandsons just showed up," Beth said. "I let them into her house. Not sure if that was a mistake or not. They make me nervous. They didn't do anything wrong, not really, but there's just something about them."

"Are we talking about kids? Teenagers?" he asked.

"Mid-twenties, maybe," she said. "Their names are Greg and Travis. I don't suppose you've heard of them."

"The names don't ring a bell," he replied. "Are you sure they're local?"

"I don't know where they're from, honestly. They showed up on their motorcycles this morning. Would you mind looking them up somehow, seeing if they have any sort of criminal record?"

"I would if I could," he said, "but I can't access any databanks with the systems down. I'll tell you what, I'll head over there personally and check them out. I've dealt with all kinds, so I'll get a sense if there's trouble, I assure you."

"Thanks, Sheriff…I mean, James," she said. "I appreciate it."

"And I hope you won't mind if I stop by and say hello, Beth. I don't want to be a pest, but it's always nice to see a friendly face."

"That would be just fine," she said.

"I'd say put the kettle on so we can have some tea, but I guess there's no stove."

"I can make tea or coffee on the grill," Beth said.

"In that case, I'll be there before you know it. See you soon, Beth."

"Okay, James. See you soon."

She hung up the phone and put it back in her pocket. Then she glanced out the kitchen window. Greg and Travis were nowhere to be seen, but the front door was still wide open.

Grandsons paying grandma a visit wouldn't leave the door like that, she thought. *That's something burglars would do.*

19

J odi had no intention of trying to balance the stupid suitcase on the frame of her bike for over a hundred miles, so she fashioned a couple of makeshift straps using duct tape and two of Mike's old t-shirts. The end result was ugly, but it fit over her shoulders and it wasn't entirely uncomfortable. While she worked on securing the straps, Owen helped Mike pack some clothes, nonperishable food, and other personal items into a JanSport backpack.

Mike also took a moment to remove the old bandage from his neck. When he did, Jodi caught a glimpse of the incision. It was longer than she'd expected, maybe six inches, running vertically up the side of his neck toward his earlobe. He washed the wound gently in the kitchen sink, cleaning off the crust that had built up over it, then he dried his hands on a paper towel.

"Does it hurt this morning?" she asked.

"For the size of the thing they chopped out of me, it's actually not the worst pain," he said, as he opened a fresh bandage. "The nausea is far worse."

"Well, don't forget to take care of it," Jodi said. "We don't want you getting infected. In our current situation, that would be especially dangerous."

"You don't have to tell me," Mike said, pressing a new gel-like bandage over the wound. "Fortunately, the constant stinging sensation serves as a good reminder that it's there."

He also took a moment to run a disinfectant wipe around the plastic port in his arm. When he was done, he picked up the backpack, as if to sling it over his shoulders.

"Let me carry it," Owen said. "You don't need the extra burden, Uncle Mike."

"Are you sure, kid?" he replied. "You're already lugging around that big duffel bag."

"Yeah, I'm sure," Owen said, taking the backpack from him. "I can handle it."

"I'm sure you can. I appreciate it." Mike stumbled over to the couch and sat down. "I have to admit, guys, while I feel better than I did last night, it's still pretty rough. I won't be able to go far without taking a break."

"We know," Jodi said. "We'll take it at your pace."

She meant it, but in truth she was frustrated. The thought of stopping every few minutes made the whole day before them seem like an impossible slog. Still, what choice did they have? She grabbed her bicycle by the handles and walked it to the door of Mike's apartment.

"Let's hit the road," she said. "We have a long way to go today."

She opened the door and stuck her head outside. It was just after sunrise, and the world seemed much emptier than the evening before. There were no crowds gathered in the parking lot or in the street beyond—not yet—just a scattering of dead vehicles and a remarkable lack of city noises. She pulled her bike down the stairs and waited for the others. Despite the backpack on his shoulders and the duffel bag hanging from his forearm, Owen hoisted the other two bikes and carried them down the steps. Mike locked up his apartment before following them.

They mounted up at the edge of the parking lot and set out single file, with Jodi leading the way and Owen bringing up the rear. Jodi kept checking the straps on the suitcase. She'd used a ridiculous amount of duct tape, but she was worried they would unravel somehow. They felt a bit loose, which made the suitcase bounce from side to side in a way that wasn't entirely pleasant.

As they made their way through Mike's neighborhood, they passed a few people out in the open: an old man sitting on a porch smoking a cigar, a couple of teenagers standing in the long shadow of an oak tree, a woman walking her dog. Everyone seemed dazed, still struggling to take in their new world. It appeared as if some of the stalled vehicles had been looted. She saw doors that had been opened, a few windows that had been smashed, and one car that seemed to have had its trunk crowbarred open.

When they reached a major street, she spotted a few vehicles weaving their way through traffic. A gas station on a nearby corner had a line of cars and trucks stretching down the street. She was tempted to ask someone for a ride to Macon, but they were carrying so much stuff now she thought it unlikely anyone would take them on.

After a few miles, Mike began to lag behind, and finally Owen called them to a halt. Jodi pulled over into the grass in front of an elementary school and stopped. Mike and Owen caught up to her a few seconds later. Mike was pale and sweaty, gasping for air, and when he stopped, he stumbled off the bike and sank to his knees.

"Just a second…just a second," he said, holding up a hand. "Let me catch my breath. I'm getting dizzy."

"It's no problem," Jodi said, fighting to keep the edge out of her voice.

She traded a look with her son, but Owen seemed not the least bit bothered by the stop. He only looked concerned for his uncle. Still out of breath, Mike mopped his face with the hem of his t-shirt and rose, wincing from the effort.

"I'm just warming up," he said. "Any minute now, I'll catch a second wind and then I'll pass both of you. Just wait and see. I ran cross-country in high school. I'm no quitter."

He climbed back onto his bike, adjusted himself, and signaled for Jodi to continue.

"Are you sure?" Jodi asked.

"I'm as sure as I can be."

She pedaled off the grass and resumed moving past the elementary school. They were in a nicer neighborhood now, heading in the general direction of State Highway 1, which Jodi knew would take them all the way to Macon. By the time they came in sight of the highway, Mike was lagging again, breathing so loudly that Jodi could hear him.

Finally, about five miles from the elementary school, they stopped again, this time pulling into the parking lot of a small Catholic Church which was right next to the highway. Mike was drenched with sweat, so Jodi headed for a couple of tall pine trees to one side of the church and came to a stop. Mike slid off his bike, catching himself against the trunk of a tree before sitting down on the grass.

"So much for that second wind," he said, grabbing the bandage on the side of his neck. "It didn't last long. Maybe I've got a third wind in me somewhere."

Though they'd left the downtown area behind, they weren't out of Augusta yet. Jodi was beginning to feel impatient to the point of distraction. As Mike struggled to catch his breath, pouring water on his face from a water bottle he'd dug out of his backpack, she tried to calculate how long it would take them to get to her mother's house. The prospects were bleak.

It's 125 miles. Under ideal conditions, we might get there in two days, she thought, *but with Mike in his current state, we'll be lucky to cover twenty miles today. That means we could be on the road for a week.*

Owen squatted down next to his uncle, swapping out the empty water bottle for a new one. They wouldn't have enough water to last a day if they swapped one out every time they stopped, but Jodi didn't want to say it. She couldn't bring herself to tell Mike what she was thinking. It wasn't his fault he was so weak. She looked at the bandage on the side of his neck. He'd changed it out that morning, but it was already stained.

This was a mistake, she thought. *Why did I ever think riding bikes to Macon was a good idea?*

"Mike, is there anything we can do for you?" she asked. "I don't want to push you beyond what you can bear."

"That third wind is coming," he said. "I just know it. I'm already feeling better than I was this morning."

"Is that true?" she asked.

He glanced at her briefly then looked away. "No, not really," he said, after a moment. "I'm human wreckage, but I'll push through the pain."

He started to get up, but she waved him back down. "Why don't you rest a little bit longer this time," she said. "Maybe we'll get farther."

"I'm fine," he said. "I can make it."

"You can't push yourself to the breaking point," she said. *Then we'll really be in trouble.*

"She's right, Uncle Mike," Owen said. "Take it easy."

Mike took a swig of water, swished it around his mouth, and spat it out. "Okay, fine, another minute or two. I'm sorry, guys. I know I'm a huge pain in the butt."

"No need to apologize," Owen said. "You can't help it."

Suppressing a sigh, Jodi set her kickstand and sat down beside Mike. She was impressed with her son's patience, but she was struggling not to act annoyed. This wasn't going to work. She had to admit it to herself. Mike just wouldn't make it.

"I don't know why I'm so weak," Mike said. "I thought I'd have a little more strength this morning."

Though Jodi wasn't sharing her real thoughts, she could tell her brother was picking up on her mood. Finally, a heavy silence fell among them. As she gazed off into the distance, she saw a few working vehicles pass on the nearby highway.

If some halfway decent individual in a pickup truck would let us pile in the back, we'd be set, she thought. Then again, they were carrying a lot of stuff: her purse, the duffel bag, the suitcase, the JanSport backpack, and three bikes. Even a pickup truck might be a tight fit. *We might have to leave the bikes behind.*

She slid the bike helmet off her head and set it to one side, tucking her hair behind her ears.

"Mom, is there some way maybe Uncle Mike could ride on my bike with me?" Owen said.

"I don't think that would be safe," she replied. "He might fall off or get his foot caught in the spokes."

"There's no way we could make it work," Mike said, "but I appreciate the thought, kid."

A vehicle caught Jodi's eye then. It was much smaller than the others, and as it approached it took her a moment to realize what it was. Not a small car. It was one of the little gray pedicabs that had become common in downtown Augusta. She normally saw them carrying couples in the parks near the Savannah River. This one was way out of its typical area. At the moment, it had no passengers, only a stocky driver with a red beanie on his head and thick glasses that caught the late morning sun.

"Stay here," Jodi told Mike and Owen. "I might have a solution."

She rose, put her bike helmet back on, and approached the sidewalk as the pedicab drew near. When she waved at the driver, he waved back. That was a good sign. As he came within shouting distance, she called, "Hey, you carrying any passengers today?"

The pedicab was essentially a bicycle attached to a two-person padded bench. She thought if they piled the luggage on one side and put Mike on the other, they could make it work. The driver pulled up beside her and stopped.

"Oh, yeah, I've had plenty of passengers," he said. "We're ferrying people all over the place, especially with so many cars out of commission. Where are you headed?"

"Actually, I'd like to buy the pedicab from you," she said, opening the purse that still hung from her shoulder. She fished around inside for her money clip. "I'll trade you one of our brand-new mountain bikes, plus…" She pulled out a wad of cash. "Two hundred dollars."

The pedicab driver stared at her in disbelief. "Ma'am, the pedicab belongs to the company," he said. "They've got a tracking device installed, so they know where it is at all times. I can't just sell it to someone."

"I imagine the tracking device got fried like everything else," Jodi said. "Just tell the company someone stole the pedicab from you. Look, I hate to put you in this position, but we're kind of desperate." She held up the money. "You don't have to tell the company about the two hundred dollars. Keep it for yourself."

The driver looked from Jodi to the money to the bikes. "Let's say two-fifty, one bike, and…uh, what else do you happen to be carrying in your suitcases there?"

In the end, they settled on $250 plus Mike's bicycle and some of the first aid supplies from the duffel bag. As the pedicab driver rode away on the mountain bike, Jodi thought she heard him whistling a tune. Mike took a seat on the back bench, the suitcase, backpack, and duffel bag piled beside him. Jodi left her bike beside the tree and took the driver's seat of the pedicab.

Maybe I should have given him two bikes, she thought, looking regretfully at the Schwinn propped against the tree. *Seems a waste to leave one behind.*

"This was a good idea, Mom," Owen said. "I hope that guy doesn't get in trouble with his boss."

"I doubt it," Jodi replied. "At least we made it worth his while. Honestly, he got a pretty good deal."

Pedaling the pedicab proved a bit more difficult and taxing than the mountain bike, but now that Mike didn't have to stop, they made better time. Owen followed behind, and though he didn't say anything, he seemed relieved not to be lugging around the duffel bag. They turned onto Highway 1 and made their slow but steady way across Augusta. By late afternoon, they'd reached the outskirts of the city. Buildings gave way to endless trees, which lined either side of the road as far as the eye could see.

Jodi tried not to think about how much farther they had to go.

20

S andy Springs wasn't far out of their way, for which Shane was grateful. Debra could have asked him to take her to Athens, and he would have had a hard time saying no after what she'd done for Violet. As it was, they would only have to deviate a few miles from their route. There wasn't a seat for Debra, so she'd pulled one of the buckets forward, settling it just behind the spot where Ruby liked to lie, and used it as a seat.

The woman smelled quite strongly of sweat and dirty clothes, but she proved to be good company for Violet. She chatted, asked questions, and told funny stories, which left Shane free to concentrate on avoiding vehicles and hitchhikers on the road.

"So, Violet, what are your hobbies?" Debra asked. "What do you like to do for fun?"

"I read books," Violet said. "I like historical fiction mostly."

"Wow, you can read books? I'm impressed."

"I mostly listen to them on my audiobook player," she explained. "I can read in Braille, if I have to, but it's not as fun. Reading Braille for a long time makes my arm feel kind of tired."

"That's interesting," Debra said. "I'm not a real good reader, so you're probably smarter than me. The most I read is maybe a text message from a friend."

The further they got from Resaca, the more problems Shane encountered on the highway. Just past the Calhoun exit, he encountered a massive pileup that seemed to have been caused by a fuel truck overturning. It had slid sideways into other vehicles and sparked a fire, which had blackened the road all around it for a good twenty yards. Shane spotted a couple of bodies draped in sheets on the shoulder.

He would have pulled into the northbound lanes and risked driving against traffic, but the median dipped deeply here, making it impassible as far as the eye could see. He was forced to come to a stop, though he looked carefully to make sure no one was waiting to ambush them. There was a strip of grass beyond the outside shoulder, but it sloped down into a ditch that ran along the edge of the tree line.

Without meaning to, Shane cursed under his breath, and Violet immediately quit talking and turned to him, pushing her sunglasses up the bridge of her nose.

"We're stuck again, aren't we?" she said

"Well, there's one way past," he said, "but it's not pleasant. We've got some…uh, people on the road."

"Dead people?" Violet said, loudly.

"Seems like it."

"How much ground clearance does this van have?" Debra asked, leaning forward to peer at the bodies through the windshield.

"Ground clearance isn't the problem," he said. "I don't think the wheelbase of the van is wide enough. I think I'm going to have to get out and move those…people…into the ditch."

"Don't do it," Debra said. "Could be others hiding in the trees or behind the vehicles, waiting to jump out. You've got a lot of good stuff in this van, from what I can tell. You're a prime target."

Shane shuddered, recalling the aggressive hitchhikers from the previous day. He couldn't decide which was worse: risking an ambush by getting out of the van, or driving over the bodies.

"I think you can clear them," Debra said. "Go for it."

"And what if I can't?"

"Speedbumps," she said, with a hard edge to her voice. "Roll right over them. They won't mind—they're dead. You've got a daughter to think about. Don't take unnecessary risks."

Shane made a disgusted sound.

"Dad, please don't get out of the van," Violet said.

That settled the matter. Gritting his teeth, he put the van in drive and eased onto the shoulder. "Fine. Just cross your fingers that we don't get stuck."

"We won't," Debra said, "if you go fast enough. Look, it'll be over before you know it. You're not going to hurt their feelings."

"Oh God," he groaned.

He hit the accelerator and picked up speed as he approached the bodies. Three of them, they were lined up side by side. Maybe it was a whole family.

I'm so sorry, he thought. *Forgive me.*

Right before he hit them, he tensed, huddling over the steering wheel and tightening his grip. The van went over them far easier than he expected—*thump, thump, thump*. Indeed, as Debra had said, it was just like hitting speedbumps a little faster than usual. Buckets rattled in the back, and Debra bounced on her makeshift seat. Ruby whined, and Violet gasped.

And then they were past the bodies and moving south again.

"See?" Debra said. "No big deal."

They encountered a second and more serious obstacle outside the town of Emerson. Just beyond an overpass, they crested a hill and came upon a massive pile of debris spread across all four lanes of the highway and the median, leaving only the right shoulder open. As Shane drew closer, the pile began to seem deliberate, a breastwork comprised of tires, lumber, trash, even furniture and cinder blocks. He spotted a vehicle upside down in the ditch beyond the debris, and he was pretty sure it was a blue Georgia State Patrol car.

"What happened here?" he muttered.

Why had someone blocked every lane and then left a single shoulder open? It looked like it had been made recently, possibly that very morning, but Shane didn't see any sign of people anywhere. That didn't mean much, however, because the trees that ran alongside the ditch were dense, with plenty of shadows in which to hide.

"This looks bad," Debra said.

"Yeah, I'm not slowing down," Shane replied. "Everyone hold on."

"Gun it," Debra said.

Debra braced herself against the back of Violet's seat, and Violet grabbed the handle of Ruby's harness in both hands. Shane gunned the engine and flew through the gap in the crude wall. As he did, he caught movement out of the corner of his eye, people racing out of the trees beyond the ditch. When he sailed past them, he heard the loud crack of a gunshot. He floored the accelerator, racing at a dangerous speed along the gravel shoulder. The steering wheel felt loose in his hands, his control of the van shaky at best.

As he approached a bend in the highway, he pulled back into the right lane. A second gunshot chased them around the bend, and Shane dared a glance at Violet to make sure she hadn't been hit. She was huddled over Ruby, holding on for dear life.

"Everyone okay?" he asked.

"I'm fine," Violet said.

"Fine," Debra added.

Only when he was well out of sight of the wall did he dare to slow down.

"The power went out *yesterday*," he said, "and people are already going insane."

"Civilization was a lot flimsier than anyone realized," Debra said. "You gotta be ready to fight for yourself and your family at a moment's notice."

"Where's the government?" Shane wondered aloud. "Aren't they doing anything about this?"

No one had any response to this, but Debra made an unhappy face and sat back on her bucket seat.

Once they reached the outskirts of Atlanta, Debra began directing him toward Sandy Springs. They left Interstate 75 in the town of Cumberland, cutting east on I-285. After a day spent skirting wreckage and ruins, Shane's nerves were on edge, and he kept drumming his fingers on the steering wheel. He was beginning to hate this little detour, even if it was only a few miles out of the way. Any delay felt dangerous now.

After a few minutes, Debra suddenly leaned forward and began waving frantically toward the upcoming exit.

"Take that exit," she said. "That's the one we need."

Shane saw nothing remarkable in that direction, but he moved into the exit lane anyway, cutting over to the shoulder briefly to avoid an overturned motorcycle. Once they were on the access road, Debra directed him down a narrow street that cut through a dense forest.

"Are you sure this is the right way?" Shane asked.

"I'm sure," Debra replied. She seemed tense, constantly knitting her eyebrows and rubbing her hands together. "I double- and triple-checked. You should see a sign for the camp in a second."

Sure enough, almost as soon as she said it, Shane spotted a small green sign beside the road. As they got closer, the words became clear: "Fulton County Juvenile Boot Camp." In smaller letters beneath, it said, "Be Prepared to Stop."

"Juvenile Boot Camp," Shane said. "What does that mean?"

"It's a place the court sends troubled kids," Debra said. "An alternative to juvenile detention reserved for boys the judge thinks are…you know, *redeemable*."

"And this is where your son is located?"

"Yes," she replied. "He's not a bad kid, though. He just got in a little bit of trouble. Nobody died or anything."

"Will we have any difficulty getting in to see him?" Shane asked.

"No, I don't think so. I'm his mother. How are they going to stop his mother from seeing him?"

They drove out of the trees into a large clearing, and before them, a high chain-link fence surrounded a large camp. Enormous stop signs with flashing lights stood on either side of a gate. Beyond the gate were recommissioned military vehicles in a parking lot and two rows of buildings stretching toward the back fence. A single striped gate arm barred the way, a security guard in a black uniform standing to one side with a clipboard in his hand. When he saw them coming, he raised a hand to signal them to stop.

"Well, security's pretty light," Shane said, "so it shouldn't be too much trouble."

"We'll get in," Debra said. "Trust me. I can handle rent-a-cops like this guy."

Shane came to a stop in front of the gate, rolling down his window as the man in uniform approached. He was holding a clipboard with a stack of papers attached to it.

"Can I help you, sir?" he asked.

"I'm not sure what—"

Debra leaned across Shane, reached out to grab the frame of the door, and spoke over him. "Sir, I'm here to see my son. He was sent here by the court last week."

"What's his name?" the soldier asked.

"Corbin Graves," she said.

The soldier flipped through the pages on his clipboard, stopped a few pages in, and slid his finger down a block of small print. He read something for a moment, his mouth moving silently, then shook his head.

"I'm sorry, ma'am," he said, his voice tightening. "He's not allowed any visitors at this time. You'll have to turn your van around."

"But he's here," she said. Not a question, Shane noted. "My son is here."

"Ma'am, no visitors are permitted for new entrants to the camp," the soldier said. "You'll have to turn back right now. I'm sorry. You can call the office later to arrange visitation, assuming the phones are back up."

"I'm his *mother*," she said, sharply. "How can you keep me away from my own child? Can you at least bring him to the fence and let me speak to him?"

"You'll have to leave," the guard said sharply, jabbing a finger in their direction. "I'm telling you, he is not allowed visitors at this time."

"Okay, get back," Shane said to Debra, trying to gently move her out of his personal space. "He's not going to let us through."

"No, they're keeping my son from me," she said, her voice shrill. "They can't do that! The whole world is falling apart. I *deserve* to know he's okay."

"Dad, let's just leave," Violet said. "Just turn around and leave."

Before Shane could react, Debra's other hand whipped up and thrust her pistol out the window, pointing it at the solider. It was a .44 Magnum, and it seemed massive when it was inches from Shane's face. Shane grabbed her forearm and tried to pull it back, but she was surprisingly strong.

"Open the damn gate," she shouted. "Now! Right now. Don't test me, you pig."

The soldier saw the gun and stumbled backward, raising the clipboard in front of his face as a shield. Shane was still struggling with Debra when the pistol fired. The sound was so loud in the van that it stabbed into his skull. Every other sound disappeared completely, leaving a world that seemed to be buzzing. The stench of gunpowder filled his nostrils.

Stunned, Shane saw the soldier fall backward, grabbing at his chest with both hands. The clipboard clattered onto the street, papers coming loose and scattering in the wind. A distant screaming voice broke through the buzzing, and he recognized it as his own daughter.

"What did you do?" he said. "Why did you do that?"

"Drive through the gate," Debra said. She leaned back out of his reach. He barely made out the words. "We're going in there. They won't keep my son from me."

"No," he said. "Are you out of your mind?"

When Shane went for his Glock, Debra shifted her gun and pointed it at Violet. Shane's daughter was curled up in her seat, arms wrapped around Ruby, who writhed as she tried to get out of Violet's grip.

"Drive through the gate," Debra shouted, pressing the barrel of the gun against the back of Violet's head. "Now!"

Shane didn't think he could get his own gun out of the holster in time, and he certainly didn't think he could knock the gun out of Debra's hand.

"Okay, whatever you want," he said. "Don't hurt my daughter."

His heart pounding, his ears still ringing, he nodded and put the van in drive. Then he stomped on the accelerator and braced himself for impact. They hit the gate arm straight on, ripping it away from its mooring. It flipped over the top of the van and flew off to one side as they raced into the camp.

21

"We just blasted our way into a military camp," Shane said. "You realize that, right?"

"It's not a military camp," Debra said. "It's just a stupid county program for juvenile offenders. Guy wanted to play Mr. Big Shot and keep me away from my son; well, he got what he deserved."

"Do you actually think we're going to be able to find your son and get him out of here alive?"

"If we act fast enough," Debra replied. She sounded out of breath, and her lips were pulled back in an animalistic grimace. "Just do what I say. Head for that big building over there."

Old trucks and Jeeps had been parked haphazardly in the parking lot. Beyond them, Shane saw two long rows of pole-barn buildings stretching toward the back fence. In front of them, a similar but much larger building appeared to be the main structure of the camp.

Surprisingly, Shane didn't see a lot of personnel at first. No one in the vicinity of the main building, no one moving between the rows of buildings in back. However, as they raced across the parking lot, he spotted a number of people in a far corner of the lot around some exercise equipment. It appeared to be an obstacle course.

"They must've heard the gun," Shane said, fighting to stay calm, though every nerve cried out.

"We'll be out of here before they think to look for it," Debra said.

"Do you know where your son is?" Shane said.

"No, if he's not out in the exercise yard, he'll be in one of the barracks," she said. "I intend to find out. Park right there." She pointed at the main building in front. "Out of sight on the east side. It seems to be the headquarters. Someone in there is going to tell me where to find him."

"This is ridiculous," Shane said. "There has to be a better way—a safer way."

"Too late for that," Debra said tightly. "This is what we're doing." She still had the gun pointed at the back of Violet's head, but she'd moved back enough to be out of Shane's reach. As for Violet, she was still bent over a squirming Ruby.

Shane drove past a couple of trucks and an old Jeep, trying to move fast without drawing attention, and pulled in along the east wall of the main building. This side of the parking lot was practically deserted. Before he'd even come to a complete stop, Debra flung open the side door of the van and gestured with her gun.

"Violet, get out of the van," she said through clenched teeth. "You're coming with me."

"No, you can't do that," Shane said. He wanted to lunge at her, but he restrained himself.

Violet wrapped herself even more tightly around Ruby, who was whining and trying to back out of her grip.

"Violet, you come with me, or I'm afraid I'll have to do your father like I did that guard," Debra said. "Let's go."

"Violet, don't listen to her," Shane said.

But Violet lunged suddenly toward her door, opened it, and stepped outside.

"I have to, Dad," she said, voice cracking with emotion. "She'll do it. She'll shoot you!"

"I won't shoot either of you if you play nice," Debra said.

She swung her door shut and grabbed Violet by the arm. Ruby tried to follow, clambering up on the passenger seat, but Debra kicked the passenger door shut. Shane could see that Violet was shaking, her hands clasped tightly in front of her. Ruby put her face to the window and began to whine.

"Keep the engine running," Debra said, loud enough that he could make it out.

She held the gun out, rocking it from side to side as a warning. Then she moved around behind the van, pulling Violet along with her. Shane tried to track them in the side-view mirror, but they quickly moved out of sight. Ruby ran toward the back of the van, but the back windows were blocked by the buckets. This sent her into a panic, as she began to leap from one side of the van to the other, whimpering and barking and trying to find a way out.

Boiling with rage and fear, Shane slammed his fist against the steering wheel. He was tempted to go after them. If he snuck up behind Debra, he might get a clear shot at her, but the thought of putting Violet in the middle of gunfight was too much.

If only I was a better shot, he thought. *If only my gun training wasn't limited to three minutes in the lobby at work with Landon.*

He smacked the steering wheel again. Distantly, he heard the sound of a door with unoiled hinges swing open and then swing shut. Ruby approached his seat, knocking Violet's bucket over in the process, and whimpered in Shane's face.

"Sit tight," he said. "Nothing we can do, girl."

I should have taken a shot at her anyway, he thought. *It's a risk, but not as big a risk as letting her drag Violet into that building.*

He cursed himself, gently pushing Ruby out of his face.

"You can't go out there," he said.

Suddenly, he heard shouting. It seemed to come from the building— at least two voices. The shouting built to a crescendo, then ended suddenly as a gunshot rattled the thin metal walls of the building. Fear burned in the back of Shane's throat. He put the van in drive but kept his foot on the brake.

A moment later, he heard the scuff of shoes on pavement, and Debra reappeared in the side-view mirror, dragging Violet behind her.

Violet struggled to keep up, on the verge of falling. As soon as Ruby sensed them coming, she leapt onto the passenger seat and started barking again. Debra opened the side door and climbed in, pulling Violet in after her. When Ruby turned and came toward them, Debra wrapped an arm around Violet and pulled her in between them.

"Got what I needed," Debra said. She pointed through the windshield toward the rows of buildings in the back. "He's in the barracks. The second one on the right, building B. Drive there. Quick."

"Dad, do what she says," Violet said, fumbling at Ruby to keep her back. "Hurry."

Shane didn't wait for Debra to shut the door. He let his foot off the brake and drove toward the buildings in back.

"Did you shoot someone else?" he asked.

Debra was sweating, her hair wilted and wet, eyes tinged with madness. She kept the gun pointed at Violet, but she was casting her gaze about.

"Don't worry about what I did," Debra said. "Just hurry up."

He raced across the parking lot and pulled into the gravel beyond it. The barracks were flimsy structures, little more than khaki-colored aluminum with cheap windows set into the sides. Some of the doors were open, and Shane spotted what appeared to be a security guard in a dark-blue uniform watching them. He seemed alarmed but unsure of what to do. As the van approached, he said something over his shoulder.

Shane stopped the van in front of the second building—it had a small

B painted in white near the corner—and Debra backed out of the side door, dragging Violet along with her.

"Stay here," she said. "Be ready to high-tail it out of here the second we get back."

She shut the door in Ruby's face. Swinging around, she ran toward the door. There was a moment when Debra's back was to him, and Shane grabbed the handle of the Glock, pulling it halfway out of the holster. Still, he didn't trust his aim, and she was moving too fast. She disappeared through the open door into the building.

It occurred to Shane that if someone spotted him with a drawn weapon, they could see him as the bigger risk and take a shot at him. He slid the gun back into the holster and hunkered down in his seat. The security guard in the doorway a few buildings down stepped out onto the gravel lot, gesturing toward the van. A second guard appeared in the door behind him.

"Come on, you idiot," Shane muttered. "Get your son and let's go. Hurry up."

A few seconds later, Debra came running out of building B, Violet stumbling to keep up with her. A young man followed at her heel, an acne-ridden teenager in a gray t-shirt and camo pants. He had a hideous grimace on his face. Debra waved him into the van first, and he climbed in, scrambling over toppled buckets. He gave Shane the briefest of glances, saying nothing as he moved to an open spot near the back of the van.

Ruby leapt from the passenger seat to the floorboard and back into the seat. Shane had never seen her so frantic or so uncertain about what to do. Debra shoved Violet through the side door. Shane's daughter fell, caught herself on the floorboard, and her sunglasses went flying. She started to feel around for them, then seemed to change her mind and climbed up onto the passenger seat. Ruby hopped into her lap, licking her face.

"I'm fine. I'm fine," Violet told the dog.

"Get us out of here," Debra shouted, waving the gun at Shane. "Back through the gate. Quick as you can."

She had one foot on the running board when they heard shouting from somewhere behind them.

"Security! Stop!"

Many people were streaming out of the buildings now, moving in their direction. Debra hoisted herself into the van. At that moment, Shane saw the security guard draw his pistol and take a shot in their direction. Debra cried out, falling into the van.

"Get going, you idiot," she yelled.

Shane took his foot off the brake and hit the accelerator, cutting a broad arc through the gravel. As he did, Debra reached back and pulled the door shut. The young man who had followed her—presumably her son—started to move toward her, but she waved him back angrily.

"Stay low," she growled. "They're shooting at us."

A second shot rang out, and Shane heard a distinctive *ping* as it hit the side of the van. He floored it, bouncing back onto the parking lot. Another guard was standing at a corner of the main building, shouting at them, her gun drawn and pointed at the van.

"Violet, duck down," Shane said. "Keep your head below the console."

She bent down as far as she could go in her seat, wrapping her arms around Ruby. A third bullet hit the frame of windshield, leaving a small spiderweb of cracks in the corner above the passenger seat.

"Just go. Just go," Debra said. "Back through the gate."

Shane adjusted the rearview mirror to get a look at her. She was slumped against the side door, her left hand clutching her side. He saw dark blood seeping through her fingers. She still held the gun, and she had it pointed at him, the barrel trembling slightly. As Shane watched, she moved her left hand, revealing a ragged hole in her shirt. It looked like she'd been shot just below the ribs. A dangerous spot for a bullet.

Just bleed out and leave us alone, he thought.

"Get us out of here, and we all survive together," Debra said, meeting his gaze in the mirror.

Shane raced behind the building and sped through the open gate. A final gunshot chased them as they turned east and made for the highway.

"Mom, what did you do?" the young man asked.

"What I had to," she replied.

22

By the time they reached the city limits of Augusta, a mass exodus had begun to form on the highway. Most of the people were on foot or riding bicycles. A few drove motorcycles or ATVs, but gridlock on the highway was so bad it was practically impassable for larger vehicles. Numerous wrecks had blocked the lanes, forcing people to either turn back or abandon their vehicles. Whole families were marching along, carrying backpacks and bags, pushing strollers.

This made it a bit of a challenge for the wide-body pedicab. At times, Jodi had to wait for people to move out of her way. Other times, she had to apologize when she pulled in front of someone. Within three hours, she'd been cussed out by at least a dozen people. Everyone's nerves were on edge.

Finally, she came to a stop at a spot where all four lanes were blocked and a large family moving at a snail's pace had blocked the shoulder. She turned in her seat to face Mike as Owen rode up beside them and stopped.

"All of these people are making me nervous," she said. "I wish we could get off the highway. What do you guys think? Mike, you know the area best."

"It would help if I had a map," he replied. He was nestled against the stack of their luggage, one arm wrapped around the pile to keep it from toppling out the back of the pedicab. "We can always leave the highway and take to the backroads, but I'm not sure that would be any better—we could easily get lost wandering those small towns without a map."

"Okay, let's keep our eyes out for a convenience store so we can buy a map," Jodi said.

She resumed pedaling, though it took her a few seconds to build up speed. The weight in the back seat was beginning to wear on her, and the pedicab wasn't very maneuverable. Still, she was determined to endure to the point of collapse. She wanted to get far away from Augusta before night fell.

Eventually, she spotted a small, run-down gas station. Quite a few people were gathered in the parking lot, and they all seemed restless and irritable. One older woman was wagging her fingers in a child's face and scolding him. As they drew closer, Jodi realized the store was closed. A poster had been taped to the backside of the glass door, the words "Closed Indefinitely" written in large red letters. A crack ran from one corner of the glass to another. Maybe someone had read the sign and attempted to take out their frustrations on it.

"There goes that idea," Jodi said.

"There will be other stores," Mike said. "Some smart capitalist will find a way to run a store with no power. Even if the customers are on edge, there's still money to be made. And when there's money to be made, people find a way."

"I'm sure you're right, Mikey," Jodi said.

After a few miles, they became aware of a commotion up ahead. It sounded like someone was shouting. A group of people were moving back and forth in the middle of the road, as if a fight had broken out. Jodi saw an older gentleman in a vest running as fast as he could along the shoulder, his arms wrapped around his head, as if to protect himself. Suddenly, with a cry, he dove into the ditch, landed in a puddle of muddy water, and began crawling through the grass. Others were gathering on the shoulder now, pushing and shoving to get past each other.

"What is going on up there?" she wondered aloud.

"Fighting over something," Mike said. "It's the new American pastime, sis. Let's avoid them like tooth decay."

The left lane was open, so Jodi steered the pedicab off the shoulder, past an abandoned semi, and into the open lane. As she did, she felt a sudden sharp stinging sensation in her right arm. Thinking it was a bee or wasp, she brushed at her arm, and her fingers swiped through something wet.

She glanced down at her arm and saw blood pouring freely from a small hole in her forearm. The initial sting quickly gave way to a painful heat radiating up her arm and a tingling in her fingertips.

"What...?" Suddenly light-headed, she pulled over to the inside shoulder and came to a stop. "What was that? Mike, did something hit me?"

"Jodi, look at that guy," Mike said. He didn't seem to notice her arm. He was staring up the road, gesturing at something. "Do you see him there?"

Jodi realized now that a single person was shouting at the top of his lungs, and as the crowd in front of her scattered, she spotted him. He had wild hair sticking out in greasy tangles, an old Army surplus jacket that was at least two sizes too big hanging from his shoulders, and black boots. As he marched east in the left lane, he shouted at anyone in sight. Though she couldn't make out the words, she saw the glint of a silver pistol in his hand. In the midst of his ranting, he raised the gun and took a wild shot into the distance. Then he turned toward a group of people moving past him on the far side of the road and took a shot at them as well.

Her whole arm now felt like it was on fire, but Jodi dropped from the seat and landed on the warm asphalt, crawling toward the nearest vehicle. Mike moved to follow her, knocking their stack of luggage over in the process. He grabbed the JanSport backpack in passing and slung it over his shoulders. The vehicle was a stalled Camry that had t-boned a 70s-era station wagon and caved in the side. Jodi pressed herself into the angle where the two vehicles met, her right arm flopping into her lap. She had left a meandering trail of blood behind her.

"Mom, are you *shot?*" Owen said, crawling up beside her. "Oh, my gosh, Mom, you're bleeding like crazy!"

Though it hurt to lift it, she examined her arm, turning it back and forth. There was a hole on either side, so the bullet had passed through. She was amazed at how small the holes were. She would have expected a bullet wound to be larger. Heat was giving way slowly to raw pain, so she set her arm down again on her lap.

"You have to do something about all that blood," Mike said, crawling up behind Owen, already out of breath. He'd clapped a hand to the bandage on his neck. "Does it hurt?"

"Not as much as you might expect," she said.

At least there was no bullet inside of her. For some reason, that made her feel marginally better about the situation. Her purse was still hanging from her shoulder, but she let it drop now. With her left hand, she rooted around inside and produced a handkerchief, pressing it to the exit wound, which seemed to be bleeding worse.

The shooter was close enough now that they could hear him. He sounded like he was both praying and ranting, alternatively speaking to God and to anyone who would listen. His voice had already started to go hoarse, as if he'd been doing this for quite a while.

"Don't you understand," he shouted. He also seemed to be crying. "It's the Rapture! They warned us! The holy men warned us! We've all been abandoned. We've been left behind! God, why did you take her from me? She's gone. Like all the others, she's been taken, and we've been left. Oh, God, help me! I can't be here. I don't want to be here. Someone kill me! Go ahead. Someone kill me! There's no hope for any of us."

And with that, he took another shot. A woman screamed, and the panic of the crowd intensified.

"I have to get out of here," he shouted. "I have to be with her! God took all the good people and left the scum. Swept them out of the earth with his mighty hand. What use is it to stay here? Kill me! Someone kill me. Come on, you cowards!"

As he got louder, it became clear that he would pass right next to the vehicles where they were hiding.

"Mom, what do we do?" Owen said. "He's getting closer."

"Well, it's clear we can't reason with him," she replied. She cast about, looking for some way out. Could they crawl across the median without being spotted? She didn't think so.

"No, not me. Please, not me." A woman pleading for her life. "I didn't do anything."

Her voice was silenced by another gunshot.

"Do you want to stay here in this world?" the man ranted. "The devil owns the world now. God has left us! Don't you get it? Don't any of you get it? We're the trash he intends to burn!"

He was very close now, just on the other side of the car, and, to Jodi's horror, it sounded like he was coming around the front end of the station wagon. She signaled for Owen to climb under the Camry, but he shook his head.

"Can't fit under there," he said.

Almost on top of them, the madman took another shot into the distance. "Blood and weeping. That's all you've left us, God! Blood and weeping! Why won't someone kill me? All you disgusting cowards! I hate you all."

"Okay, I've had enough," Mike said suddenly. He dumped the backpack onto the street and unzipped it, thrusting his hand deep inside.

"Mike, don't do anything stupid," Jodi said. "Just hide. Try to get as low as you can. Maybe he won't see us when he walks by."

"Nope," Mike replied. "Someone has to stop this loser."

When he drew his hand out of the backpack, he was clutching a .38 Special. He cocked the hammer and rose. Jodi gasped as he stood up on shaky legs. At that moment, the stranger appeared above the hood of the station wagon. He had jumped onto the car, and he looked down at them now.

"Don't you understand," he cried, teeth bared. His greasy hair stuck out at all angles from his head. He had specks of blood splashed across his right cheek and temple. "It's the end! It's the end! For you, for me, for everyone."

As he brought his gun around, Mike raised the .38 and fired. A single shot, it caught the madman just above the right eye. Jodi saw a sudden dark hole in the man's forehead, and then he fell backward, his words becoming a momentary gurgle. She heard him slam against the hood of the station wagon and then hit the street on the other side with a dull thud.

And then he fell silent.

"Whoa, Uncle Mike, you got him," Owen said with a gasp.

"Mike, where did you get that gun?" Jodi said.

Mike slumped down onto the road, grimacing. "It's mine," he said, out of breath. "I bought it a month ago. You know the neighborhood I live in."

"You never told me," she said. "I thought you were all about gun control."

"I wasn't going to say anything." He dabbed the sweat from his forehead and cheeks. "Some punk kid robbed me on my way home from my second chemo treatment, so I made sure it wouldn't happen again."

"Is he...dead?" Owen asked.

"If he's not, he soon will be," Mike said. "I don't hear him ranting."

As if in reply, the madman gave what sounded like a last shaky breath. Despite his flippant words, Mike looked deeply shaken. He shoved the gun into his backpack and zipped it up tight.

Jodi, sick to her stomach, forgot all about her arm for a second. She started to stand up, but then she felt trickles of blood on her fingers. She sat back down with a groan.

"What are we going to do?" Mike said. "Look at you, Jodi. You're hit bad."

She picked her handkerchief up from the ground, but it was soaked through.

"I can help."

The new voice came from the back end of the Camry. A group of people had appeared there. A woman stepped forward. She was small but sturdy, her hair cut very close.

"You just saved a whole bunch of lives," she said. "Let me help you."

She came and knelt beside Jodi, gently lifting her injured right arm.

"Who are you?" Jodi asked.

"I was a medic in Afghanistan," she said. "I just wish I had a first aid kit with me."

"We have so many medical supplies," Jodi said with a laugh. "Didn't think I'd have to use them so soon. Owen, get the suitcase."

He nodded and ran back to the pedicab, returning shortly with the suitcase. When he opened it, bandages, pill bottles, and syringes spilled out.

"Excellent," the medic said. "Do we have any water?"

Mike pulled a bottle out of his backpack and handed it to her. She proceeded to wash the entry and exit wounds, a process which stung like hell. Jodi bit her lip to keep from crying out.

"Well, at least it went straight through," the medic said. "Looks like it passed between the bones. That makes you incredibly lucky. The bullet's not still in there."

She cleaned the wounds, disinfected them, and finally covered them with a generous number of butterfly bandages.

"Keep the wounds clean," she said, standing up. "Change the bandages regularly, and you should be okay."

"Thanks," Jodi said.

The medic gave her a curt nod. "I'd better help others. I saw quite a few get shot."

She thanked them again, and, with no fanfare whatsoever, she grabbed a fistful of wrapped bandages and disinfectant and left. Jodi didn't try to stop her. She couldn't hoard their supplies if people needed immediate medical help. When the medic was gone, Owen shoved everything back inside the suitcase and closed it.

Jodi looked at poor sweaty Mike, who had turned a shade green. She looked at her son, who had abject horror etched onto his face.

"No time to reflect on our near death," she said. "We have to get back on our bikes."

Neither Mike nor Owen moved.

"Sorry, guys," she said. "Despite everything, we have to hit the road again. We need to make many more miles before nightfall."

"Are you sure you can ride with your arm like that?" Owen asked. "Mom, you literally just got shot."

"I can because I have to," she said, struggling to get to her feet. "I *literally* have to. Son, you'd be amazed at what you can do when you have to do it."

23

They wound up taking a circuitous route around Sandy Springs. Though Debra was slumped against the door, her eyes dull and glassy, she still had the gun firmly in her grip. Shane doubted she could do much with it, but he didn't want to take any unnecessary risks.

"I'm sorry, Shane," she said, after a few miles of silence. They had reached the other side of Sandy Springs at a point where I-285 bent south to circle Atlanta. "I wasn't really going to hurt your daughter. They made me desperate, that's all. I overreacted. I can admit that now."

Shane didn't have anything nice to say in response to this, so he gritted his teeth and kept driving. He glanced in the rearview mirror and saw Debra's son, Corbin, pressed up against the stacks of buckets at the back of the van. He appeared absolutely distraught.

"You can pull over now," Debra said. "We're far enough from Sandy Springs, and I doubt they'll know which way we went."

He looked at her in the mirror. Her face had gone an awful yellowish color, and when she raised her right hand, he saw that it was covered in blood.

"Pull over, please," she said again.

"We should keep moving," Shane said. "The farther we get away from the camp, the better."

"Please." It came out as a long groan this time.

He leaned back to get a better look at her and saw blood everywhere. It had soaked through the side of her shirt and down into her jeans.

"Okay, we're pulling over," Shane said.

Violet turned to him and looked like she was about to say something, but then she shook her head and remained silent. Shane took the next exit and pulled onto the shoulder of the access road. He took the key from the ignition, stepped out of the van, and ran around to the side door. When he opened it, Debra flopped backward into his arms.

"Corbin, help me," he said, wrapping his arms around her. "We have the stop the bleeding, or she's not going to make it."

Corbin crawled forward and grabbed Debra's legs, lifting her and helping Shane carry her out of the van. They found a soft spot beside the road to lay her down. As Corbin examined the wound, Shane went back to the van and grabbed one of the buckets that was marked "First Aid." He popped it open and pulled out a wad of bandages and small packets of disinfectant wipes.

Corbin had lifted Debra's shirt, revealing the small, neat hole in her side. He wiped the blood away with his hand, but more quickly oozed out. Shane tore open one of the disinfectant wipes, bent over Debra, and began to clean the area around the wound.

"I'm sorry," Debra said. She finally let go of the gun and it clattered on the gravel shoulder beside her. "I'm sorry for what I did. Tell Violet I didn't mean to scare her."

"Okay, okay," Shane said. He opened one of the bandages and pressed it against the wound, but blood seeped through almost immediately. "We've all made some terrible choices since this whole thing began. No sense talking about it now. Lie still and let me see what I can do."

"Please…please…" Her eyes seemed unfocused now, unable to find his face. "Don't leave Corbin behind. Don't blame him for what I did. He's…he's a good boy. He's always been a good boy, and I didn't deserve him."

"Mom, stop that," Corbin said, tears running down his face. "You're coming with us."

Shane pressed a fresh bandage to the wound. The blood looked dark, almost black. He knew that might be an indication the bullet had pierced her liver. If so, there was little they could do for her. Even if they got her to a hospital, her chances were slim.

When he was on his third bandage, Debra tipped her head to one side, as if seeking something. Her hand came up, fumbled in the air, and found Corbin's shirt.

"I want you to keep being a good boy," she said. "I know you didn't mean to get in trouble. It was just a bad choice. I've made plenty, but I need you to make good ones now. Don't be a taker no more. Be a helper."

"Don't talk like that," Corbin said. He was crying, his face twisted with grief. "You're coming with us. I told you that."

"I should have been there for you." Debra's voice was scarcely a whisper now. "Should've put down the bottle a long time ago. When you were little. You've become such a good man. Like your father. I'm proud of you. I sure didn't have anything to do with it, but…"

Her hand slid off his shirt, leaving a smear of dark blood.

"Can't you help her?" Corbin said to Shane.

"I wish I could." He put the third bandage, thoroughly soaked, next to the others.

"When things went bad, I just had to see you," Debra whispered, as her eyes slipped shut. "I messed up. Oh, Corbin, can you ever forgive me?"

"Of course," he wailed. "Stop saying stuff like that, Mom."

"At least I'm here with you now, right? At least I'm…I'm…"

The words faded, became a final expulsion of breath, and then she was gone.

"Mom?"

Corbin covered his face and broke down, sobbing bitterly. Shane patted him gently and rose, wiping his hands on a fresh bandage. The smell of blood was so strong in his nostrils, he thought he might vomit. As he stepped back, leaving Corbin to grieve, he realized Violet was standing outside the van.

"She shot people," Violet said softly. "Innocent people. They might be dead now."

"I know," Shane replied, "but it was his mother. Let him grieve."

"There was a guy behind a desk in the building," Violet said. "When he wouldn't tell her where her son was, she just shot him." Violet snapped her fingers. "Just like that. Like he was nothing at all. I heard him groaning on the floor, and she left him there. I know she helped me at the gas station, but she was a bad lady."

"I know." He hugged his daughter. "And she's gone now."

He doubted Corbin heard them. The young man seemed utterly lost, bent over his mother and howling, rocking back and forth. Shane stooped down and grabbed Debra's gun, tucking it under the passenger seat in the van.

It was the perfect time to leave. Corbin was so consumed by his grief, he probably wouldn't notice until they were long gone. Maybe it was the right thing to do. The last time Shane had trusted a stranger, it had almost gotten them all killed. He knew nothing about Corbin. Did he really want to put his daughter at risk again?

Shane leaned in close to Violet and spoke just loud enough for her to hear. "Get back in the van. Put your seatbelt on."

Violet jerked away from him, as if shocked by what he'd said. "You're going to leave him behind? What his mom did isn't his fault."

Instead of answering, Shane gently turned her toward the open passenger door. She hesitated a moment and finally climbed in, pulling Ruby onto her lap. Shane shut the door behind her. Then he grabbed the side door and slid it shut, trying to make as little noise as possible.

Corbin had ceased his loud sobbing. When Shane looked at him—intending it to be his last look before driving away—he saw the young man resting his cheek on his mother's stomach. Debra's mouth hung open, her head tipped back, eyes half-lidded. Her right hand lay in a pool of her own blood on the ground.

She's a killer, Shane thought. *She brought this on herself. She brought it on both of them. I don't owe either of them anything, not after what she did.*

He almost walked away. The first step came easy. What did he owe this young man? Corbin could hitchhike, or else guards from the camp would come along and pick him up.

But Shane hesitated. Corbin was holding his mother's bloodless left hand and patting it.

"I barely knew her," he said with a sniff, "and now she's gone."

He wiped his cheeks and looked up at Shane.

"I know she wasn't a good person," he said. His face was blotchy and red from crying. "She did a lot of bad stuff. She hurt a lot of people, including my dad. My whole life she was like this ghost, floating out there in the world somewhere. Suddenly she shows up in the camp... and now this. I shouldn't even be so sad, but I can't help it. What's wrong with me?"

Shane didn't have an answer for him. This kid didn't have the hardness in his eyes that his mother had. He was practically an innocent, and a wounded innocent at that. When Corbin bent over the body again, Shane approached and laid a hand on his shoulder.

"Corbin, it's time to go," he said. "Come on."

24

S hane opened the side door and tried to beckon Corbin to get in, but the young was still kneeling beside his mother, his hands clasped in front of him.

"We can't bring her with us," Shane said. "You understand, I hope. I'm sorry, kid."

Corbin scrubbed his face with his hand.

"I can't just leave her by the side of the road," he said. "Even if she did bad stuff, we should at least bury her, shouldn't we?"

"There's no place to bury her," Shane said, "and we can't haul the body in the van with us. The best we can do is wrap her in a blanket and leave some identification with her. There's an old blanket behind the driver's seat that we can use. Someone will come along eventually."

Corbin seemed to consider this, but then he shook his head. "No, that's not right. I don't want to do that, leave her body on the ground like roadkill. Even wrapped up in a blanket just doesn't seem right. I think I'll have to stay here and keep watch. It seems like the right thing to do." He rose and stood at parade rest, as if this had become his new post.

Shane was tempted to leave him to his self-appointed task. It was what Corbin wanted, after all, and why should Shane talk him out of it? He had enough to worry about, and quite frankly, he was still angry about the attack at the camp. But he felt sorry for the kid. Corbin was not his mother, that was clear.

"Look, Corbin, I'm not leaving you here," Shane said. "This isn't what your mother wanted. Practically her last words were to ask me to take you with us. Do you honestly think she'd be okay with you standing here keeping watch over her body?"

Corbin seemed to consider this, and his posture slumped. "I don't know why you want me to come with you. After what my mother did back there, I deserve to be left."

"You are not your mother," Shane said.

"Well…that's true." He looked at his blood-spattered hands. "Okay, you're right. I can't stay here. There's no point. What's done is done." With that, he turned and walked toward the van, dragging his boots in the gravel as he came. As he climbed into the van, Ruby turned to face him, but she didn't bark or growl. She sniffed at his face, at his shirt, at his hand, then she lay back down on the floorboard. He found a spot near the back and sat down, looking red-eyed and miserable.

Landon had a blanket rolled up and tucked behind the driver's seat. Shane pulled it out now and unrolled it. It was a handwoven green blanket of a kind usually seen at souvenir kiosks in Mexican tourist towns. Shane had no idea where or when Landon had acquired it, but he hoped it didn't have any sentimental value. The blanket wasn't quite big enough, but he draped it over Debra's body, leaving only her shoes to stick out of the end.

Before he fully covered her, he dug into her pockets and found her driver's license clipped to a credit card along with a big wad of cash. He took the cash and card and put the ID back in her pocket. In her other pocket, he found a small bottle of Advil and some gum. He grabbed the Advil. Then he flipped the blanket back in place and went to the van.

"Corbin, it only seems right that you take these," he said, thrusting the credit card and cash at him.

Corbin looked at the money and shook his head. "I don't want it. There's no telling how she came by that cash. For all I know, she robbed someone. Use it for gas or something."

"Are you sure?"

He nodded vigorously. "Absolutely."

"Fine," Shane said, pocketing the cash.

He grabbed her gun from the place he'd dumped it earlier and put it with the credit card in the glove compartment. Though he hoped they wouldn't need another gun, it seemed wasteful to leave it behind. Before he closed the passenger door, he gave Violet another hug.

"Are you okay?" he asked.

"I will be," she replied. "It's good we didn't leave him behind. I think it was the right thing to do."

"Yeah, I think I agree."

He got into the driver's seat, started up the van, and pulled away. As he pulled back onto the highway, he glanced at Corbin in the rearview mirror. The young man was folded up in the midst of the buckets, looking completely lost.

Not much I can do for him, Shane thought.

He turned his gaze to the highway. Their current path skirted the edge of Atlanta, and as they drew closer to the city, conditions on the road worsened. A massive pileup had blocked the northbound lanes for miles, with hundreds of vehicles lined up behind the wreckage and abandoned. A few people still lingered in the area, including a family that had set up a small tent by the side of the road.

As the afternoon wore on, Corbin said not a word. He didn't move from his spot in the back, folded up and turned inward. Eventually, Violet started speaking, and it took Shane a second to realize she was talking to Corbin, trying to break him out of his terrible silence.

"Did you like being in that camp?" she said.

Corbin flinched, as if she'd startled him. "What? What was that?"

"Did you like being in that camp?" she asked again.

"Oh, sure," he said bitterly. "It was a blast. Wake up at five and do jumping jacks for half an hour while some guy yells at you. Better than going to jail, I guess. They only sent me there because my grades were decent. Judge said I needed help in life."

"How did you get in trouble?" Violet asked.

"It's not worth talking about," he said, but then he continued anyway. "I borrowed my neighbor's car without asking. He had a '52 Chevy. He said I could drive it a while back, but then he never kept his word. I just got mad, I guess. It was dumb. He left the keys in it, so I was just going to drive around the block, but I lost control and plowed into this hardware store's front window. So stupid." He smacked the side of his head. "My dad was embarrassed. That's the worst part of it, because he's the only one who was ever on my side. I wish I'd never done it. It was just a stupid impulse, and it was the last thing my dad ever knew about me. He had a heart attack while I was waiting for my trial date."

It wasn't the worst crime of all time, certainly not as bad as Shane had feared. Corbin didn't seem like a lost cause. Angry, yes, and probably deeply wounded, but he wasn't a hardened criminal.

"Corbin, where would you like to go?" Shane asked. "If you want to go back to Sandy Springs, I can drop you off close, and you can hike back to camp."

"No," Corbin replied. After a moment, he added, "I don't ever want to go back there. They murdered my Mom. I know she provoked them, but I'd rather get thrown in juvenile detention than go back to that place. I'm done with it, and I'll never do anything to wind up in a place like that ever again."

"Where do you want to go then?" Shane asked.

"Can I...can I come with you?" he asked.

When Shane hesitated in answering, Violet spoke up.

223

"Of course, you can," she said. "There's plenty of food and supplies for everyone where we're going."

Not wanting to contradict his daughter, Shane let the offer stand. He didn't fully trust Corbin. Quite frankly, he still didn't really know him. However, he'd heard enough and seen enough to not fear him.

"Thank you," Corbin said, and he sounded close to crying again. "I won't be a bother, I promise."

Shane was finally forced to leave the interstate just outside the town of Northlake due to another massive pileup in the southbound lanes. He cut over to Tucker and then turned south. This slowed their progress, and the afternoon wore on toward evening. They wouldn't make it to Macon, that was clear. Delays, problems, and lunacy had held them back once again. Shane fought back his anger. There was no one to direct it at now anyway, and no use being in a bad mood.

When they stopped to take a bathroom break, taking turns behind an empty warehouse, Shane heard Violet yawn. He looked over and saw her swaying on her feet.

"I suppose we'd better stop for the night soon," he said.

The sun burned a dozen shades of orange on the horizon. Shane looked for the northern lights but didn't see them. Maybe they would come later.

"Is there a motel nearby?" Violet said. "I could use a real bed. Even if the mattress is hard, it would be nice to have a pillow and a blanket."

"I'm sorry, sweetheart, I don't think we should use a motel," Shane said. "I don't want to leave the van unattended. I'm afraid it would get broken into while we were in the room. I'm sure working vehicles are high priority target."

"Okay," Violet said, sadly. "I understand. Too bad we can't fit the van inside the motel room like you did at the power plant."

"They don't make motel rooms that big," Shane said.

He gave her a hug. When Corbin came back around the corner from relieving himself, Shane shared the plan with him.

"We'll find a quiet place to park," he said. "Corbin, you can sleep in the back. Violet and I will tip our seats back and make the best of it."

"Doesn't seem safe," Corbin said. "What if someone tries to rob us? There are plenty of bad people out there. We'll be sitting ducks."

Shane patted his holster. "These ducks are armed. I'll sleep lightly, ready to draw at the slightest sound. I know it's a risk, but it's better than waking up in a motel room to an empty parking lot with all our supplies gone."

"Can't argue with that," Corbin said. "I probably won't sleep much anyway, not after today."

"Well, I'm gonna sleep," Violet said, stifling a yawn. "I'm gonna sleep like crazy."

They got back in the van and kept driving until they found a secluded parking lot beside an empty shopping center on the outskirts of a small town. They pulled over and prepared for the evening. Shane cracked open one of the supply crates and found some purified water and MREs for dinner. He opened Ruby's bag of dog food and poured a small pile for her on the floorboard. He also took the extra gun from the glove compartment and placed it in the door pocket beside his seat.

The truth was, he had no intention of going to sleep as long as Corbin was awake. He didn't seem like a problem, but he was still an untested entity. Shane would not be naïve again. He'd trusted Debra blindly and put his daughter at risk, a lesson he wouldn't soon forget.

When it came time to sleep, Violet leaned her seat all the way back. Ruby worked herself into the footwell beneath her seat, curling into a little ball on the padded mat. Corbin stretched out in the back, his hands tucked behind his head.

"Is everyone comfortable enough?" Shane asked.

"I'm fine," Violet replied. "I'm tired enough that it doesn't matter."

"It's okay," Corbin said. "The bunks at camp weren't much better than this anyway. At least I don't have twenty other guys in the same room snoring and farting and moving around."

Violet giggled at this.

Shane shut off the engine, put the key deep in his pocket, and cracked his window just enough to let in some fresh air. As casually as possible, he adjusted the rearview mirror so he could see Corbin. Then he tipped his seat back enough to cross his arms.

The town was dark, too dark, like a great well of bottomless night, but the insects and night creatures sounded twice as loud. Frogs and crickets and any number of things began chirping, croaking, and yowling loud enough to wake the dead.

Maybe they've decided it's their chance to take over, Shane thought.

Despite Corbin's assurance that he wouldn't sleep, he was softly snoring within minutes. By the faint moonlight shining through the windshield, Shane saw that the young man's eyes were closed. Violet followed not long after, curled on her side, her sunglasses forgotten on the floorboard.

Shane settled in for what he knew would be a long, lonely night.

25

F rom time to time, as Mike edged toward exhaustion, he would feel a violent wobble and come bolting out of near-sleep only to realize Jodi was fighting to change lanes. Her right arm was covered in bandages from elbow to wrist, and she kept the arm tucked against her side, which made steering awkward.

So glad I bought that gun, he thought. *It could have ended a lot worse.*

Buying a gun hadn't been an easy decision. Mike was uncomfortable around firearms. He always had been. In fact, until he was robbed two blocks from his own apartment, he'd been pretty staunchly opposed to them. In the end, raw animal fear had forced him to compromise his political views and purchase the .38 Special, and now it had saved their lives.

The irony was not lost on him. As they rode along, he reached into the backpack and pulled it out. The gun was still warm, and he smelled a hint of gunpowder. For no particular reason—except that he liked the feel of it—he spun the cylinder, popped it out, popped it back in, and spun it again. Then he tucked the gun under the suitcase on the seat beside him, making sure it was within easy reach.

He was so tired he could barely think straight, despite the fact that he'd done less work than either Jodi or Owen, and he certainly didn't have a gunshot wound to contend with. Still, he felt himself edging closer to collapse, and, to top it off, his butt was sore from being crammed in the seat beside the pile of luggage. He couldn't move around or shift positions.

Eventually, after a few grueling miles in which Jodi pedaled slower and slower, Owen came up beside her and asked to change places.

"Mom, you need a break from pulling the heavy load," he said. "Let me take over."

She didn't protest, which Mike knew was out of character. Wordlessly, she climbed down from the pedicab and took Owen's bike. It made Mike feel rather pathetic and useless. He should be helping Jodi bear the load, instead of *being* the load. Why should his injured sister or his teenage nephew have to haul him around like dead weight?

Mike, on the verge of feeling sorry for himself, began sinking into that dark little pit he'd discovered after his cancer diagnosis.

Don't forget, buddy, you just stopped an active shooter situation, he reminded himself. *You were far from useless then.*

It made him feel better, but only marginally so. The realization that he'd taken a life made him queasy, and the image of the bullet hitting the man above the eye was seared into his mind.

It had to be done, he reminded himself. *It was his life or the lives of your loved ones.*

They left the highway in the town of Blythe when the mass exodus proved to be too much. Jodi seemed scared that they might encounter other lunatics in the crowd. As they wound through the countryside, passing farms, isolated homes, and small towns, they encountered far fewer people.

Finally, as afternoon gave way to evening, they entered a tiny town called Keysville. Owen pointed out a small convenience store by the side of the road. The rain canopy above the gas pumps had a sign that read, "Mom and Pop's Country Store." Surprisingly, the store appeared to be open, with lamplight flickering through the small windows on either side of the door.

"Pull in," Jodi shouted from behind the pedicab.

Owen came to a stop under the large awning in front of the door, and Jodi pulled up beside him. As she stepped down off her bike, she grimaced in pain.

"Does it hurt a lot, Jodi?" Mike asked.

"It has gotten worse," she said. "I need to fish some painkillers out of our medical supplies. Wish we had something stronger than ibuprofen. Should've had Erica get us into the pharmacy somehow."

Mention of the attractive nurse made Mike feel a moment of wistfulness.

"Why don't we try to find a real vehicle?" Mike said. "You need a break. This bike riding is too much."

"Yeah, I think you're right," she said, tucking the injured arm against her belly, "but it'll have to be big enough to haul the bikes. I don't want to abandon them. We might need them again."

Owen opened the front door of the store, holding it for Jodi.

"Should I stay out here and guard the stuff?" Mike asked.

Jodi shook her head. "You find a roadmap. I'll stay in sight of the door and keep an eye on things."

In truth, she didn't seem like she cared all that much whether or not their things got stolen. She looked absolutely miserable and only about half-conscious. As Mike rose to follow her, he grabbed his .38 out from under the pile of luggage and jammed it inside his backpack. Then he slipped the backpack over his shoulders and went into the store.

There wasn't much to Mom and Pop's Country Store. Two aisles ran the length of the small building, with coolers in the back, and a cash register on a glass counter on the right. A handful of customers roamed the aisles. An older couple—presumably Mom and Pop— were perched behind the register, the old man wearing thick glasses and a bright red sweater, the woman in a quaint floral-print house- dress. Light came from a kerosene lamp near the cash register, and by that weak light, Mike noticed an old mechanical credit card reader on the counter. He pointed it out to Jodi.

"You take credit cards?" she asked the old man.

Pop gave her a big grin and nodded. "Turns out the old-fashioned ways are the better ways. I take Mastercard and Visa."

"Fantastic," Jodi said, and then to Mike she added, "I didn't want to keep using up our cash. Never know when we might need it in an emergency."

"We've already embraced the value of bribing people," Mike said, "and bribes are cash only."

Jodi gave him an exasperated look and waved him down the aisle. "Try to find a roadmap, something local enough to include back roads." Then she gestured at her son. "Owen, grab us some food and water and whatever other supplies you think we might need for the next few days."

Mike trudged down the emptiest aisle toward the back of the store, his thumbs tucked under the straps of his backpack. He finally spotted a rack of maps near a non-functioning ATM at the back. The rack had almost been picked clean, but he found a single remaining map of Georgia at the bottom. Bending over to grab it took him a couple minutes of careful balancing, and when he finally snagged it, it felt like quite an accomplishment. It was a jumbo-sized paper map, and he made the mistake of unfolding it. It took him a while to get it folded again.

Cutting over to the second aisle, Mike found Owen picking up cans of food and bottles of water, balancing them in the crook of his arm.

"Need some help there, kiddo?" Mike asked.

"No, I've got it," Owen replied. "You should go sit back down, Uncle Mike."

"I'm hobbling along just fine," Mike said. "I've got at least twelve good steps left in me."

He made his slow way to the front of the store, avoiding the handful of customers picking through the shelves. When he got there, Jodi was chatting with the couple behind the cash register.

"It's been a rough day," Pop said. "Worse than we expected. We thought we were providing a great service by staying open today but everyone has been so darn rude. Some people treat us like the power loss is our fault, and they argue with each other at the drop of a hat. I thought a couple of gentlemen were going to come to blows earlier. What do you think they were fighting about? The last case of beer."

"We're thinking about not opening tomorrow," Mom said. "It's just such a hassle."

"Why should we put up with rude behavior?" the old man said. "I don't need to be called names when I'm trying to serve customers."

"I'm very glad you're open right now," Jodi said, "but I'll be honest with you. It might be a good idea to close the store and save what you've got in stock for yourselves. I heard from a fairly knowledge-able person that it could be years before they get the power grid back up and running."

"Years?" the woman said, glancing at her husband. "You can't mean it."

"Let's not expect the worst," Pop said. "Not yet."

Mike could tell by the way the old couple looked at each other that they didn't quite believe Jodi. They thought she was being alarmist. He didn't blame them. It wasn't easy to accept that all the concerted efforts of the corporate world, the government, the military, and volunteers couldn't somehow rush the rebuilding and get everything up and running soon. Still, this poor couple would suffer for their optimism. Now was a time for realism and preparing for the worst. Mike had learned that if he'd learned anything.

"You have to take care of yourselves," Jodi said. "That's all I'm saying."

"I'd hate to leave people in the lurch," Pop said. "Our regulars count on us. We're the only store in town. Still, we'll think about what you said."

"We could put a few things back, I guess," Mom said, in a tone that suggested she did not intend to do any such thing.

Owen came back then and dumped a bunch of stuff on the counter. Mike added the map, and the store owners added it all up. When Jodi handed them her credit card to pay for it, the old man used the manual credit card machine to make an imprint of the card on a double receipt. He took the top copy and handed Jodi the bottom. Mike marveled at this. He hadn't seen such a crude device since his childhood.

"It's like watching someone demonstrate an antique machine in a museum," he said. "If only you had an old kinetoscope and one of those love tester machines."

"I always kept my credit card machine under the counter," Pop said, handing Jodi her credit card. "I figured I might need it someday."

"Were you three planning to spend the night?" Mom asked.

"We hadn't thought about that, to be honest," Jodi said. "I imagine we'll park in a field somewhere."

"There's a park on the south side of town," Mom said. "You'll see it just a mile past the store. It's a safe enough place. Well, it used to be. No telling what it's like now. People have been so different today. I just don't understand it. If they'd grown up way out in the country like me, maybe it wouldn't be such a big deal."

As she spoke, she bagged up their items, using a paper grocery bag. She started to hand it to Jodi, then spotted her bandaged arm and handed it to Owen instead.

"Are you okay there?" Pop asked. "Looks like you took a fall."

"I'm fine," Jodi said tightly.

"You don't look fine. It sure looks like a lot of blood and bandages."

"It is," Jodi said, "but I'm fine. Thanks for asking."

Mike eased up to the counter, leaning against the cold glass. He felt stiff and sore from riding in the back of the pedicab for so long, and a slight nausea was starting to roil in his belly again.

"Hey, you fine folks wouldn't happen to know someone who would sell us a truck, would you?" he asked.

The couple seemed to consider his question, and the old man was just about to answer. Before he got a word out, the front door swung open and banged off the wall. Mike heard heavy boots stepping into the room, and he turned around. Four men sauntered into the store, all of them big, hefty guys in leather jackets. They wore boots and raggedy jeans, and one of them had a large spider tattoo on his left cheek. Their jackets had skull patches on the left breast.

As they entered the store, they spread out and looked around, as if sizing up the place. The biggest of the men was a huge grizzled creature with jowls like a bulldog and hateful, beady eyes. He looked at Mike, and his lip curled, revealing a hint of cigarette-discolored teeth. The man raised his hand and jammed it deep into the pocket of leather jacket.

26

The grizzled man produced a handgun and racked the slide. As if that were a signal, the other men drew guns from their pockets. He stepped forward and thrust the gun in the direction of the counter. Jodi and Mike instinctively drew aside, but the gun was not meant for them, not yet.

"Hey there, Pop," the grizzled man said, aiming for the old man behind the counter. He had a rough voice, like sand and pebbles. Mike noted that his knuckles were crisscrossed with scars, old and new, his fingernails bitten down to the nubs. Clearly, he'd lived a hard life.

"Who are you?" Pop asked, sounding far more angry than scared. "How dare you come in here waving guns around."

The grizzled man shook his head, filthy strands of black hair coming untucked from behind his enormous red ears. "Let's don't get off to a bad start. We're going to make this real simple. We've come to take whatever we want, and you're not going to do anything about it. Is that clear?"

"You're out of your mind," Pop asked. "We're a small business. We don't carry a lot of cash."

Instead of answering, the grizzled man flicked his hand at his men.

"Snake, take the left aisle," he said. "Kade, take the right. Grab anything of value. Pick those rubes clean."

"You got it, Big Bill," Snake said.

Snake had thinning dishwater hair combed back from a high, sun-wrecked forehead. He shook out the sleeves of his jacket and strode to the left aisle, where three customers were caught in the act of picking over the shelves. A man and two women, all in their late fifties, they froze, staring at Snake like deer caught in headlights.

"Empty your pockets," he said, gesturing with his gun. "Fast. Don't waste my time."

The man turned out his pockets first, tossing a set of keys, a wad of cash, and some coins onto the floor. One of the women was carrying a small leather purse. She tossed it down the aisle, so that it slid toward Snake's feet. The third woman pulled keys and a couple of credit cards out of a jacket pocket and flung them away from her, as if they were hot coals.

"That's good," Snake said. "Real good."

He stooped down and picked up the purse without taking his eyes off the three. Then he unzipped the purse with his teeth and overturned it, dumping everything onto the floor. Tubes of lipstick, photographs, keys, tissues, an assortment of random papers, and about thirty other unidentifiable things rained down.

Kade, the one with the spider tattoo, went down the right aisle. The man had a wiry beard beneath a rather large nose. He seemed permanently sunburned, the skin around his eyes lighter, as if he often wore a large pair of sunglasses. A single customer halfway down the aisle backed away at his approach. She was a young woman, small and timid, cowering like a cornered mouse.

"Don't hurt me," she said. "Please, take whatever you want."

He towered over her, pointing his gun at the top of her head. "You'd better show me something good then. I want jewelry, cash, credit cards, something."

While Snake and Kade robbed the customers in the aisles, the other two thieves turned to confront the people in the front of the store. Mike felt their hateful and gleeful eyes pass over him.

"I want all of you to get down on the ground," the grizzled leader said. "I'm going to make this as easy as possible, so you just do what I say, don't make any trouble, and we won't have to kill everybody in this place. How does that sound?" With his free hand, he smacked the spiky-haired thief in the chest. "Keep a good eye on 'em, Dale. Anyone makes a move to resist, deal with it. Got me?"

Dale nodded. "You bet, Big Bill. What, are y'all deaf? He said get on the ground!"

Jodi gestured for Owen to get on the ground, then she followed him. They lay flat, arms and legs splayed. Mike glanced in the direction of the store owners. The old woman went down, disappearing behind the counter. Pop did the same, but he moved creakingly slow. As he went, Mike saw him reach to a shelf behind the counter and push a small box out of the way, revealing the wooden stock of a shotgun.

Don't do it, Pop, Mike thought, as he dropped onto the floor. *Don't be a hero.*

The second Big Bill turned away, Pop swept the shotgun off the back shelf and swung it around, banging it against a corner of the glass counter in the process. The man standing beside Bill, the one named Dale, was the smallest of the four, leathery and fierce, with spiky black hair. He spotted Pop's gun first and pointed.

"No, you don't, old man," he said. "I see you there."

Pop was a fraction of a second too slow on the draw. Maybe the trigger was a bit of a hard pull for him. Mike saw him straining, saw his liver-spotted hands quaking from the effort. Then the spiky-haired thug opened fire with his pistol. Pop took a step back and turned, dropping the shotgun and raising his hands in front of his face, as if he might shield himself. His wife screamed as he fell behind the counter. Mom rose, frantic, and made a mad dash for it, stepping over the body and trying to run toward an open door at the end of the counter.

"Bad move," Big Bill said. He tracked her with his pistol and shot her in the back twice. With the first shot, she kept running. With the second, she fell, hit the doorframe, and slid out of sight. Bill smiled and gave his friend a friendly punch on the arm. "Good catch, Dale. Old Pop thought he was slick."

"Old Pop's arthritis got the best of him," Dale said. "You warned him, and he tried something anyway."

Snake, Kade, Big Bill, and Dale, Mike thought. *What a group of winners. Wish I could get to my gun.*

Unfortunately, they had the upper hand. Mike lay down beside Jodi and pressed his hands to the cold linoleum floor. It took him a few seconds, as the movement caused the incision on his neck to hurt. He reached up to touch the bandage, making sure it hadn't soaked through with blood. It still felt dry to the touch.

"Now, let's not try to follow Pop's example," Big Bill said to the rest of the room. He swept his gun in the direction of Owen, Jodi, and Mike. "I've got a bullet for anyone who wants to try some smart move. What about you three? Want to pull any stunts like old Pop there?"

Jodi and Owen kept their heads down, for which Mike was grateful, but he noticed that Owen had eased in front of his mom, as if to shield her with his body.

Good kid, he thought.

The four thieves went through the store, grabbing anything they wanted. Big Bill stepped behind the counter and emptied the register. Mike could practically feel the weight of the .38 in his backpack, but he knew there was no chance he could move fast enough to grab it without getting shot. In his current state, he wasn't much faster than poor old Pop. Instead, following Owen's example, he eased over to Jodi, trying to position his body slightly on top of her.

"Dale, pick those three clean," Big Bill said from behind the register. "Pick up the pace."

Mike stiffened when the spiky-haired thief, Dale, approached and knelt down behind them. He began with Owen, digging into his pants pockets one by one. He didn't find much: a few coins, a crumpled five-dollar bill, some pocket lint, a school ID. He kept the coins and the bill and tossed the ID on the floor.

"Pathetic," he said.

Owen scowled at this, as if offended.

Though Jodi was next in line, Dale skipped her and knelt behind Mike. Something cold touched the back of Mike's neck. He flinched, certain it was the barrel of the gun.

"Just hold still, buckaroo," Dale said, laughing under his breath. He reeked of cigarette smoke, leather, and road dust, and Mike, in his frail state, had to suppress his gag reflex. "Let's just see what goodies you've got for me here."

Mike tensed as Dale unzipped the backpack. Though tempted to fight over the gun, he knew it would be a useless gesture. Dale could take whatever he wanted, and Mike couldn't do a thing about it without getting a bullet through the neck. He felt a hand rooting into the big pocket of his backpack. Clothes spilled out onto the floor, followed by a water bottle, which rolled off Mike's shoulder and bounced toward the door.

Dale grabbed a pair of Mike's boxer shorts, and he cursed under his breath, flinging them away. This caused him to give up on the big pocket, and he unzipped the smaller pocket on the backpack instead.

In there, he only found a bottle of Mike's after-chemo pills. He shook the bottle, seemed to consider it for a second, then—to Mike's surprise and alarm—he shoved the pills in his jacket pocket, as if he thought they were something that could get him high.

"Whole lot of nothing," Dale muttered.

Without emptying the rest of Mike's backpack—therefore, without finding the gun jammed in the bottom of the big pocket—he rose and stepped over to Jodi, the great cloud of stench swirling in his wake. Mike breathed a sigh of relief.

Dale squatted down over Jodi next, but he actually sat down, his large posterior cradling the small of her back. When he brought his weight down on her, she clamped her eyes shut and uttered a small, annoyed sound. Owen glanced at the thief with fire in his eyes, but Jodi gently grabbed his wrist.

"Let's see what we got here," Dale said.

Mike noticed that Jodi's purse was nowhere in sight. He assumed she had hidden it beneath her body. Dale had no access to her pants pockets because he was covering them with his enormous thighs, but it soon became clear that her pockets weren't his primary interest. His grubby sausage fingers stroked her hair, and Mike saw her tense up. He dared a glance at the guy and saw a hungry look in his eyes. Dale had watery eyes, bags beneath them like fat parentheses. For a few seconds, his fingers moved through Jodi's hair, then they glided down her back.

I have to stop this, he thought, *but if he sees me going into the backpack, I'm a dead man.*

Seething, Mike dared to reach toward his backpack, his left hand snaking up along the side, scrabbling at the coarse canvas. His sister was visibly grinding her teeth, clearly struggling not to respond, but Owen seemed on the verge of lashing out.

I'd better do something stupid before the kid does, Mike thought.

He managed to get his hand inside the big pocket, but as he did, his fingers brushed the zipper and make a soft but distinctive sound. Dale glanced up, raising his pistol.

"Stop messing with that girl," Big Bill shouted from behind the counter.

When Dale didn't immediately respond, Bill picked up the credit card reader and tossed it at him. It bounced off his back, and Dale shouted in alarm. He flinched, reaching back, and in the process, he inadvertently fired his gun. The bullet hit the floor not six inches from Jodi's head, splitting the linoleum and ricocheting into the far wall.

"Watch yourself, stupid," Big Bill said. "Get in gear. Load up and let's go. There are plenty of pretty young things waiting for us down the road."

Dale grunted loudly, as if offended, and rose.

"I think we're done here," Big Bill said, stepping out from behind the counter. He was carrying a paper grocery bag that he'd folded over many times. When he moved, the bag jangled with coins and cash. "What did you guys get?"

Snake approached from the left aisle. "Wallets, watches, phones, cash, cigarettes, lots of good stuff," he said.

"Same here," Kade added, coming down the right aisle, "and a nice diamond ring. Look at this thing. It's like a chunk of rock!" He held up a generously-sized diamond ring, turning it back and forth in the lamplight.

"Don't drop it," Big Bill said. "Put it in your pocket and let's get out of here."

Mike heard the mousey woman in the right aisle quietly crying. Had Kade taken her wedding ring? He thought so, and it made him burn with anger. When he looked in her direction, he saw her curled into a ball on the floor, her face in her hands.

Oh, yeah, I'd love to shoot these guys, he thought.

He didn't think he would have the chance. Instead, judging by the way Big Bill's eyes were flitting about the room, it seemed like the thieves were about to do the shooting. A nice way to eliminate any witnesses in a world where police would be very slow to respond.

Bill waved his men to the front door with his gun, and they came lumbering along bearing armfuls of stolen items. Kade turned to survey the room, his spider tattoo seeming to shift and move in the flickering lamplight.

"Clear the room, Big Bill," he said.

This is it, Mike thought. *This is the moment we all die.*

Even then, Mike tried to ease his hand into his backpack. The angle was all wrong. He could feel the bulge of t-shirts and socks poking out of the open pocket, but he couldn't dig in deep enough to get the .38.

"Clear the room," Kade said again. "They've got it coming. Why not?"

Big Bill swept the barrel of his gun across the room, letting it linger on Jodi for a second.

"Nah, I'd rather save the ammo," he said, after a moment. He grabbed the handle of the front door and pulled it open. "We'll need it when we hit the next place. Guys, there's a thousand targets out there and not enough police to matter anymore. This is our time to shine!"

"This dump is small potatoes," Dale said. "Let's hit a bank next."

"Nah, banks have their own security," Big Bill said. "These gas stations got nothing. They're sitting ducks. We can pick them off one by one, and nobody will do a thing about it."

Snake, Kade, and Dale laughed at this like it was the funniest joke Bill had ever told.

To those lying on the ground, Bill said, "Don't any of you move until we're on the road. It's your lucky day. I don't feel like killing anyone else, but one move could change my mind."

As if testing their resolve, he stared hard for a few seconds. Mike froze, his left hand awkwardly bent back and brushing against his backpack. Then Bill laughed with his friends and left. They strode out of the store together, letting the front door bang shut. Mike didn't dare move or speak. A few seconds later, he heard the revving of motorcycle engines as Big Bill's gang roared away, heading north.

Jodi was the first one up. She pushed herself off the floor and stood surveying the room. "They're gone," she said, loud enough for the whole store to hear. "You can get up. It's over."

Mike got up, half his backpack spilling onto the floor in the process. He pulled the gun out, tucked it under his belt, and rushed to the counter. A number of customers in the aisles were crying now, trying to comfort one another. Mike leaned over the counter and saw Pop curled up on the floor in the narrow space there. He was definitely dead.

Slipping behind the counter, Mike looked for the old man's wife. He found her sprawled in the open doorway at the end of the counter. When he approached, he heard labored breathing. Despite his exhaustion, he knelt beside her. She'd been hit twice in the back—he saw the puncture wounds cutting though her cotton dress.

"Ma'am, are you alive?"

He tried to roll her over, but she groaned in pain.

"Is he dead?" she said softly, blood trickling from the corner of her mouth. "My husband, Harold, did they kill him?"

"I'm so sorry, ma'am," Mike said. "I don't think he made it."

She uttered a gentle moan. "It doesn't matter now. Take the keys... from his pocket." She winced in pain.

"What can I do to help?" Mike said.

"Nothing," she replied. "Take the truck. It's parked in back beside the trailer. Take it and go. Get out of here before they come back."

"I don't want to take your stuff," Mike said. "You need a doctor."

"No..." She took a sharp, pained breath. "I don't need anything. Take it and go...while you can." And then she let the breath out slowly.

Jodi came up beside him then, her injured arm curled against her stomach. "Get the keys," she said to Mike. "I'll see what I can do for her."

Mike went back to the counter and stooped over Pop. The stench of blood and gunpowder made him sick. With one hand, he pinched his nose shut. With the other, he dug into Pop's right pocket and found a hefty set of keys attached to a small silver fob. In the process, he got blood on his hand, and he grimaced in disgust.

"Sorry, Pop," he said. "Wish I could do something for you. You seemed like a decent fellow."

When he stood up again, he found both Jodi and Owen trying to help the man's wife. Jodi had pulled a bandage out of her purse and was attempting to staunch the blood flow, but it was a futile effort.

"She's gone," Jodi said, after a moment, tossing the bloody bandage aside. "Shot to death for absolutely no damn reason." She looked at Owen in disgust, and her son nodded sadly.

Mike jangled the keys, and they both turned to him. Other customers were leaving now. Mike heard the door open and close twice. A sobbing woman fled in tears.

"What do we do with the bodies?" Owen asked.

"Bury them out back, I guess," Mike said. "Seems like the civilized thing to do."

"No," Jodi replied wearily. "It's too late at night. We can't linger here, and digging two graves would take too long. We'll cover the bodies. That's the best we can do."

"Seems like a shame," Mike said.

"It is," Jodi replied. "It is a shame."

In the end, they covered the bodies with emergency travel blankets they found discarded in an aisle. They'd been taken off the shelf by one of the customers but left behind in the aftermath of the robbery. They briefly discussed taking some supplies off the store shelves, but in the end, they felt too bad for the poor store owners. It didn't seem right taking anything. Mike felt a pang of sadness as they blew out the kerosene lamp and left the store, Pop and Mom dead on the floor of their own business with only thin metallic sheets draped over them.

"It's not right," he said. "I'd like to track those four scumbags down and plug 'em all full of holes."

"I don't blame you," Jodi said. "Just be glad anyone got out of there alive."

They wheeled the pedicab and the bike around behind the store, where they found what Mike estimated to be an '85 Chevy Silverado. It was an ugly two-tone color, yellow on the bottom and a pukey cornflower-gold on top, but it seemed like it was in good condition.

Mike and Jodi, working together, lifted the bike into the bed of the truck. As they were doing that, Owen figured out how to fold up the pedicab.

"It's got a little lever here on the side," Owen said, as he picked up the folded pedicab and set it in the back.

"Wow, good eye, kid," Mike said. "I never would've seen that. I was about to recommend getting a tow strap and dragging the thing."

They stuffed their luggage in the gaps in back, though Mike brought the backpack with him into the cab. As Jodi started the truck and pulled onto the street, he tensed, pulling the gun out from under his belt and pointing it at the floorboard. He expected to see the bikers lurking somewhere just down the road, but as they drove away from the store, he saw nothing but miles of empty country road stretching out before them. They blew past the little park the old woman had mentioned and kept going into the night, heading south. Mike finally jammed the gun into his backpack.

27

The sound invaded her dream. She was frantically trying to drive wolf spiders the size of housecats out of her garden, swinging a shovel back and forth. They were coming from all sides, and they zigzagged as they came, dodging her blows. When the shovel finally connected to one of them, it shattered, making a sound like a window being broken by a rock, and flew apart into glittering fragments.

Beth opened her eyes in the darkness and realized the sound had followed her out of sleep. Staring up at the well of shadow that was the bedroom ceiling, she heard glass tinkling on a granite counter. She rubbed her eyes and sat up, throwing her blanket back. She almost called out to Kaylee, but she thought better of it and bit her tongue.

Moving as quietly as possible, she reached behind the nightstand and grabbed the double-barrel shotgun from its place in the corner. It was a Fox Model B, a hefty piece of metal and wood, and she liked the feel of it in her hands. Practically an antique, it had once belonged to her father. Fortunately, she'd thought to load it before going to bed. She knew not to trust the nighttime during a crisis.

She eased her bedroom door open and stepped into the hallway, seeing a faint light shining in the direction of the dining room. Beth tightened her grip on the shotgun, planted the butt against her shoulder, and moved quickly down the hall. If it was an intruder, she wanted to catch them off guard before they could react. Ironically, though Bauer hadn't awakened immediately at the sound of glass breaking, he began to bark furiously when Beth passed the door to Kaylee's bedroom.

When she came in sight of the dining room, she didn't see anyone, but she heard noises coming from the kitchen. Hushed voices, the clatter of cans beings moved around. Bauer was losing it now, sliding back and forth against Kaylee's bedroom door as he tried to get through.

Beth rushed into the dining room, turned toward the far corner of the kitchen, and aimed the shotgun.

"Nobody move," she shouted.

Two figures were bent over her open pantry, one in a denim jacket, the other wearing a filthy, stained t-shirt. They rose together and looked at her. Despite the gun in her hands, they seemed more annoyed than scared.

"Greg. Travis," she said. "What the heck are you guys doing in here?"

Shards of glass were scattered across the counter. They'd come in through the window above the sink, smashing it with the concrete cherub from Mrs. Eddies' statuary garden. The cherub lay on its side beside the toaster. Greg shook out his denim jacket, as if shaking off a fly, and set a couple of cans back into the pantry.

"What are you doing?" Beth said again.

"Hey, calm down," Greg said, waving a hand at her. "Put that gun down, lady. There's no reason for hostility. We're just borrowing some food. Our grandma's pantry was pretty much empty. Looks like she was living on potted meat and bread the last few days."

"The food in her fridge is already starting to smell bad," Travis added, clutching a jar of corned beef hash in both hands as if it were a treasure. "We've been on the road for a few days. We're hungry!"

Beth lowered the shotgun so it wasn't pointed directly at them, but she maintained a firm grip, her finger near the trigger. "If you were out of food, you might have tried *asking*," she said. "As it is, I'll thank you to get out of my house. I don't appreciate the broken window."

"I'm sorry you feel—"

Greg stopped speaking mid-sentence and rushed at her. She raised the shotgun, her finger slipping under the trigger guard, but Greg was surprisingly fast. In three strides he entered the dining room, swung his arm, and knocked the shotgun aside. She almost dropped it, and as it wobbled, he grabbed the barrel with both hands and yanked it away from her. Beth was dragged toward him in the process, but he put a shoulder against her and shoved her into the dining room table.

Bauer was going crazy in Kaylee's bedroom, scrabbling at the door and barking himself hoarse.

"Take a seat," Greg said, gesturing at the nearest chair.

Travis came up beside him, smiling, still clutching his can of corned beef hash. Beth pulled the chair out and sat down, desperately trying to think of some way to get the gun back. Her collarbone hurt where Greg had hit her.

"Guys, there's no need for this," she said. "I have food to spare. All you had to do was ask."

"Shut up," Greg said. "Am I going to have to shoot that stupid dog?"

"He's behind a door," Beth said. She couldn't see any way out of the situation except to be docile, give the men what they wanted, and hope they left. "He won't do anything to you. All bark, no bite."

"What about you?" Greg said. "Am I going to have to shoot you, or are you going to cooperate with us?"

"Just take what you want and go," Beth said. She figured if they looted the entire kitchen, she still had the hidden storage space beneath the basement. It would be enough.

Greg and Travis both stared at her for a few tense seconds, then they laughed, Travis elbowing Greg in the ribs.

"I don't think we're going anywhere," Greg said, walking past her. He made sure to bump her with his elbow in passing. They went into the living room and dropped onto her couch. Travis swung one of his legs over the padded arm.

"We could just make ourselves at home, if we want to," Travis said. "Smells a lot better over here."

"Yep," Greg agreed, pointing the shotgun toward the dining room. "I do believe I catch a whiff of lavender and maybe Pine-Sol? Very nice."

This made Travis grin.

"I'll tell you what, old lady," Greg said. "Why don't you bring us a beer? Help us get nice and drunk, and we'll think about moving on."

Beth sighed. "I don't have any beer. I don't drink."

"Did you hear that?" Greg said to Travis. "She doesn't have any beer. What do you think about that?"

"I don't like it," Travis said with a scowl.

"Show me how much you don't like it."

Travis rose, cracked his knuckles, and came toward the table.

"Sorry, guys," Beth said. "I don't drink alcohol. Maybe a glass of wine on special occasions, but that's it."

She didn't see the punch coming. Her head rocked back, and she saw stars. A sudden numbness and tingling spread from her lips into her jaw, and she realized Travis had slugged her. To make matters far worse, a second later she heard Kaylee crying.

"Now, now," Greg said. "Don't break the lady's jaw."

Tears in her eyes, Beth looked toward the hallway and saw Kaylee standing there in her pajamas. Acting on instinct, Beth rose from the table and rushed to her, hoping it wouldn't get her shot. Greg tracked her with the shotgun as she placed her body in front of Kaylee.

"Uh-oh, the kid's getting riled up," Travis said. "If she starts wailing, she'll wake the neighbors."

"She's just scared," Beth said. Her lips had begun to sting, and she was pretty sure they were swelling. "Calm down, guys." She turned to her granddaughter, wiping the tears off her cheeks with her thumbs.

"Grammy," Kaylee said. "What happened?"

"Go back to your room," Beth said. "Is Bauer still in there?"

"She wanted to run out," Kaylee said. "I didn't let her."

"Keep her in there. Go on. It's fine."

"Grammy, no."

Beth grabbed her shoulders and pulled her close. "Pumpkin, it's okay. I'm just hanging out with the neighbors. We have to talk about some things, but everything's fine. Go to your room right now."

"Are we sharing with them?" Kaylee asked. "You said we had to help people."

"I did say that," Beth replied. "Yes, we're sharing. Let me take care of it."

"But, Grammy, it sounded like you were arguing."

"We had a misunderstanding, that's all. Now, you go to bed right now. Listen to your grammy."

Sticking her lower lip out, Kaylee pouted back down the hall to her room. Beth caught a glimpse of Bauer trying to get past her, but Kaylee gently pushed the dog back into the room with her foot and shut the door behind her.

As soon as the bedroom door shut, Beth went back into the living room, fighting not to show the pain she was feeling in her lips, her gums, her jaw. The boys were lounging on the couch, Greg balancing the shotgun in the crook of his arm.

"Okay, guys, here's what I'll do," Beth said. "I'll get a cardboard box and pack you some food from my pantry. I don't have beer, but I have bottled water, plenty of canned meat, vegetables, fruit, staples like flour and rice."

Greg pulled a face and shook his head. "Old lady, you don't get it. We're not leaving."

"We don't need a box of food," Travis added. "We've got all the food we want right here. No reason to haul it next door to that dusty old place. Never much liked it there anyway."

"Cans of vegetables don't interest me," Greg said. "It's been a long time since we had real home cooking, and now that Grandma's gone, who is going to pamper us? Even with that tube in her nose, she still made us nice dinners and poured us drinks. She was a sweet old lady."

"Consider us adopted," Travis said. "We'll call *you* Grandma from now on."

"I like the sound of that," Greg said.

Beth listened to them with growing alarm. They weren't here to loot the pantry. They were here to move in. And still, as stubborn and resourceful as she was, Beth thought there had to be some way to get rid of them.

"I see the wheels spinning," Greg said, tapping his forehead with his free hand, "but you're not getting rid of us, and unless you want that kid of yours getting hurt, you won't try anything. Is that clear?"

When Beth didn't answer right away, he said it again, louder and more sharply.

"Is that clear? Keep the kid safe and behave, Grandma."

Beth nodded. For once, her clever mind had failed her. She saw no way out of this situation. All she could do was hope her family would arrive soon and somehow realize there was a problem.

28

Shane hadn't expected to fall asleep. He was a nervous wreck, and he sat wide awake for at least a couple of hours, staring out the windshield at the dark countryside. Ruby, Violet, and Corbin all snored softly like some kind of strange, discordant symphony, and the noise made sleep seem even more unlikely.

When it came, it came suddenly. One moment, he was staring at the crescent moon through the windshield, the next moment he was waking, his cheek pressed against the cold glass of the driver's side door. He felt crisp morning air coming through the open window as he opened his eyes. When he sat up, his stiff back cried out in protest. Judging by the position of the sun, it was late morning. He'd slept much longer than he'd intended.

A sudden loud *crack* split the still morning air. Shane knew that sound too well now. Every vestige of sleep dropped away like a cloak that had been tossed off and he sat up, wide awake and instantly alert. He turned toward the passenger seat. Violet wasn't there and Ruby was missing. Hooking his arm around the armrest, he checked the back of the van. No Corbin.

A second later, he heard a voice. Though he couldn't make out the words, he knew it was Violet. Heart racing, he opened the driver's door. As he hopped out of the van, he clumsily drew the Glock, fumbling with it a second before getting a firm grip. In front of him, he saw the empty parking lot. A rickety fence ran along the edge, but it was so full of gaps that he could see the overgrown field beyond. No one there. On his right, a shopping center sat empty, "For Sale" signs posted in the windows.

He heard a second shot, and this time it was clear that it came from the other side of the van. Racing around the front end of the van, he found Corbin and Violet standing side by side, facing away from him. Corbin was holding his mother's gun, the one Shane had put in the door pocket before going to sleep. He had it pointed at the fence along the back of the building, where a crude circle had been traced on the dry wood in chalk. Ruby lounged at Violet's side, and while she seemed anxious, she stayed in her position despite the noise.

"Put it down," Shane said, pointing the Glock at the ground. "Put it down right now."

Corbin glanced over his shoulder, a confused look on his face. He hesitated a moment, then bent over and set the gun on the pavement.

"I was just showing Violet how to shoot," he said. "I figured it might come in handy if we get in trouble on the road."

Shane holstered his gun, fought an urge to cuss the kid out, and approached. "Teaching her how to shoot? Corbin, she's visually impaired."

"He showed me by feel how to line up a shot in front of me," Violet said. "I'm not useless, Dad."

"I didn't say that, Violet. I would never say that."

She scowled at him. "He showed me how to work the safety, how to hold the gun properly, and how to pull the trigger. He says I hit right in the middle of the circle."

Shane swooped down and picked up Debra's gun. "Okay, I get it," he said. "It just startled me, that's all. Where'd you learn to shoot, Corbin?"

Corbin shrugged. "I used to go hunting with my dad all the time before he died. I didn't enjoy it as much as he did, but it's how we spent time together. I learned to use rifles, pistols, shotguns, even a compound bow."

Embarrassed by his outburst, Shane handed the gun to Corbin. "Show me what you can do."

With a nod, Corbin grabbed the gun, cocked the hammer, and pointed it at the fence. Shane noted that he had perfect grip. It was what Landon had tried to show him, but somehow Shane couldn't get it quite right. Corbin fired two shots at the fence, the sound echoing far into the distance. The bullets hit dead center within the chalked circle.

The kid nodded, as if satisfied, and lowered the gun, looking at Shane.

"You're good," Shane admitted. "I don't suppose you could teach me. I understand the basics, but I feel clumsy."

"Yeah, sure," Corbin said. "Draw your gun and show me how you hold it."

Shane pulled the Glock and pointed it at the circle on the fence, doing his best to copy what Landon had showed him.

"No, that's called a teacup grip," Corbin said. "It's all wrong. Here, let me help."

He grabbed Shane's hands and started moving them around.

"Don't cross your thumbs," Corbin said. "Stack them like this. You want to keep your thumbs out of the way."

When he seemed satisfied with Shane's grip, he gestured for him to aim. Shane pointed the gun at the circle, feeling more confident. He pulled the trigger, and the bullet hit within the circle, punching a hole in the dry fence board.

"That's not bad," Corbin said. "You're a better shot than you should be without any experience, but you need to keep practicing."

"Thanks, Corbin. Sorry about before. Next time, warn me before you take the gun."

"I will," Corbin said.

"You slept a long time," Violet said. "We were bored."

Though he felt better about the situation, Shane put the gun in the glove compartment. Violet and Ruby climbed into the passenger seat, and Corbin resumed his place in the back of the van. For breakfast, they ate some leftover crackers from the previous night's MREs. Shane didn't have much of an appetite.

They were just about to get underway again—Shane had put the key in the ignition—when his phone began to ring. It startled him. He'd assumed the battery was dead, but when he pulled it out of his pocket, he saw that he still had around 20 percent left.

"Is it Mom?" Violet asked.

"Seems like it," Shane said.

He answered the call. As she spoke, he could hear the throaty rumble of an old truck in the background.

"Jodi, where are you?" he asked.

"On some country road," she replied, "trying to stay roughly parallel with State Highway One."

"Is everything okay?"

She didn't answer for a second, and he took that as her answer. "We're fine today. Had some trouble yesterday. Problems on the highway forced us to divert."

"Is anyone hurt?"

Again, she hesitated. "There've been some injuries, but I'll tell you all about it when we get to Mom's house."

If she won't tell me, it must be serious, he thought, but he wouldn't press the issue. Clearly, she was trying not to think about it.

"Where are you, Shane?" Jodi asked.

"Somewhere south of I-20," he said. "We're cutting down to I-75. Assuming we can find a clear lane all the way, and barring any serious problems, we should get to Macon tonight or tomorrow."

"Well, you'll arrive ahead us," Jodi replied. "Possibly a day or two. It's been slow going, and these back roads are rough."

"Do you have enough food, water, and fuel?" he asked.

"I think so. Shane, I can't get hold of my mother. I've called her repeatedly this morning, and she just won't answer. I want to think it's a bad connection, but what if there's a problem? I'm worried about her and Kaylee."

Shane felt a flutter of anxiety. He fought not to imagine the worst. "Just keep trying," he said. "Maybe Beth is busy."

"I hope so. How's Violet? Can I speak to her?"

Shane passed the phone to Violet, tapping her against the arm so she would take it. Violet still seemed to be brooding about Shane's earlier outburst. He knew he'd embarrassed her.

"Hey, Mom, how's it going?"

Jodi had been injured. Shane was sure of it. Something in her voice, something in the hesitation. She wasn't one to react to minor injuries. What if it was serious? Would she tell him? He wasn't sure.

I should divert course and meet her on the road, he thought. *She might need help. Owen and Mike are with her. What if they're all hurt?*

He tried to map out an alternate route in his mind, one that would quickly bypass Macon and find Jodi somewhere off Highway 1 on the other side.

"Are you okay, Mom?" Violet asked. "It sounds like something is wrong."

Violet's question only confirmed his fear. His daughter was good at picking up on verbal cues.

If we're lucky and don't encounter any serious blockage, we could push our speed a little, he thought, *and meet Jodi somewhere east of Macon.*

The thought of Kaylee stopped him. If Jodi was hurt, it wasn't bad enough to prevent her from speaking. Kaylee's condition, on the other hand, was a mystery. He couldn't drive around Macon without checking on her. It was a terrible choice all around, but he knew Jodi could take care of herself most of the time.

"Bye, Mom, be careful today," Violet said. "I love you, too."

She passed the phone to Shane. When he went to speak to Jodi, he found she had already hung up. He jammed the phone back into his pocket and started the van.

"Are Kaylee and Grandma in trouble?" Violet asked. "Mom can't get ahold of them."

"I'm sure it's just the phone," Shane said. "Maybe her battery ran out. We should get there today or tomorrow, depending on highway conditions."

He dared a little more speed that morning, slowing only as they approached curves in the road. When they reached the interstate, it was worse than he'd hoped. Dead vehicles and wrecks cluttered the lanes, and people were camped on the shoulder along the way. They were headed southeast now, following a straight course toward

Macon, but Shane found that he could rarely travel above twenty miles an hour for fear of running into someone or something.

Gas was a concern. They were approaching half a tank, burning through fuel far faster than he'd expected. The weight of supplies in the back had something to do with it, he was sure. Still, he didn't want to push their luck. As soon as he could fuel up, he intended to do so. After all, if they came to a major blockage, they might be forced to take to the backroads.

At every exit, he slowed to a crawl and looked for an open gas station, but almost every business was closed. Most of the gas stations had large signs saying they were out of fuel.

Seems like the economy has screeched to a halt, he thought.

By late afternoon, the van had less than a quarter of a tank. Shane was starting to feel true dread. He took the exit at Forsyth. It seemed like a sizable town, and he could see people milling in the parking lot of a Walmart. Surely, someone in town would have diesel. When he pulled into town, he saw a long street lined with fast-food restaurants. None of them were open, but as he approached an intersection, he spotted a police officer standing at a corner of a McDonald's parking lot.

Shane had Violet roll down her window, as he pulled up next to him.

"Officer, anyone selling diesel around here?"

"Straight ahead," the officer said. He was young and seemed weary beyond belief. He'd probably had a couple of rough days trying to keep order in this town. "Take a left at Railroad Avenue and go past the museum. You'll see a small place on the right. I'm pretty sure they're open today."

"Thanks."

Shane followed his directions, but it proved to be farther than he'd expected. Finally, as the van's fuel gauge danced dangerously close to empty, he came in sight of a small gas station near a high school. It wasn't until he pulled into the parking lot that he saw the sign posted on the window: "Hours 10 am to 4 pm."

He couldn't blame them for wanting to close before evening settled in, but it put him in a predicament. He pulled up to the front of the building and stopped.

"Dad, what are we doing?" Violet asked. "Are we stuck again?"

"No, we're not stuck," he said, "but I think we're done driving for today. We need gas, and we can't get it until tomorrow." *Assuming the business owners show up.*

"Are we ever going to get to Macon?" Violet said, leaning her head back.

"Of course."

But her question lingered in his mind.

29

With a groan, Mike flopped to one side, sliding against Owen's chest before mashing his face against the passenger window. It startled Jodi, and she inadvertently swerved the truck. For a moment, the back right tire dug into dirt on the shoulder. She moved back into their lane, even as she slowed down.

"Uncle Mike, are you okay?" Owen asked.

Mike sat up, gripping his forehead. "Motion sickness is killing me. The chemo makes it worse, but these darn winding roads are miserable. If I had anything at all in my belly, it would come right up. I don't suppose we could take a break. Sitting still for a few minutes would settle my stomach."

Jodi glanced at him. "Okay, I'll find a place. To be honest, I wouldn't mind stretching my legs. It's getting cramped in this truck, and I'm still sore from all that bike riding yesterday. I barely slept last night while we were parked in that field."

"Yeah, that was the worst night's sleep I've had in maybe...ever," Mike said.

She spotted a small dirt turnaround beside a stand of pine trees, so she pulled off the road. They bumped and thumped over the uneven ground and came to a stop behind the trees, out of sight of any oncoming vehicles.

"Mom, I could drive for a while, if you need a break," Owen said.

"No, that's fine," Jodi said, opening her door. She stepped outside, stretching her arms above her head.

"I have my learner's permit," Owen reminded her, "and Dad had been teaching me to drive. He even let me drive to the grocery store last week."

"Now is not the time for driving practice," Jodi said. "Road conditions are unpredictable. Anyway, it's a manual transmission. You've only practiced on an automatic. You guys stay here. I'll be right back."

Before he could press the point, she walked off behind the trees, fishing her phone out of her purse. First, she tried calling Shane again, but this time she didn't get through. Coverage had gotten bad, and she was running out of battery. When Shane didn't answer, she tried calling her mother. It was perhaps the fifteenth time she'd tried to call that morning. She wouldn't have worried quite as much if she'd gotten a "cannot complete" message. Instead, it just rang and rang. Why wouldn't her mother answer?

She hung up the phone and stood there for a minute, soaking in misery. She felt utterly alone and out of her element. Suddenly, it seemed like they would never make it to Macon, and if they did, maybe it would be too late.

Don't think that way, she chided herself.

She was about to call her mother again when she heard the distinctive sound of gears grinding from the other side of the trees. Jamming the phone in her purse, she rushed back toward the truck, pushing through tree limbs. Owen was behind the wheel of the Silverado, Mike sitting next to him and apparently giving him instructions. The truck made an awkward circle in the turnaround and came to a shuddering stop beside Jodi. Owen beamed at her through the windshield, grinning, even as Jodi stormed toward the driver's door.

Flinging open the door, she leaned in, ready to scold him, but Mike quickly spoke, "It was my idea, sis. Don't yell at the kid. He's pretty good. He was shifting gears and everything."

Jodi stepped back, grumbling under her breath.

"Look, you can't do all the driving," Mike said. "You're worn out, you're wounded, and I can tell you're struggling. Shifting gears with a bloody arm is no good. Give the kid a chance. You can rest and take it easy for a few hours."

Jodi glanced at her bandaged arm. She'd changed the bandages that morning, but the arm hurt a lot. She had a constant ache that throbbed up her arm to her shoulder.

In a moment of weakness, she held up her hands in a gesture of surrender. "Okay, fine. Owen can drive for a while."

Owen gave a whoop of excitement and bounced on his seat as Jodi walked around the truck. She climbed into the passenger seat, squeezing in beside Mike, and pulled her seatbelt into place.

"Mike, it's up to you to navigate while he drives," she said. "I'm not up to it."

"I've got it covered," Mike replied. "Just relax. You've done enough of the heavy lifting on this miserable trip."

She couldn't argue with that, so she leaned back into the corner where her seat met the door, resting her wounded arm on her purse. Owen gave an enthusiastic, "Woo hoo!" and put the truck into first. He added a bit too much gas, so when he let off the clutch, the truck jerked forward violently. Owen gave his mother a sheepish grin.

"You've got it, kid," Mike said. "Just remember what I told you."

Jodi grabbed the door handle and held on tight, praying the poor clutch would hold out long enough to get them to her mother's house. Once they got back on the road, Owen did fine. In fact, he was a surprisingly smooth driver, despite the winding back roads.

"See, your kid is decent," Mike said, when they were a few miles down the road.

"Yeah, good job, Owen," Jodi said.

"Thanks, Mom."

Jodi was so sleep-deprived that she might have dozed off if she hadn't been so worried. As it was, she couldn't stop thinking about her mother. This put her in a state of near delirium as she leaned against the passenger window and stared at the passing scenery. Owen took it slow, which intensified her anxiety. From time to time, Mike would unfold the map to check their progress, and each time Jodi was disappointed at how much farther they had to go. The back roads weren't clear of obstacles either, so occasionally they had to slow to a near stop to navigate a stalled or abandoned vehicle or some other road debris.

Eventually, it became clear they were going to have to stop again for the night. Although they passed a few houses, Jodi didn't want to approach strangers to ask for shelter. As the sun was setting, they rounded a bend and spotted a lonely red barn set back from the road.

"That'll do," Jodi said. "Pull in there."

Owen pulled off the road, navigated an overgrown dirt driveway, and pulled into the barn. Most of the roof was gone, and one of the walls had fallen down. However, enough of the structure remained to hide them from the road.

It had been a long, quiet day, and Jodi was restless. Talking to Shane and Violet in the morning had helped, but she hadn't been able to get ahold of them since then. She really wanted to hear from her mother.

She swapped places with Owen, and he settled into the passenger's seat for the night. As she reached down to recline her seat, she paused.

Try one more time, she thought.

Digging her phone out, she saw she had 5 percent of her battery life left. In the morning, the phone would be dead, unless she turned it off, but turning it off meant she might miss a call. She dialed her mother's number and put the phone to her ear.

On the second ring, Beth answered.

"Hello? Hello?"

Jodi was so shocked she'd answered that she stuttered for a second before speaking. "M-Mom…Mom, there you are!"

"Oh, my goodness, Jodi," Beth said. "It's so good to hear from you. I was just thinking about the time Michael took us to the beach at Marco Island. Do you remember?"

"Michael?" She didn't know the name. Jodi's father had been named Mitch. How could Beth get the name wrong?

Head trauma. That was Jodi's first thought.

"Remember when we were walking on the beach," Beth continued, "and we ran into those awful Carrigan brothers? They were very badly behaved. We didn't know what to do, and they wouldn't leave us alone." And then, strangely, she laughed, but it sounded forced.

"Carrigan brothers? Michael? Mom, what are you talking about?"

"Oh, they were a handful." Her tone of voice was all wrong. "We couldn't get them to leave the beach."

"Mom, how is Kaylee doing?" Jodi asked.

"Kaylee is sleeping. Nothing to worry about there. Nothing at all."

Something was definitely wrong, and it wasn't head trauma. Jodi was sure of it now. There was an undercurrent of fear, a slight tremor at the edge of every word.

"Is everything okay, Mom?"

Beth hesitated just a second before saying, in an overly excited voice, "Oh, everything's *great*."

"Okay, well, barring any complications, Shane and Violet should arrive to—"

Beth interrupted her, speaking over her loudly, "I love you, dear, and I'll see you in a few days. I have to go now. I'm very tired. Good night."

And then the phone went dead.

Jodi glanced over at Mike and Owen. Her son had already leaned his seat back, and he was either asleep or close to it, hands tucked into his pockets. Mike, however, was wide awake and watching her.

"What's wrong?" he asked.

Jodi looked down at her phone again. She was tempted to call back. "Mom seemed confused. Calling people by the wrong names, and just…I don't know. She called our father Michael instead of Mitch, and she mentioned something about the time we went to Marco Island when we were little and ran into the Carrigan brothers. Does that name ring a bell?"

"No," Mike replied, "but I do recall running into some weirdos on Marco Island who kept pestering us. They were drunk, as I recall. We definitely didn't get their names."

"Why would she bring that up?" Jodi asked.

"No idea," Mike replied, "but calling our father by the wrong name is a red flag. She called the old man a lot of things over the years, but she never forgot his name. I would say she's losing it, but dementia doesn't set in overnight. Seems intentional."

"Maybe she hit her head," Jodi said. "What if she slipped and fell trying to carry supplies out of her basement?"

"It's possible," Mike said.

"Shane will get there before us." She opened her phone contacts and flipped to Shane's name. "I'd better warn him."

She dialed his number and let it ring, but he never answered. She tried again and got the automated message: "All circuits are busy now. Please try your call again later." After a couple more tries, she gave up and opened her messages instead, dashing out a quick text: "Something might be wrong with Mom. She might be wounded, ill, or in danger."

She sent the message then put the phone back in her purse. It would have to do.

30

S hane slept better that night, mostly because he was more
exhausted, but partly because he was beginning to feel more
comfortable around Corbin. That made it all the worse when he was
rudely awakened by a sharp *tap, tap, tap* on the window. In his
groggy state, it sounded like someone banging a gun barrel against
the window, so he fumbled for his Glock as he sat up. He couldn't get
it out, so he opened his eyes and looked at the window.

An unfriendly face glared back at him. It was an unkempt older
gentleman with a short graying beard. He gestured for Shane to roll
down the window, but Shane kept a grip on his pistol and spoke
through the glass.

"What do you want?" he said.

"What do *you* want?" the man replied, twice as loudly, giving the
window another tap. Shane saw that it was a wedding ring that had

made the sound. "You're camping on my property, pal. I didn't give you permission to sleep here."

Shane rubbed his face, trying to rouse himself from the fuzzy-minded residue of sleep. When he lowered his hands, the bearded fellow was still glaring at him with unfriendly green eyes. Violet continued to sleep in the seat beside him, snoring softly.

"We need diesel for the van," Shane said. "You look like one of the few gas stations still open for business."

The man gestured for him to get out. When Shane didn't immediately respond, he snapped his fingers and gestured again. Finally, Shane unlocked his door and eased it open, as the stranger backed out of the way. On edge, his right hand hovering near his holster, Shane climbed out of the van.

In an attempt to ease the tension, he extended his left hand and introduced myself. "Shane," he said. "Sorry about parking at your building. We're just low on gas and figured we'd catch you first thing this morning."

The stranger stared at him for a second, then nodded and shook his hand. "I'm Andy. I own this place. Look, I have diesel, but you'll have to pump it manually."

"How much are you charging?" Shane asked, tensing for the bad news.

"I kept raising the price per gallon and people kept coming," Andy replied, a smile playing at the corners of his mouth. "When I hit thirty dollars a gallon, I sort of stopped."

"Thirty..." Shane almost choked on the word.

"Sorry, that's just the nature of supply and demand," Andy said. "You understand. If I hadn't raised prices, I'd have run out fast."

With a nod, Shane dug his wallet out of his back pocket and produced a credit card. When he tried to hand it to the gas station owner, the man waved it off.

"No, thanks. That does me no good," he said.

"You can't take a credit card?"

"I can take it," Andy said, crossing his arms over his chest, "but money is pretty close to worthless now. People paid through the nose yesterday, and what can I do with all that cash? Hardly any businesses are open. Grocery stores have been picked clean."

Shane couldn't argue with this, so he put the credit card back in his wallet. "Okay, in that case, how do you feel about bartering?"

"I like it," Andy said. "What have you got?"

"Food," Shane said.

"What sort of food? Show me."

Shane went to the back of the van, opened the door, and pulled two buckets off the top of the wall of supplies. One was mostly MREs, the other contained Spam and other canned meats. He brought them back and set them at Andy's feet.

"How much fuel will this buy me?" he asked.

Andy popped open the lids one at a time and looked inside. He pulled out some of the MREs to read the labels, then dropped them back into the buckets.

"Five gallons," he said.

"That's it?"

Andy just stood there with his arms crossed. Shane hated to give him more. After all, he didn't know how much food Beth had in stock. What if they needed all these buckets? He was tempted to try to barter a bit more aggressively, but the gas station owner clearly had the advantage.

Shane heard the passenger door slam shut, and a moment later, Violet and Corbin walked up beside him. He put his arm around Violet.

"You know," Andy said, narrowing his eyes. "I do have *other* needs." His eyes flitted back and forth from Shane to Violet.

"You're disgusting," Shane said, fighting an urge to lash out as he stepped in front of Violet.

Andy's eyes widened. "What?" He smacked his forehead. "I wasn't talking about your kid, you idiot. What the heck is wrong with you, suggesting a thing like that." He gave Shane a look of withering disgust. "I'm building a root cellar behind the store, but my shoulder is killing me. I can't dig anymore. If you and the boy there will dig the rest of it for me, I'll give you a full tank of gas plus a ten-gallon jerrycan as backup."

Embarrassed, Shane stepped aside and looked at Corbin.

"What do you say, Corbin?"

"Sure, why not?" Corbin said. "I've dug trenches and stuff with my dad. It's not hard."

"Okay," Shane said. "We'll do it."

As it turned out, Andy's house was a small shack behind the gas station. It looked to be about a hundred years old, a crumbling shotgun home with a weedy garden in back. Andy led them to the spot where he'd begun digging the root cellar. It was shallow, maybe two feet deep by five feet long, and the soil beneath look tough and unyielding.

"Only got one shovel," Andy said. "If you and the boy trade off, I'm sure it won't take long."

He handed the rusty old shovel to Shane and motioned them into the trench.

"Let's get this done," Shane muttered.

As the man had suggested, Shane and Corbin took turns. Even Ruby helped occasionally, hopping into the trench to dig into the hard soil with her paws. Violet carried the buckets of dirt for them, dumping them in a field behind the fence. The work was backbreaking, and Shane felt mounting frustration as the hours passed. So much wasted time. He just wanted to get on the road.

"How deep does it need to be?" Shane asked.

It was somewhere close to noon, and he was covered in dirt and soaked with sweat. Ruby had given up helping them when the pit got too deep for her to easily hop out of. She was now standing dutifully beside Violet, panting.

"I was thinking about ten feet," Andy said.

"Ten feet," Shane echoed, stifling a groan. He looked around at the pit they'd dug. If they were lucky, it was maybe five feet deep.

"It won't take that long," Corbin said, grabbing the shovel from him. "My dad's yard was all hard clay. It was a lot tougher to dig out than this."

Corbin still seemed to have plenty of energy, and he definitely had a much better attitude. It put Shane to shame, and he bit back any complaints. As Corbin continued to dig, Shane passed the buckets to Violet. They were forced to take frequent breaks for water, and they ate a quick meal in the early afternoon, though Shane wolfed down the food as fast as he could.

"It's coming along great, boys," Andy said, pacing back and forth on the edge of the deepening pit. "This'll do real good. Couple more feet, I think. Shouldn't take much longer."

They didn't get deep enough to satisfy Andy until sometime in mid-afternoon. By then, even Corbin was scowling, his gray t-shirt turned about two shades darker with sweat. Andy helped Shane out of the hole, then Shane helped Corbin. As they turned to survey their handiwork, Shane massaged his aching right arm.

"That's excellent work, gentlemen," Andy said. "It would've taken me at least a week to get that done, and my back might never have recovered."

Taking turns with the shovel, they'd managed to dig a seven-foot by seven-foot hole. If it wasn't ten feet deep, it was close. Shane couldn't help thinking that it looked a little like a mass grave. He handed the shovel to Andy.

"You earned your fuel, boys," Andy said. "Come on."

Shane did his best to knock the dirt off his hands, sleeves, and pant legs. It was a futile effort. He chugged an entire bottle of water while Andy hand-pumped diesel. Once the van's tank was full, the now-friendly gas station owner filled an old metal jerrycan for them as well.

"You're all set," Andy said. "An honest day's work for a full tank of gas. Feels like a fair trade to me."

"Enjoy your root cellar," Shane said, trying to keep the bitterness out of his voice.

"Oh, I'll get a lot of use out if," Andy said. "Maybe the next customers that come along can build me walls and a roof."

"Good luck with that," Shane said.

He dragged the food buckets back into the van. He expected Andy to argue, and he was ready with a response. *You got almost an entire day of work out of us. That's enough. We're keeping the food.* But Andy didn't say anything. He just kept smiling like an idiot as he watched them load up.

As Shane went to climb into the driver's seat, Andy gave him a hearty handshake as if they'd somehow become the best of friends. Shane forced himself to smile in return.

"That was weird," Violet said, as she climbed into the passenger seat.

"Yeah," Shane agreed.

"Is that what a barter economy is like?" she asked. Ruby hopped up onto her lap, then jumped down onto the floorboard.

"I guess so."

"It sucks a little bit," Violet said.

"Yep." Shane shut his door.

"Could've been worse," Corbin said, taking his seat at the back of the van. "He could've just refused to give us fuel. Then we'd be forced to walk."

"Good point," Shane said.

"He's just lucky we're nice people," Corbin said. "We could've taken the fuel if we'd wanted to. We're armed, and we outnumber him."

"We don't do stuff like that," Shane said.

"I know. That's what I'm saying. But we could have."

Would it really have been so wrong? Shane only entertained the thought for a second, and he felt bad for doing so.

Every joint creaked, every limb throbbed, and his lungs burned. He was coated in layers of sweat. Without another word for their new friend, Shane started the engine and quickly backed out of the gas station. He had a last glimpse of Andy standing in front of the fuel pumps grinning like he'd just played the world's funniest prank.

Shane drove away, looking at the lowering sun and cursing under his breath. They'd wasted so many hours. As he headed back to the interstate, he heard a soft beep from his pocket. It surprised him. How had the cell phone lasted so long? He fished it out and held it up. One percent battery power left. In its last moments, the phone had decided to work one last time. Shane saw that he had a text message from his wife.

He unlocked the screen and opened his text messages, but at that very moment, the phone died.

"Was it Mom?" Violet asked.

"Yeah, but I didn't get a chance to read it," he replied. "Hopefully, everything's okay."

He jammed the phone back into his pocket. Thanks to their little digging project, they wouldn't make it to Macon that day. He just wasn't willing to drive at night—too many hazards on the road. Hopefully, Jodi would get there first.

31

Beth grabbed her face, tears springing into her eyes. Her cheek felt like it was on fire. Greg dumped his plate of food on the edge of the grill and raised his hand like he meant to slap her a second time. Beth managed to avoid flinching. She would accommodate them, but she wouldn't cower.

"While I was busy yelling at you for taking so long to cook breakfast," Greg said, "my food got cold again. Heat it up, and this time don't stand there like an idiot."

"You wanted biscuits and gravy," she said. "I have to cook them on the propane grill. It takes time."

"I don't care what it takes," he said. "Hurry it up, or I'm going to smack you around some more. I woke up in a bad mood, Grandma. Don't test me."

He slapped her on the back of the head, shoving her against the grill lid, before stepping back inside the dining room. Beth opened the grill again and dumped his food into the cast-iron pan.

"Honestly, sometimes I think you want to be hit," Greg said. "You do stuff *just* to tick me off, and I thought we were going to have a pretty good morning. Our first grandma knew her place. Even if she wasn't feeling good, she dragged herself out of bed and did her work. Meals were always served prompt and hot. Got it?" When she didn't respond, he said it louder. "Got it?"

"Yes, yes," Beth replied. "I'll do better."

"If we don't eat, your grandkid doesn't eat," Greg said. "That's the rule."

Just then, Travis came stumbling into the dining room from the living room, yawning loudly and scratching his belly.

"Hey, I want something to eat, too," he said. "Why does *he* get everything? Couldn't you wake me up at least and see what I wanted?"

"Okay," Beth said. "Just a second."

She reheated Greg's biscuits and gravy until the gravy had a yellowish burned edge, then she scooped it back on his plate. Her mind wandered to the pills in her medicine cabinet. She had a big bottle of Coumadin in there somewhere. It was used to prevent blood clots, but she knew the active ingredient, warfarin, was also used as rat poison. She was pretty sure a massive overdose would be fatal. She imagined crushing up a bunch of pills and stirring the powder into their gravy. Would Greg and Travis even know the difference? Though she had no idea how many pills it would take to be lethal, she doubted she could get the pills discreetly, much less crush them to powder and sneak them into the food.

Travis was pounding the ends of a fork and spoon against the table. Beth dumped some grilled biscuits and overcooked gravy into a second plate, then she carried both plates into the dining room. She set the reheated food in front of Greg, and he pulled it away from her before she'd let go.

"It's about time," he said. "You need to try a little harder, Grandma. We're sick of your attitude. You wouldn't get knocked around so much if you were a bit more attentive."

"She wouldn't get knocked around so much if she had some booze in this house," Travis added. "That's the real problem here. It's making me irritable."

Beth set the second plate in front of Travis. In pounding the silverware against her nice dining table, he'd left about twenty little ding marks in the polished wood. Seething, Beth struggled to hold her tongue. Ruining the table seemed like unnecessary cruelty. For some reason, it bothered her even more than getting slapped.

"This gravy looks weak," Travis said, swiping her hands away from his plate. "I'm not impressed. You can't cook half as good as our other grandma."

Maybe Jodi had sensed that something was wrong. Beth would have said more if her captors hadn't been listening on speakerphone. All she could get away with was some subtle hints.

And where is Sheriff Cooley? she wondered. *He said he would stop by.*

"I need more coffee," Greg said. "Quit standing there like an idiot and pay attention. Can't you see my cup is empty?"

"Be a good grandma," Travis said. "Good grandmas don't get beat up. What's it going to take to get you trained right?"

She grabbed Greg's coffee cup and took it to the back porch, where she had some weak coffee percolating on the grill. She poured him a cup, stirred in plenty of sugar, and brought it back to him.

"Tastes like water from a stopped-up sink," Greg said, after the first sip. "You need to work on your old lady skills. Our first grandma made great coffee."

"And good gravy," Travis said. "Not this dough-water."

He flicked a spoonful of gravy at her. It spattered against the sleeve of her shirt. She grabbed a napkin and wiped at it, but it only made a much bigger stain.

"I missed," Travis said. "I was aiming for your face."

"Quit making us be mean to you," Greg said. "Just do it right."

"Don't you have any bacon?" Travis said. "Personally, I like bacon with my biscuits and gravy."

"We ate all the bacon yesterday," Beth said. "It would have spoiled. The gravy is thin because we don't have any milk. I only had water."

"Excuses," Travis said. "Our other grandma would've found a way. When we asked her for something, we always got it."

"That's right," Greg said. "We had her trained real good. She'd lug her oxygen tank into the kitchen and make anything we asked for."

"This one's got a long way to go." Travis said. "She'll be nothing but bruises by the time she gets there."

"I'm okay with that."

At that moment, Beth heard the sound of an engine revving outside. It seemed to be coming from the driveway. She didn't wait for permission, hurrying to the front door. Bauer resumed barking furiously from Kaylee's bedroom.

Sheriff, that better be you, Beth thought. *You said you'd drop by. You're two days late, but better late than never.*

She approached the small window beside the front door and eased the curtain aside. The driveway was just to the left of the door, at the edge of what was visible, but she saw a strange van parked there. It was an early 70s model Volkswagen van, the kind hippies and surfers cruised around in during Beth's childhood. Definitely not the sheriff. Then the driver's door opened, and Shane, her son-in-law, stepped out. Beth's heart raced. She caught a glimpse of Violet in the passenger's seat.

Oh no, I have to warn them, she thought. *They can't come here.*

Before she could think of what to do, she felt something clamp onto her arm like a vice. Crying out in pain, she was yanked backward by Travis. Just before the curtain fell back in place, Beth saw Shane stiffen, as if he'd heard her.

"Who is it?" Travis said. He had the shotgun in his right hand. She briefly considered trying to wrestle it away from him, but he'd already proved to be far stronger than her.

"Just a…friend," she said. The lie didn't come quickly enough.

"Family, I'm guessing," Greg said from the dining room. "Make her get rid of them."

Travis shoved her toward the front door. "Find a way to make them leave. Don't rouse any suspicion, or your granddaughter *and* your stupid dog will get it. You say whatever you have to say. Don't test me, Grandma."

Greg dashed across the living room and moved down the hall toward Kaylee's bedroom as Travis stepped back out of sight of the front door and raised the shotgun. They'd kept Kaylee and Bauer in the bedroom at the end of the hall since the night before, only allowing them out to use the bathroom. They were forced to eat in there, and even when Kaylee cried and begged for Grammy to come get her, they hadn't let Beth speak to her.

As Shane stepped onto the porch, Beth opened the front door, filling the gap so he couldn't get through. He stood there a second, eyebrows raised.

"Oh, Steve, it's so good to see you," Beth said. "It's been so long. Why, I believe the last time we ran into each other was at the company picnic when you used to work for my husband, Michael."

Shane glanced over his shoulder at the van. Beth saw two people staring back: Violet and an unidentified young man. When he turned back to her, he started to say something, but she quickly interrupted him.

"I'm sorry you've come all this way," she said. "It's not a good time for visitors. I just don't have much in the way of food or supplies."

Out of the corner of her eye, she saw Travis waving the shotgun, motioning for her to hurry up. If Shane heard it, he didn't react. He stood at the end of the porch, giving Beth a probing look.

Come on, Shane, Beth thought. *This one time, please pick up on what I'm really trying to say. Don't do anything stupid.*

"If you've come to me for help, I have none to give," Beth said, sharply. "You'll have to leave. I'm sorry. That's just the way it is. Tell your sweet wife, Margaret, I said hello. Goodbye now."

She widened her eyes at him, willing him to understand. Then she stepped back and slammed the door in his face, loudly setting the deadbolt. Leaning against the door, she prayed he wouldn't say or do anything to give her away.

"That's enough," Travis said.

He stepped forward and grabbed her arm, his fingers clamped down on the spot where he'd already left bruises. She bit her lip to keep from crying out in pain, as he dragged her away from the front door and back through the living room. He shoved her against the dining room table, which caused her to hit one of the plates, splattering gravy all over the tabletop. Before she could recover, he grabbed the collar of her shirt and marched her into the kitchen.

"Stay in here and keep quiet," he said. And with that, he planted the sole of his shoe against her backside and shoved her toward the sink. "You just better hope they drive away. Cross every finger and pray every prayer."

She stumbled, flailing her arms, and caught herself against the edge of the counter. She felt a sharp sting on her pinky, and when she turned her hand over, she saw that she'd cut herself on a shard of glass. Grabbing a wad of paper towels, she pressed it against the wound and waited until she heard Travis walking back across the living room.

When he was gone, she swept some of the glass out of her way with her sleeve and leaned toward the broken window above the sink. From this angle, she could see the far edge of her driveway. She waited, holding her breath, and a few seconds later, she heard the van's engine rumble to life. It backed down the driveway and turned, and she caught a glimpse of both Shane and Violet through the windshield. They were speaking to each other, and both of them looked distressed.

Just get out of here, Beth thought. *Don't come back.*

When they finally drove away, she breathed a sigh of relief. At least they hadn't been hurt.

But you're never getting out of here, she thought. *Greg and Travis have no intention of leaving.*

32

Shane meandered through the neighborhood, turning down streets at random, unsure of where to go. They got a few strange looks from people hanging out in their yards. Finally, after a couple of miles, he reached a cul-de-sac and came to a stop. He sat there for a minute, the engine idling. Violet was turned toward him, her head cocked to one side as she did when she was listening carefully.

"Will you tell me now, Dad?" Violet said. "What happened at Grandma's house?"

"Something's wrong," he said. Was this what Jodi had tried to tell him? Now, he desperately wished he'd had a chance to read her text. He even pulled the phone out and tried to turn it on, hoping against hope that somehow the battery might have a bit more charge. It was dead. Irritated, he tossed it onto the floorboard.

"What is it?" Violet asked.

Shane turned in his seat so he could see Corbin in the back. The young man was propped up on one knee, as if ready to charge out of the van.

"I don't think Grandma was alone at the house," Shane said. "Someone was in there with her. She was acting under duress."

"You think someone's holding her hostage?" Corbin said.

"It's possible," Shane said. "She was pretending like I was someone else, a friend of her father's, but she called her father by a different name. So either she's had a stroke, or she's trying to warn us about something. I think the latter is more likely. Beth is pretty sharp. Even if someone was pointing a gun at her head, she would try to find a way to signal for help."

Violet gasped. "Pointing a gun at her head! Dad, do you think it's that serious? Who would do such a thing?"

"There are a lot of desperate people out there these days," Shane said. "We know that firsthand, don't we? Maybe someone figured out she has supplies stored away in the basement, and they've come to loot the place. I just don't know."

Corbin made his way to the front of the van, bracing himself against the backs of the seats. Ruby felt him and looked up, curious but not concerned. In the short time he'd been with them, the lab had come to trust him.

"We have to rescue her," he said. "Here's what I think we should do. Line up your van with the front door and just *punch it*. Ram through the door, and then we come out guns blazing. They won't expect it, and they probably won't have a chance to respond. We'll be like commandos—kill the bad guys and rescue the hostages before anyone knows what hit them."

Shane glanced at the kid to make sure he wasn't joking. "I think that's a bit extreme. The thing is, we're *not* commandos. Too many things could go wrong."

"You have to tell the police," Violet said.

Her suggestion was far more reasonable. The only local police Shane knew was the county sheriff. Sheriff Cooley was sweet on Beth, and if he learned she was in trouble, he would definitely help.

"I think you're right, Violet," he said. "We have to get the police involved."

He turned around in the cul-de-sac and headed out of the neighborhood.

"Police will be too busy to help us," Corbin said. "They'll ask how you know she's being held hostage, and what are you going to say? 'She seemed confused. She called her husband by the wrong name.' They won't come."

"You might be right," Shane said, "but it's the safer course of action."

"You know everything you need to know to use that gun, sir." Corbin gestured at the Glock. "Your aim is decent. All you have to do is rush in there, pick your target, and unload. What's so hard about that? It'll be over in ten seconds."

"It *might* be over in ten seconds," Shane replied, "but there's no guarantee we won't all be dead. We have no idea what we're dealing with."

Shane worked his way back to the highway and headed into town. The sheriff's office was a small yellow building across the street from a mechanic's shop. It wasn't far, but every mile made him restless. What if it was too late for Beth and Kaylee? What if Corbin was right, and their only chance to save her had been to rush the house, guns blazing?

"Dad, what about Kaylee?" Violet asked. "Did you see her when you went to the door?"

"I did not," he replied.

"They wouldn't hurt a little kid, would they?"

"I don't know, honey. I don't know who we're dealing with here. I don't know if we're dealing with anyone at all."

When he reached the sheriff's office, he was disappointed to see there weren't any cars in the parking lot. He decided to pull in anyway. Maybe the sheriff had been forced to abandon his car on the road somewhere and walk to work. He parked in front of the building and opened his door.

"Stay here, guys," he said. "I'll be right back."

"Be careful in there," Corbin said. "You never know."

Shane nodded at him and stepped out of the van. As he approached the front door, he rested his hand on the hilt of the Glock, ready to draw. He was surprised to find the door unlocked. He entered the building, stepping into the stuffy warmth of an unairconditioned and unventilated building.

"Hello?" he called. "Is anyone here?"

He found himself in a small and unremarkable lobby. A sliding window revealed a reception desk and a cramped office beyond. As he approached the window, he saw a phone propped on the counter with a trifold sign beside it that read, "To report a problem, call dispatch. An officer will get to you as soon as possible."

A small piece of paper with the word DISPATCH in bold red had been taped beneath one of the speed dial buttons on the phone. Shane picked up the phone and pressed the button. However, after a click, it went straight to voice mail.

"Please leave a message, and we'll get back to you soon. Thank you."

He hung up the phone and stood there for a second, numb with indecision.

I have to do something, he thought. *No one is available to help us.*

He turned and found Corbin standing in the doorway, his hands on his hips.

"No answer?" he asked.

Shane shook his head.

"I'm not surprised," Corbin said, giving Shane a grave look. Under different circumstances, Shane would have found the seriousness of the kid amusing. He was so young, yet he looked like he was fully prepared to go to war. "Police can't help us now. It's up to us to get the job done."

Shane couldn't argue with him. What choice did they have? He waved the kid back to the van and followed him. Violet and Ruby were waiting anxiously.

"It's an empty building," Shane said. "No sign of the sheriff."

Violet pressed a hand to her mouth. Corbin climbed into the van and squatted just behind the front seats.

"Well, what's the plan?" he said.

"We're not ramming through the front door," Shane said. "I can tell you that."

"You could sneak in at night," Violet suggested. "Wait until they all fall asleep, then sneak in through the back door. Even bad guys have to sleep sometime."

"Not a bad idea," Corbin said. "Do either of you know how to pick a lock?"

"We won't need to," Shane said. "I know where Beth keeps an extra key for the back door."

It was definitely a better plan, but he didn't feel good about it. On the contrary, he felt a deep sense of dread. They were ordinary people, not some ragtag special forces team. None of them had ever been in combat. Corbin's time at a juvenile boot camp certainly didn't count.

"Okay, Corbin, we'll go in together," Shane said. "Through the sliding glass door in back. We'll have to assess the situation quickly. Be ready for anything, but don't shoot unless you know for sure you're not shooting at an old woman or a child."

"I can handle it," Corbin said. "I have a quick eye."

Shane reached past Violet and opened the glove compartment. He fished around inside until he found Debra's revolver, then he pulled it out and handed it to Corbin.

"Be careful with that," he said.

"I will," Corbin replied. He ejected the cylinder and removed the empty shells. "Only three shots left. Do you have ammo for this?"

"I don't think so," Shane said. "That's a .44 Magnum."

"Fine," Corbin said. "I'll choose my shots carefully."

"Dad, I want to help," Violet said.

The thought of bringing Violet into the house almost caused Shane to respond too harshly. He considered his words carefully.

"We can't bring Ruby with us," he said. "It's not safe for her, and she won't like being left in the van alone. I think the best thing you can do is stay with her and keep her calm. If she barks, it'll rouse suspicions."

"I can shoot," she said. "Corbin taught me how to aim. I don't want to stay in the van. Let me help take down the bad guys."

Shane looked at her in astonishment. Did she really expect him to say yes to this? She reached up to her face, as if to push her sunglasses up the bridge of her nose, but her sunglasses were missing. She'd dropped them in the back of the van and never bothered to pick them up again.

"I know you can shoot," he said, "but we only have two guns."

"You have rifles in the hidden compartment," she said. "You take the rifle, and I'll take the handgun. I'm a better shot than you. Corbin said so."

"I'm sure you are, but still…" Shane rocked his head back.

"Violet, you're a very good shot," Corbin said, speaking softly, "but I had to help you know where to aim. Remember? I'm not saying that to be mean, but it's true. When we enter the house, we have to move fast. I won't be able to help you."

Violet frowned and seemed on the verge of tears. After a moment, she nodded. "You're right. I'll stay in the van."

Shane reached out and patted her on the back, but she flinched. In truth, he was annoyed that she had taken Corbin's word over his. He had no doubt she would have continued to argue with him if Corbin hadn't jumped in. At least she'd agreed to stay. Shane wanted to ask Corbin to stay behind as well. He wasn't comfortable with the idea of bringing this teen boy into a gunfight. But Corbin was the better shot. He couldn't afford to leave him behind.

Adolescence is probably a fading concept in this brave new world anyway, he thought. *We have to use whatever skills we have, no matter who we are. Kids are going to have to grow up way too soon.*

"Okay, we have a plan," Shane said, putting the van in reverse. "A slightly less stupid plan."

"You just have to be brave," Corbin said. "Don't overthink it. Rush in there and do it. That's the way."

I'm sure that's the attitude that helped you steal that car, Shane thought.

"We'll park down the street," Shane said, pulling out of the parking lot, "sneak into the backyard and make sure everyone is asleep."

"Just be ready to act," Corbin said. "You can't get scared in the moment. You just have to pull your gun, point it, and do what needs to be done."

"Yeah, I got it, kid. I got it."

He wiped a fresh sheen of sweat from his forehead with a shaky hand, turned the van west, and headed for Beth's neighborhood. There were hours until sunset. He had no idea how he was going to pass the time. He felt like a nervous wreck.

Maybe we're wrong, he thought. *Maybe she's not being held hostage. Maybe she hit her head.*

He wanted to believe it, but he knew it wasn't true.

33

They found a quiet and empty street a few blocks from Beth's house, so Shane could pace without drawing undue attention. He was a nervous wreck. Corbin suggested he practice drawing and aiming the Glock, so he did. The results weren't promising. The first time he tried, he dropped the gun, and it clattered on the street.

Can I actually shoot someone? Will I hesitate at a pivotal moment?

He wasn't confident in his own abilities. Though Corbin assured him his grip on the gun was correct, it didn't feel right. Everything felt clumsy and uncertain. Violet sulked in the van, but Shane didn't know what to say to make her feel better. At one point, she walked Ruby into a yard, and Shane approached her.

"With a little luck, this will all be over soon," he said.

"I know," she replied. "I just wish I could help."

He hugged her. "You'll have plenty of chances to help in the days ahead."

"Just don't get shot," she said. "Remember what Corbin and Landon both showed you."

"I will."

By then, the sun was getting low, and the whole sky had turned an ominous shade of purple. Shane thought he saw a hint of the northern lights dancing above the horizon. Corbin gave him a meaningful look, and Shane nodded.

"It's time," he said, heading back to the van.

"When the moment comes, don't hesitate," Corbin said. "Don't second-guess yourself. Just aim and pull the trigger. You can feel bad about it later."

"I won't feel bad if we shoot the right people," Shane said. "Take care of yourself, Corbin. Don't do anything reckless."

To this, Corbin merely smiled.

They got back in the van, and Shane crept his way through the neighborhood, heading back to Beth's house. He went slowly enough that it was fully dark by the time they reached her street. He felt a mounting sense of dread. They had no idea what they were getting into. They'd made a lot of assumptions based solely on Beth's strange behavior.

But their course was set.

Shane switched off the headlights and used only the parking lights as he moved down the street. He came to a stop a few houses away and killed the engine. In the silence that followed, he heard Corbin's slow, deep, deliberate breaths.

He's not as confident as he pretends to be, Shane thought.

"Violet, keep the doors locked," Shane said. "Help Ruby stay calm. If she starts barking, it could give us away."

Violet pulled Ruby onto her lap and wrapped her arms around the dog. "Dad, be careful. Please, don't get hurt."

"We'll do our best," Shane replied.

"Don't worry," Corbin said. "We got this."

Opening his door as quietly as possible, Shane stepped outside. He heard the soft swish of the side door as Corbin followed him. The kid came around the front of the van, nodding at him. He seemed eager, too eager.

Shane made sure the van doors were locked before shutting them. Then he started down the street, stepping lightly but trying not to look suspicious in case any neighbors happened to peek outside. Corbin tried to take the lead, but Shane snagged a fold of his t-shirt and gently pulled him back.

"Follow me," he said.

They moved through the neighbor's front yard, cutting diagonally toward Beth's fence. The house was utterly dark and still. All the blinds were shut. If Shane hadn't known better, he would have assumed it was abandoned. When they reached the gate, he was afraid to unlatch it. He knew from experience that those clunky metal latches were loud, so he decided to climb it instead. He put his gun back in the holster, hopped up, and grabbed the top of the nearest post. The wood creaked as he swung his legs up and over.

He dropped down onto the grass in the backyard and pressed himself up against the bricks of the house. Corbin followed a moment later, making nary a sound as he leapt like a cat into the high grass. Sliding along the wall, Shane moved to the corner and peered around the edge. He saw Beth's big propane grill. It was open, as if she'd been cooking, a platter and an enamelware coffee pot on the shelf beside it.

Drawing the Glock, he adjusted his grip until it felt right, and moved toward the sliding glass door. Corbin kept pace with him, leading with the barrel of the .44 Magnum. Shane had to admit, in that moment, the kid did look a bit like a commando.

He knelt beside a large flowerpot at a corner of the porch. Tipping it with his shoulder, he felt underneath, his fingers cutting through spiderwebs until they found the cold metal of a spare house key. He pulled it out, rose, and stepped around the grill, approaching the back door. The vertical blinds were open, and he saw the dining room on the other side. Dirty dishes were scattered across the tabletop, food slopped onto the surface, as if a food fight had ensued.

Beth would never leave such a mess in her house, Shane thought. *Not if she had a choice.*

He felt for the keyhole. The dark framework of the glass door made this a bit tricky, and when he tried to insert the key, he made some rather loud scratching sounds. Corbin put a finger against his lips, and Shane nodded. When he opened the door, though he moved achingly slow, it made an audible *whoosh*.

Corbin ducked under his arm and slipped through the door first, moving fast and quiet. Shane entered the house behind him, spun toward the living room, and raised the Glock, pointing into the darkness. The house reeked from a combination of Pine-Sol, old food, and possibly body odor. As Shane stepped past the dining room table, the sole of his shoe slipped on something wet. He slid, caught himself against the wall, and his foot thumped against the baseboard. From the other side of the table, Corbin frantically tapped his finger against his lips.

Rushing to the end of the dining room, Shane ducked behind a chair, waiting and listening to make sure he hadn't roused anyone in the house. Every room seemed to be holding its breath. He moved out from behind the chair in time to see Corbin swing around the corner into the living room, the Magnum thrust out in front of him.

The cushions on the couch were all out of place, some of them on the floor, and there was an overturned cup and a big stain on the beige carpet. Shane signaled for Corbin to wait, but the kid didn't see. Moving low, Corbin entered the living room, sweeping his gun from side to side. Shane followed, approaching the couch. The condition of the cushions made no sense. Had someone lain on the couch and gotten up suddenly, scattering them in the process? Why would they do that unless—

He heard a single footstep and a slight expulsion of breath. It came from a dark corner near the front of the house. As Shane spun to face it, he saw a vague shape spinning through the air, tracing an arc toward Corbin. The kid didn't see it coming. He'd turned to face the foyer and the dark hallway beyond.

"Watch—" was all Shane managed to get out.

The small object hit Corbin in the right shoulder with a dull thud that suggested it had real weight to it. Crying out, the kid spun and fired wildly. By the muzzle flash, it looked like the gun was pointed toward the ceiling. Plaster rained down.

Whatever had hit him landed on the floor and rolled toward Shane. He had a fraction of a second to consider what it was.

A cherub?

Then a man rushed from the dark corner, closing the gap with Corbin in two long strides and grabbing his arms, forcing them up over his head.

"Greg! Greg, help!" the stranger shouted. "Get in here!"

Caught off guard, Corbin was thrown off-balance and fell toward the couch, the stranger landing on top of him. Shane pointed the gun at them, but they were a tangle of shapes. The only thing distinguishing them was a slight difference in the color of their shirts. Corbin was wearing gray, and the stranger had on some lighter color.

"Greg! Hurry up!"

From down the hall, Shane heard a toilet flush.

What if I hit the kid? he thought, aiming at the wrestling shapes.

He heard a door fly open. Only a second to react before someone else joined the fight.

Just remember what the kid taught you, Shane said.

He tightened his grip, made sure his thumbs weren't crossed, and steadied his aim. Pointing the gun at the lighter color, he gritted his teeth and pulled the trigger. For less than a second, the living room filled with a harsh yellow light. He saw two bodies moving on the couch, teeth bared, voices growling. He fired again, and one growl turned into a cry of pain.

Suddenly, the stranger went flying. Corbin had gotten his feet under the man, and he kicked him away. Stumbling backward, groaning loudly, the stranger landed on the carpet, did an awkward somersault, and wound up on his side. Even in the dim light, Shane saw blood spreading fast on the back of his shirt.

Shane had no time to recover. Hearing a second man coming down the hall, he dropped into a crouch and moved toward the couch. At that moment, an enormous *boom* filled the whole world, louder and more violent than either of the handguns. In the immediate aftermath, Shane heard glass shatter and wood splinter. He tracked a shadowy shape emerging from the end of the hallway, saw a brief glint of moonlight on the edge of twin shotgun barrels.

He tracked it with the Glock and opened fire. In the brief, bright flash of the muzzle, he saw a menacing shape standing before him, shotgun in hand, denim jacket hanging from broad shoulder. The second intruder stumbled backward as Shane fired, moving through the foyer and back down the hall. Shane ceased firing, afraid that an errant bullet might pass into one of the bedrooms. He ducked back into the living room to avoid a shotgun blast, crouching near the couch.

"We've got your people," the second intruder shouted, his voice coarse and cracking. "You hear me? We've got your people, and if you don't get out of here, we'll kill 'em all."

"Let them go, and I'll spare your life," Shane replied, intending to sound tough, but the words came out as little more than a squeak.

"No, stupid, that's not how it works," the man said. "You let *yourselves* go, and I'll let your people live. That's the deal."

Unsure of what to do, Shane froze, still pointing the gun in the direction of the foyer. How could he draw the man away from the bedroom to get a clear shot? He didn't know, but as he thought about it, Corbin sat up and crawled across the couch.

"Don't play with me, man," the second intruder said. From the sound of it, he was about halfway down the hall, near the guest room. "I'm giving you ten seconds to clear out of here before I start killing hostages."

As Corbin reached the end of the couch, he looked over his shoulder at Shane, pointing in the direction of the hall, and nodded. It took Shane a second to realize what he was planning. He tried to wave the kid off, but Corbin ignored him and climbed over the arm of the couch. With little time to react, Shane did the only thing he could think to do.

"Okay, we're leaving," he said. "We're leaving the house right now. Just promise me you won't hurt anyone."

"I'm not going to promise nothing," the intruder said. "As soon as you leave, I'll let your people go. That's the deal. You got about three seconds."

Corbin raised the .44, thrust it in front of him, and charged around the corner. Shane moved in view of the hallway to provide help. As he did, he saw the intruder standing just outside the bathroom, his body pressed up against the doorframe. He had greasy black hair perched on top of a long face. The shotgun was aimed at the foyer, but Corbin didn't give him time to react. He rushed in low, opening fire. The kid had two bullets left, and he unloaded them both from a low angle.

The intruder started to spin backward into the bathroom. As he did, he inadvertently fired the shotgun, but it blasted a hole in the ceiling near the front of the hall. Shane pushed past Corbin and rushed toward the bathroom door. He found the body sprawled in front of the sink. One bullet had caught him under the chin, the second had hit him in the chest. The intruder was already dead, the shotgun lying upon his stomach.

Ears ringing, Shane stooped down and picked up the shotgun, the hot metal almost burning his fingers. He set it on the counter.

How many more intruders are there? he wondered.

At that moment, light awoke from somewhere in the hallway, a flashlight beam moving across the walls. Shane heard two familiar sounds coming from beyond the ringing in his ears: a dog barking and his mother-in-law shouting his name.

"Beth, we're here," he said. "We're okay. Is everyone safe?"

"Everyone is safe," she replied. "You got them both."

Shane breathed a massive sigh of relief and sat down on the edge of the counter, sliding the Glock back into the holster. Corbin came into the bathroom then, staring at the body on the floor. The kid was out of breath, his mouth hanging open. Shane reached out and patted him on the chest with the back of his hand.

"We did it, kid. We did it."

The guy in the denim jacket was a lot heavier than he looked. The fact that Shane had spent almost an entire day shoveling out a root cellar certainly didn't help. Holding the dead man by his feet, he struggled to get him down the hall and across the living room.

"It's like dragging a beached whale back into the ocean," Shane said, speaking through clenched teeth.

"He's been gorging himself on my food since last night," Beth said. She stood in the foyer, hugging Kaylee with one hand to keep her from seeing the corpses, holding Bauer by the collar with the other. "But I made sure the food I cooked wasn't delicious. He only deserved slop, and he got slop. His disappointment was worth getting smacked around a little."

"That seems like a dangerous game," Shane said.

"I couldn't help myself," Beth said. "I kept it low-key, though. Trust me, I was tempted to act out in far more serious ways, but I restrained myself for Kaylee's sake."

Corbin seemed to have a much easier time dragging the other man, but as the body moved across the floor, the ratty t-shirt pulled up. Shane saw the bullet holes in his back.

"Mom, Violet is sitting in a van just down the street," Shane said, out of breath as he dragged the body across the dining room. "Can you go get her and bring her inside? She must have heard the gunshots. I'm sure she's freaking out."

"I just can't believe it," Beth said. "How did you get the jump on them?"

"I brought a young commando with me," Shane said, nodding his head in the direction of Corbin. "He helped me prepare."

"I'm so glad he did," Beth said, "but where did you find this young man?"

Shane and Corbin traded a look.

"It's a long story," Shane said.

They dragged the bodies out of the dining room and across the yard toward Mrs. Eddies' house. Along the way, Shane had to rest a few times to catch his breath.

"How's your shoulder, kid?" he asked Corbin.

"Hurts," the kid replied, "but nothing's broken. It'll probably just be a big bruise."

As they approached the front door of Mrs. Eddies' house, Shane saw a welcome mat lying among small statues nearby—a strange detail that didn't make sense. When he went to unlock the front door with a key they'd found on one of the dead men, he realized the front door was already unlocked. He opened it, pulled a small flashlight from Beth's house out of his pocket, and shined the light inside. The house was a wreck. Furniture had been tipped over, drawers emptied, books and clothes strewn everywhere.

"They must've gone through the house looking for valuables," Shane said, dragging the body through the open door.

"Their own grandma's house?" Corbin said. "Man, these guys were losers."

They dragged the bodies into the living room and cleared a space for them amidst the trash and overturned furniture. Shane found a tablecloth and unfolded it, draping it over the bodies.

"People who aren't ready to defend themselves are in a for a big wake-up call," Corbin said. "Guys like this are just going to enter homes and take over. They'll go from house to house like a Viking raid until they're stopped."

"I'm afraid you might be right," Shane replied. "I'm just glad we were prepared."

As he was speaking, he heard a sound coming from somewhere else in the house. It was a voice, he thought, but it was making a weird sound, almost an animal noise. Corbin looked at him, eyebrows climbing his forehead.

"Another one," Corbin said. He pulled the .44 Magnum out from under his belt and started to rise, but then he caught himself. Spinning the cylinder, he said, "I forgot, I'm all out of ammo."

Shane rose. He was no longer in the right mindset to confront an attacker. All the adrenaline had left him, but he forced himself to stand up and move to the hall. As he did, he drew the Glock again, dropping the magazine to make sure he still had bullets.

"Okay, Corbin, stay behind me," he said, sliding the magazine back into the grip. "Don't do anything rash."

As he moved down the hall, Shane heard the intruder again, and this time he was sure it was coming from the bedroom at the end of the hall. The door was ajar. He could see a sliver of yellow wallpaper, some debris on the carpet. A bad smell lingered in the hall—a sickly mustiness. Shane adjusted his grip and approached the bedroom.

Was the intruder groaning? Was it someone in pain? He couldn't quite tell, but it was a strange sound. Some low subhuman sound.

"Is that a dog or something?" Corbin said softly from behind him.

As he drew closer, Shane heard strained breathing. Definitely someone in pain. He lowered the gun and called out.

"Hey, is someone down there? Are you hurt?"

He pressed himself against the wall and slid up to the door, peering around the frame into the bedroom.

"Is someone in here?" he called.

He only got a raspy breath in reply. The first thing he saw was a bed in the corner, the body of an old woman in a nightgown lying exposed on a mattress. He shined the flashlight at her and realized she was dead—at least a couple days dead.

Then his light found a second person. A stocky gentleman with a neatly trimmed goatee. He was curled up in the corner, his hands pulled behind his back. He wore a khaki-colored, short-sleeve shirt that had a sheriff's patch on the left arm.

"Sheriff Cooley," Shane said, rushing to his side. "What are you doing in here?"

The sheriff had a large wound on the side of his head, and a line of dried blood running down in front of his ear. When Shane prodded him, he groaned again, and his eyes fluttered. It looked like he'd been lying there for a couple of days at least.

"They got him," Corbin said. "Those two deadbeats out there. Sounds like he's dying."

"No, he's alive," Shane said, "but I'm sure he's got a pretty serious concussion. Corbin, let's get him back to Beth's house."

They carried the sheriff back to Beth's house. He weighed far more than Greg, and Shane was on the verge of passing out by the time they got him through the sliding glass door. Beth, Violet, Kaylee, and the dog met them in the living room.

"Oh, goodness," Beth said. "Poor James. What did they do to him? Put him in the guest room. Don't worry about getting blood on the sheets. I'll clean them later."

They laid the sheriff on the bed in the guest bedroom, lit some candles to give him light, and examined his wound. Unfortunately, none of them had more than basic medical knowledge. Beth cleaned the wound and tried to give him some pain pills, but he either couldn't or wouldn't swallow them.

"Poor Sheriff Cooley," she said. "I sent him over there to check on those boys. If I'd known how dangerous they were, I would've warned him first."

"He's lucky to be alive," Shane said.

"Will he recover, Grandma?" Violet asked.

"Time will tell," Beth replied. "There's only so much we can do."

In the end, with the sheriff resting in the guest room, the rest of them wound up at the dining room table. Kaylee was quiet, clearly disturbed by her experiences with her captors, and she insisted on sitting on Violet's lap. At first, Violet had her head on the table, but she relented, sitting up and putting her arms around her little sister as Kaylee sipped apple juice. Ruby and Bauer curled up together in the corner, as if comforted by each other's closeness. Beth checked the ugly bruise on Corbin's shoulder.

"It's a good thing you came when you did," Beth said. "They were getting meaner. Lack of booze, lack of drugs, lack of *whatever* was turning them cruel."

"Sorry I didn't arrive yesterday," Shane said. "Some idiot made us dig a root cellar in his backyard for a tank of gas."

"That's what the world's come to," Beth said.

She gave Corbin a couple of aspirin and a glass of water.

"Beth, I don't suppose you've got any charge left on your cell phone," Shane said.

"Not sure," Beth said. She pulled the phone out of her pocket, unlocked the screen, and handed it to Shane. "Maybe enough for one call."

He opened up her contacts and scrolled to Jodi's number.

"You're calling Jodi?" Beth asked. "Any idea where she is? I haven't heard from her."

Shane shook his head as he dialed the number. He pressed the phone to his ear.

"All circuits are busy now. Please try your call again later."

He sighed, hung up the phone, and handed it back to Beth. "I guess we stretched our luck getting cell service to work as a long as it did."

"Mom is out there somewhere," Violet said. "Do you think she's okay?"

"I hope so," Shane replied, then added, "I'm sure she is."

Violet frowned at him. Clearly, she'd heard the note of doubt in his voice.

Jodi's hurt, Shane thought. *She's out there somewhere, and I can't talk to her. And because she's taking backroads, I can't even go and find her. What do we do now?*

A question for another day. He'd never been so sore in his life. All he needed now was a good night's sleep—without interruption—and he thought maybe, just maybe, he would manage it.

END OF CRUMBLING WORLD

SURVIVING THE END BOOK ONE

Crumbling World, 13 November 2019

Fallen World, 11 December 2019

New World, January 8 2020

PS: Do you love EMP fiction? Then keep reading for exclusive extracts from **Fallen World** and **Surviving the Swamp**.

THANK YOU!

Thank you for purchasing 'Crumbling World'
(Surviving the End Book One)

**Get prepared and sign-up to Grace's mailing list
to be notified of the next release at
www.GraceHamiltonBooks.com.**

Leave a review at:

f facebook.com/AuthorGraceHamilton

g goodreads.com/gracehamilton

BB bookbub.com/authors/grace-hamilton

a amazon.com/author/gracehamilton

ABOUT GRACE HAMILTON

Grace Hamilton is the prepper pen-name for a bad-ass, survivalist momma-bear of four kids, and wife to a wonderful husband. After being stuck in a mountain cabin for six days following a flash flood, she decided she never wanted to feel so powerless or have to send her kids to bed hungry again. Now she lives the prepper lifestyle and knows that if SHTF or TEOTWAWKI happens, she'll be ready to help protect and provide for her family.

Combine this survivalist mentality with a vivid imagination (as well as a slightly unhealthy day dreaming habit) and you get a prepper fiction author. Grace spends her days thinking about the worst possible survival situations that a person could be thrown into, then throwing her characters into these nightmares while trying to figure out "What SHOULD you do in this situation?"

You will find Grace on:

facebook.com/AuthorGraceHamilton

goodreads.com/gracehamilton

bookbub.com/authors/grace-hamilton

amazon.com/author/gracehamilton

BLURB

Family is all that matters when friend becomes foe—and the stakes are survival.

The world has become a dangerous place for Shane McDonald and his family since the solar storm wiped out the power grid. Tensions flare when it grows clear the dire situation will be prolonged and most are ill-prepared. Even the friendly small town of his prepper mother-in-law has drawn unwanted attention as word gets around about sharing their supply stores.

And strangers begin to infiltrate the once peaceful Georgia community.

All Shane can think about is where his wife and son ended up in all the chaos as the hours stretch into days since they last communicated. Jodi is far too trusting a soul, her desire to help the downtrodden a dangerous commodity among desperate and increasingly hostile citizens.

But Jodi isn't without resources when push comes to shove. When her son and cancer-stricken brother come under attack, she finds the strength to do what's necessary to ensure their safety—and inadvertently draws the attention of a menacing gang.

Now they must stay one step ahead of their pursuers in a race to reunite with family.

Before all hell rains down on them.

Get your copy of *Fallen World*
Available 11 December 2019
www.GraceHamiltonBooks.com

EXCERPT

Chapter One

The pain in her right forearm made deep sleep impossible, and she finally sat up, rubbing her eyes, then rolled down the window for some fresh air. Jodi checked the bandages on her arm. Blood had seeped through on both sides. She flexed her fingers, feeling stiffness and an ache that went all the way up to her shoulder.

Getting shot sucks, she thought. Technically, she'd found that *having been shot* was far worse than *getting shot*. The moment of impact had felt like little more than a bee sting. The real pain had followed afterward and seemed determined to linger.

The air was still and stale, so she opened the truck door and stepped outside. They were parked out of sight of the road, in the dilapidated shell of a big red barn. Mike and Owen were still crunched up in the front seat. Somehow, despite being packed into the Silverado like olives in a jar, the two of them had managed to sleep long and hard all night.

Jodi went to the back of the truck and dug down between the bicycle and pedicab that were folded up in back. She unzipped the suitcase and pulled out fresh bandages and disinfectant. Leaning against the side of the truck, with one hand she managed to remove the old bandages from her arm, wad them up, and jam them into a side pocket on the suitcase. The bullet wounds were ugly and oozing, but not particularly large considering the amount of pain she felt. The skin around them was an angry red.

Please, don't be infected, she thought, as she cleaned both the entry and exit wounds. She gingerly placed new bandages on both sides of her arm.

She just wanted to be at her mother's house. Jodi was tired of being on the road, tired and hurt and frustrated. She found herself fighting bitter tears, and she pressed a hand over her eyes and willed them away. It wouldn't do for Owen to wake up and find his mother crying. When she felt some semblance of control, she turned back to the truck and called to the others.

"Guys, I think it's time to get up," she said. "Come on, Mikey. It's morning. We should hit the road."

Mike stirred first. With a groan, he sat up, running his hands through his patchy hair. The large bandage on the side of his neck had come loose, giving Jodi a glimpse of the surgical incision. He pressed it back in place as he turned to her.

"Did you just call me *Mikey* again?" he croaked. His eyes looked sunken into his pale, damp face. "Oh, gosh, that's a habit you need to break. I'm not twelve anymore. Are we there yet?"

"You're the one with the map," Jodi reminded him.

"I shoved it under the seat a little too far," he said. "I'm not awake enough to get it."

"I'm sure we have a little way yet to go," Jodi said. "Cross your fingers that the road is clear today."

Mike shook Owen awake. "Get up, kid. We've got places to go and people to see."

Owen snorted and leaned forward, pressing his forehead against the steering wheel. "I'm awake. I'm awake." He scrubbed his face with his hands and looked around. Red marks on his cheek and temple marked the spots where he'd pressed against the side of the car in his sleep. "Morning? Mom, it's, like, barely first light. What time is it? It can't be six."

"I can't tell you what time it is because we don't have any working clocks," Jodi said, "but it's time to hit the road."

"Can I drive for a while?" Owen asked. "It makes the time pass faster. It's so boring just sitting there staring out the window, and I think I did a pretty good job yesterday."

Jodi considered this. Yes, he'd done better than expected handling problems on the road the previous day, and she was so foggy-minded she wasn't sure how well she could drive. "Yeah, that's fine. You can drive for a while. How much gas do we have?"

"More than half a tank," Owen said. "Not quite three-quarters."

"Good." Jodi climbed back into the truck and shut the door. She almost rolled the window up then thought better of it. The wind on her face might help. "That should be enough gas to get us home. Still, if you happen to see an open gas station, pull in."

"Okay," he replied. "Let's just hope it doesn't get robbed while we're there."

"Don't talk about that," Jodi said. "We were lucky to get out of the last place."

She signaled for Owen to get going, and he started the truck. The engine rumbled to life, and Owen shifted into first, backing out of the barn and easing through the high grass as he worked his way back to the road. As they'd gotten closer to Macon, the backroads had gotten worse. Now, the number of stalled vehicles had increased, so much so that Owen finally took to the shoulder of the road to avoid them, though this meant mostly driving on gravel. Jodi encouraged him to keep it slow and steady, but he seemed confident. Actually, she had to concede he'd proved to be a very competent driver, even with a manual transmission. He shifted gears as if he'd done it for years.

The sun was just rising, casting long shadows that stretched out before them. Jodi spotted people sleeping in some of the cars. A few seemed to have settled in, as if their stalled vehicles would become their permanent homes. They passed a minivan which had been pulled just off the road, the side doors on both sides thrown open. A family gathered in and around the van were cooking a meal on a campfire they'd built nearby, and they'd set up some kind of shelter at the back of the van using blankets and tree branches.

"It's getting worse," she noted.

"The world?" Mike replied.

"Yeah...well, civilization," she said. "Are these dead cars going to become permanent settlements? It seems like some people who got stranded have simply given up on going home. Will these become tent cities?"

"Maybe it'll be better for the environment," Mike said. "Less waste. More of a tribal existence, like the olden days. A return to primitive living, as it was supposed to be. I'm not saying I look forward to it. I'm just looking at it from a different perspective."

"I think you might be romanticizing primitivism," Jodi said. "Yes, it might mean less environmental damage, but it also means a lack of clean water and food, or public services like police and fire departments, at least for the time being. And what about access to reliable medical care? I can't say I'm not worried about that." She glanced at Mike's bandage then looked away. "I think before it gets better, it's going to create widespread suffering, which could provoke ever more savage acts of desperation as people try to survive."

Mike sighed. "Fair enough. I was trying to look on the bright side, Sis. I'll try not to do it in the future."

"I'm not scolding you," Jodi said. "I just lost my rose-colored glasses somewhere along the way. The future looks bleak to me."

"Mom!"

Owen's sudden cry startled her, and she swung around to find him pointing frantically into the distance. When she looked to see what he was pointing at, she spotted a man stepping out in front of their truck. An old sedan was stalled at an angle across both lanes, leaving only the shoulder open. The man stood there in the gap, waving both hands over his head. He was young, dressed in a filthy t-shirt and shorts, face shiny with sweat.

"Just keep going," Mike said. "He'll get out of the way."

Owen nodded and kept going, but a second later, he seemed to reconsider and slammed on the brakes. Jodi was thrown against her seat belt. Mike only had a lap belt, and he grabbed the dashboard to keep from hitting his head.

"I can't just *hit* somebody with the truck," Owen said.

The man had a look of desperation on his face. In fact, he seemed close to tears. As soon as the truck stopped, he approached, moving hesitantly, as if he feared for his own safety.

"Let's make sure he knows where things stand," Mike said. "If this guy is up to some shenanigans, he's going to regret it."

He unzipped his backpack and fished around inside, as Jodi gestured for the stranger to approach on her side of the truck. As the man stepped up to the open window, Mike pulled out the .38 and held it up, making sure the stranger could see. The stranger paused, gave the gun a lingering look, then grimaced and resumed moving.

"I'm sorry," he said. "I didn't mean to frighten you." He was out of breath, wheezing.

"You about got yourself flattened," Mike said. "If your goal is to become roadkill, standing in traffic is a good way to accomplish it, buddy."

Jodi held up a hand to silence him. "What's wrong? Are you hurt?"

The stranger held his hands out as if to show he had no weapons. "I'm sorry, ma'am. Look, I'm not trying to cause trouble, but no one would stop, and I didn't know what else to do. It's my wife." He gestured toward a small shed just off the road. What appeared to be a fairly new Toyota Camry was parked along the side, the passenger door wide open. "She's over there in the car."

"Mom, should I drive away?" Owen asked.

"I vote yes," Mike said. "I smell a scam."

Jodi signaled for Owen to wait. The stranger looked genuinely scared. There was a glimmer of raw terror in his eyes. Could anyone fake this? She didn't think so. Jodi considered herself a fairly good judge of character, and she'd only gotten better in the last few days. No, this was *real* fear.

"My wife...she's giving birth," the man said. "For real, the baby's trying to come out right now. I told her to wait, but she said she has no control over it. I don't know the least thing about delivering a baby. Can you please help me? It's our first child. Please!"

Jodi glanced at Owen and Mike, who were giving her hard stares in return. Owen shook his head.

"Let's just leave," Mike said. "Even if he's telling the truth, what do *we* know about delivering babies?"

"Well, one of us in this truck has given birth three times," Jodi reminded him.

"Still, is it really our problem?" Mike said. "Let's get out of here."

But Jodi couldn't do it. The man was terrified. How could she abandon him?

"I'm going to check it out," she said. "You guys stay here."

"Come on, Sis. This isn't your gig."

"He looks scared," she said. "I have to at least check it out."

Mike tried to hand the gun to her, but she waved it off. "If there's trouble, you'll need it. You're a good aim with that thing."

She opened her door and stepped outside.

"Don't try to pull any tricks," Mike said to the stranger. "I've got my eye on you, pal, and I've dealt with sorry little punks before."

"Thank you, ma'am," the stranger said, clasping his hands in a gesture of gratitude. "I was so scared, and no one would stop. One guy even took a shot at me. Thankfully, he missed."

Jodi extended her hand to him. "I'm Jodi." She at least wanted a name from him. That would make her feel better about the situation.

"Andy," he said, shaking her hand. "Please, we have to hurry. The baby is trying to come out right now."

He turned and started toward the shed. As Jodi followed him, she noted that he had a huge sweat stain in the middle of his back.

"Did you say you've helped deliver babies before?" he asked over his shoulder.

"No, I said I've given birth a few times," Jodi said.

Andy laughed awkwardly. "Oh, I guess I misheard. Well, it still makes you more of an expert than me."

When they reached the back of the Toyota, he waved her ahead of him.

"Just take a look and tell me what you think," he said. "Does the baby look like it's coming out right? Is everything okay? There's a lot of blood."

Jodi approached the open passenger door. As she leaned down to get a look inside, her last thought was, *For a woman about to give birth, the mother is being awfully quiet.* The second stranger was curled up on the front seat, but as soon as Jodi looked inside, he rose as silently as a snake, thrusting a handgun in her face. She didn't recognize the make or model of the gun, but she didn't need to. As far as she was concerned, a bullet was a bullet.

"Grab her quick," he said. He was a mean-looking fellow with slicked-back hair.

She scarcely had time to react. She stumbled backward, but both of her arms were grabbed and pulled behind her. Andy's ragged breathing tickled the back of her neck, but when she tried to pull away, his hands clamped down hard. The pain in her injured right arm became so severe that her vision dimmed.

"I was trying to help you," she said.

"Yeah, that's what I hoped you'd do," Andy replied. "Good job, Kenny."

The second man, Kenny, climbed out of the car, his gun fixed on Jodi. Andy turned her painfully back in the direction of the truck and began frog-marching her toward it, pinning both arms against her back. Jodi was genuinely afraid she might vomit from the pain. Kenny fell in behind them, so Jodi lost sight of the gun.

Mike had seen what happened, and he was leaning out the open window, the .38 pointed at Andy. In his miserable, pale, patchy-haired condition, he didn't look like much of a threat.

"I knew you were scummy, you jerk," he shouted. "You're a miserable-looking little rat. Let her go right now!"

"You guys get out of the truck right now," Kenny said. "You won't get a shot off before I kill your friend here, so don't try it. Get out of the truck."

"Don't listen to him," Jodi said. "Start the truck and drive off. Owen, do as I say."

Kenny reached around from behind and slapped her hard on the right cheek. She blacked out for a second and had to take a corrective step to keep from falling down. When the darkness passed, she realized Mike was supporting his wrist with his other hand, strengthening his grip as he prepared to take a shot. Jodi decided to help him.

"Get out of the truck," Kenny shouted. "Both of you! I will not say it again."

Jodi glanced down to see the position of Andy's feet, then she stomped on the insole of his right foot as hard as she could. He cried out in pain and let go of her arms. Immediately, she pulled away from him, spun around, and clawed at his face, trying to get her fingers in his eyes. He grabbed at her hands as she ground her fingertips into the soft skin of his eyelids.

In the midst of the chaos, she heard the distinctive *pop* of a gunshot from somewhere nearby. Kenny took a step backward, his mouth hanging open. Blood gushed from a wound on his neck as he fell backward. When he hit the ground, the gun dropped from his grasp and fell into the grass. Jodi immediately let go of Andy's face and dropped to her knees, digging into the grass until she felt cold metal.

Once she had the gun, she rose and ran back to the truck. Andy was moving behind her, but she didn't bother to look at him. When she reached the truck, Mike opened the door and slid over to make room for her. She sat down beside him and pulled the door shut, signaling for Owen to take off. He put the truck into gear and pulled away in a cloud of gravel. Only then did Jodi dare a last glimpse at her attackers. Kenny lay on his back in the high grass, a mere lump fading into the distance. Andy had run back toward the Camry, but she lost sight of him as Owen drove away.

She felt sick to her stomach, both from the sharp pain in her arm and from the sudden turn of events. On top of that, all of her nerves were on edge. This made for a potent combination, and she found she couldn't stop shaking. Rocking back and forth in her seat didn't help, so after a few miles, she turned to Owen and waved at him.

"Pull over," she said. "Quick."

"Are you okay, Mom?"

"Just pull over," she said.

Owen found an open spot just off the road and pulled the truck in. Jodi threw open her door and stepped outside, bent over and gasping for breath. Mike got out beside her and put a hand on her back.

"Take it easy, Jodi. You're fine." He rarely used her name. "Here, give me that guy's gun."

She realized she was still clutching the gun, and she passed it to Mike. He took it from her weak grasp.

"Just give me a minute," she said, struggling to catch her breath.

She heard Mike fiddling with the gun, and after a moment, he burst out laughing. "Oh, man, this is a *pellet* gun. It's got a CO_2 cartridge in the handle. Those guys were rank amateurs."

He held up a small silver cartridge. Though he seemed to find this hilarious, Jodi didn't see the humor in it. In fact, she felt like vomiting. Mike had just potentially killed someone. Even if it had been necessary, how could anything about it be funny?

"What?" Mike said, seeing the look on Jodi's face. "They tried to steal our truck with a fake gun, and they paid the price for it. I won't feel bad for protecting us, not after all the weirdos we've run into in the last few days." He jammed the CO_2 cartridge back into the handle of the gun.

"We can go now," Jodi said. "I just needed a moment to collect myself."

"Promise me and the kid you won't get out of the truck again," Mike said, as he gave her a hard look. "Not unless we all agree to it."

"I promise," she said.

"You can't believe every sad sack who comes along with a sob story, Sis. From now on, we err on the side of caution every single time."

"I know. You're right. This guy, he was really good at faking fear, but I won't fall for it again."

This seemed to satisfy Mike, and he climbed back into the truck, dumping the pellet gun on the floorboard. Jodi slid in beside him and shut the door, taking a long shaky breath.

"Let's get away from here," she said.

Owen put the truck into gear and pulled away.

Get your copy of *Fallen World*
Available 11 December 2019
www.GraceHamiltonBooks.com

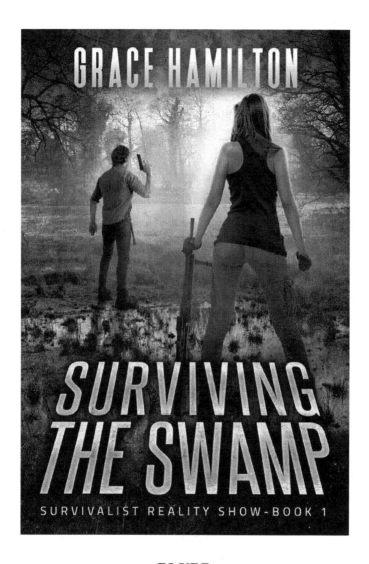

BLURB

Skin of Your Teeth Survival is a reality show made famous for pairing part-time survivalists with a real-life survival situation. Always carefully planned out by world-famous Prepper and Survivalist Wolf Henderson, season ten promises to be different This time none of the contestants are survivalists. They've all been picked to fail.

But when an EMP hits, the cast scatters and Wolf is left to care for a husband and wife team, a quietly scrappy chick, and a bumbling scientist. At the spur of the moment, Wolf offers them safety at his island bug-out location and takes off with his ragtag team to move through the wild and dangerous swampland of Florida.

The loner of the group, Regan, isn't sure what to do. She can't survive on her own, but she also doesn't work well in a group. She believes she has a better shot in one of the major cities on the coast than in the swamp, so she joins the team with every intent of striking out on her own once the opportunity arises. But with the world around them growing more dangerous every day, she has to figure out whether she's better off with the group or alone in the post-EMP world.

And whether Regan or Wolf realize it, the dangerous journey through swampland will soon become a literal fight for survival once they reach the chaos of 'civilized' South Florida.

Grab your copy of *Surviving the Swamp.*
www.GraceHamiltonBooks.com

EXCERPT

Chapter One

Regan Goodfellow wasn't a quitter. This last week had tested her strength and her will to survive, but she'd taken on every challenge willingly. More than anything, she wanted to prove to herself how tough she really was. Facing off against a dangerous swamp with deadly animals was a great way to do that. Maybe not the most practical or conventional method, but exciting, nonetheless. If only it wasn't so damn wet. Of course it was wet; it was a *swamp*, complete with endlessly boggy ground, damp hand-holds, and humidity like she'd never imagined.

Moving through it was brutal, and easily the hardest thing she'd ever done in her life. She stopped yet again, to drag in several deep breaths, her lungs sorely lacking oxygen after the breakneck pace she'd set for herself through the dense foliage that kept slapping her face. Thankfully, she had worn a lightweight, long-sleeved shirt. It was certainly coming in handy now, even if it was snagged and torn in places.

With her feet sinking into the muck that counted as ground in this area, three inches below water and settling into mud, her legs felt like they had a million pins pricking her flesh, tingling as they did from overexertion. She was so close to making it to dry ground. Or, drier ground. There was no way she was going to stop now. She had to get her feet out of the water.

Most people would have been terrified to be alone in the Everglades, and she knew that might be the rational mindset, but it wasn't hers. She had something to prove to herself and all the people who had tried to keep her down over the years. No Florida swamp was going to beat her. People thought that because she was a bit on the small side, and didn't look like one of those badass chicks from any of the movies, she would fail. They were wrong.

"Keep moving," she whispered to herself, willing her legs to carry her through the swampy bog.

She had once thought running on sand was tough, but this marsh was a completely different challenge. Every step was a battle. Her hiking boots sank into the mud, making a sucking sound as she pulled each boot out and took another step. So much of the land was muddy ground, much of it covered by at least a few inches of water—and every bit of it fought her forward momentum. Thankfully, it wasn't overly hot. Although, the humidity made it uncomfortable even in the shade. Florida humidity had turned her skin into a sticky glue that bugs and debris clung to. It was gross, and the first thing she was going to do when she got out of this swamp was take a long, hot shower. Maybe the weather wasn't bad when you could lay out on beaches and then jump in the ocean, but this journey she was on was a long way from any beachside vacation.

"Focus," she reminded herself when her mind started to acknowledge her physical discomfort yet again.

Shifting her weight, she took in another deep breath and grimaced as the sucking sound of the mud beneath her feet responded to her renewed attempts to move forward. She had to get to dry land. She'd never make it through another week if she had to stay in the thick swamp with its millions of mosquitoes and other bugs feasting on her body. Every sting reminded her that she had used the last of her bug repellant earlier that morning when things had gone from bad to worse.

The worst of it all was, her feet were wet, something she knew was bad. Wolf Henderson would lecture her for days when he found out she had lost her spare socks somewhere along the way. When they'd first set out on this little adventure, he had warned them all about foot rot. Human skin was not meant to be wet; he'd told them more than once. And now she knew why. Running was rubbing her toes and heels raw despite the fancy socks she had on. If she ever managed to find him and the others, she was fully prepared to be called out. He could complain and lecture all he wanted so long as he had some dry socks for her.

A small clearing ahead greeted her when she glanced up from the boggy ground to take new stock of her surroundings, and she pushed her body more upon seeing it. The clearing would provide options. At the very least, she wouldn't be smacked in the head with the branches that came from every direction, creating the dense canopy of the swamp. The shade was great—the bugs that came with it, not so much.

"Stop it!" she scolded herself aloud. "I can do this. And someone will come looking for me if I don't check in. Right?"

Her sinister laughter in the quiet swamp sounded funny to her ears. Everything about this situation was so wrong. Why had she ever thought a reality survival show would be a good time? It wasn't supposed to be like this. She'd been ditched by her partner earlier, and now she was alone. And yeah, of course, that's what she'd *said* she wanted, but now....

Reaching the sandy ground of the clearing, Regan gave herself a moment to enjoy the solid footing and take in her surroundings, weighing her options and calculating what path made the most sense. There was a wide pond in front of her, and going through it would be the quickest, shortest route to where she was trying to get to. Heading left would lead her deeper into the swamp, and she was not going back the way she'd come. Her eyes drifted to her right, where a steep hill of a rock stood ominously above her, stretching a good twenty feet into the sky. Going that route would take her a little out of her way, but she could circle back and get to her rendezvous point. It didn't look insurmountable, but it was steep. Especially considering her soggy footwear.

She let out a long sigh. None of her options promised she would make it to safety. The pond covered with floating green algae actually looked like the easiest choice, but Regan knew simplest was not best, especially in her case. Who knew what was under that algae, creature-wise? The tree that stretched out over part of the pond, keeping it in the shade, was also a problem. There was a wasp nest hanging over the area. That was a major deterrent. Even being in the vicinity of the nest was freaking her out. One sting and she would go into anaphylactic shock, and she couldn't exactly pull out an EpiPen while swimming. Her allergy was no joke. That had been a hard lesson learned when she'd been a little girl, and the single EpiPen she carried wouldn't be enough to save her if she was stung by more than a few of those horrible wasps.

Standing around and debating what to do could get her killed, too. She had to keep moving. She looked at the murky water, knowing it would likely be a safer option in some ways, but there was always a chance there'd be a deadly snake waiting to clamp down on her leg. Snakes were one of her least favorite animals on earth. The swamp-lands of Florida were rife with snakes; a fact she should have thought more about before signing up to do this stupid survival show. Sure, only a fifth or so of Florida snakes were venomous, but in her mind, snakes were snakes.

She stared at the water, shaking her head and cursing the rain they had been dealing with all week. It had made the swamp extra treacherous, which was never a good thing when survival was the goal. Staying upright had been her main goal as she'd traversed slippery rocks made deadly by the layers of moss and slime covering them, and remaining on her feet hadn't even been easy on what counted for solid ground around here, given the mud and the water.

"Relax, Regan. You've been in worse situations," she said aloud, trying to calm herself down.

She had to stay calm and think rationally. It was how she had stayed alive as long as she had. She couldn't lose her head now at the thought of a snake brushing by her.

Finding herself staring up at the slippery hill of rock that could lead to safety, she groaned. It was her best option. She knew it. The risk of being stung was too great. She had to avoid the wasps at all costs. Could she climb the rock wall alone? Having a partner would have made this path an easier prospect, but it was too late for that.

Besides, depending on other people always ended badly. Another hard life lesson she had learned over her twenty-seven years. People sucked. They were unreliable, and they always promised to help and be there for support, and then when you actually needed them, they screwed you over. Regan was done with all that. Being on her own had been a lot easier. She never had to worry about people letting her down or inserting their drama into her life, like her first partner on the show had done. Little Miss Sunny had been a nightmare. Regan had wanted to kill the producers for pairing her up with the school teacher. Thankfully, Sunny had been booted off, leaving Regan with a new partner. And while anyone was better than Sunny, her so-called partner was now nowhere to be found. *Typical.*

"You can do this. You don't need anybody. This is all you. Get your butt up that slope!"

The rock-covered hill was a slippery mess and her boots were coated with mud, making it even more difficult for her to get a strong foothold. Having clambered five feet above the base, she closed her eyes and focused on the goal. Getting to the top. It wasn't all that high. A couple stories, if she'd been trying to scale a building. Not something she had actually done, but she easily imagined jumping out of a second-story window and the height involved there—*that*, she had done.

With renewed strength, she stretched an arm up, felt around, and found the smallest hint of a ledge. It would have to do. With all the power she could muster in her five-foot, five-inch frame, she used her leg muscles to propel herself up the hill several inches. When she got a good foothold, she breathed a sigh of relief.

"You can do this," she repeated to herself.

Then Regan made the mistake of looking up. She had barely made it half way up, and there was nothing to hold onto.

"Come on!"

She was only a few yards off the ground, which wasn't a big deal, but if she did jump off the hill, she risked twisting an ankle or falling into the nasty, bug-infested pond. There was also the chance that she would hit her head on the way down, given the slick slope involved. It wasn't like she could run to the hospital to get patched up or take a couple Advil to relieve the pain of a head or ankle injury. The swamp wasn't exactly the best place to take risks.

"Well, this sucks," she muttered, holding onto the side of the hill and not knowing whether to keep trying to climb up or admit defeat and jump down.

Grab your copy of *Surviving the Swamp*.
www.GraceHamiltonBooks.com

Made in the USA
Columbia, SC
06 December 2023

27862293R00196